Cardinal
Love in Los Angeles Book 4

By Racheline Maltese and Erin McRae

Avian30
New York, New York
2018

This is a work of fiction. Names, characters, places, and incidents either are the product of the author's imagination or are used fictitiously. Any resemblance to actual events, locales, organizations, or persons, living or dead, is entirely coincidental and beyond the intent of either the author or the publisher.

Avian30
New York, New York
Cardinal by Erin McRae and Racheline Maltese
Copyright 2018
ISBN: 978-1-946192-13-4
www.Avian30.com

First Avian30 Printing: November 2018
Printed in the USA

1

The sky has grown dark by the time Alex drives up to his house. Of course, this is Iceland and it's March. It's always dark. Tonight, though, the lights are all on, and there's an ugly turquoise Nissan Quest in the driveway. Alex is relieved that whoever drove the thing here from the airport parked facing into the wind. The crew for *Saga*, the film in which he gets to play an awesome Viking anti-hero, are keeping a running tally of how many people get the doors blown off their rentals. People not from Iceland need a lot of information on how to survive Iceland. He's glad someone warned his family about the wind.

He pulls his own car up alongside the minivan and parks. Before he turns the ignition off, Paul's silhouette appears in one of the big windows overlooking the hill. Irrationally, all Alex wants to do is sit in his car for another moment and enjoy the reality of having a family again. But Paul, and everyone else, is waiting for him.

So he braces himself for the smack of cold air, gets out of the car, and picks his way up the path to the house. Paul yanks the door of the house open and pulls him into a hug right there in the doorway. Alex laughs and buries his face in his shoulder. Ali, who at seven hasn't the manners of either of her parents – and since her father is Liam that's saying something – attaches herself to his side.

Alex tries to shuffle forward. "We're letting the cold in," he protests. "Where are the babies? And Liam?"

Carly gets up from the couch to close the door and detach Ali from Alex's leg. Paul isn't letting go, which is perfectly fine with Alex, but he really does want to see his daughter.

Paul finally lets go so Alex can hug Carly too.

"Hi Alex," she says, both fond and sarcastic. "Our flights were great, thanks for asking. Liam's sleeping off the jetlag and the babies are in the playpen and no longer screaming because planes are terrible. How was work?"

♦

Alex picks Claudia up only to have her turn her face away from him and reach for Paul. Which he knows is fair. She's only nine months old and, near-daily video calls aside, she hasn't seen him in two months. But her rejection still hurts.

Finally, after a lot of quiet conversation with Paul, Claudia gets used to Alex enough to babble at him very seriously from the safety of Paul's lap. Finally, to Alex's inexpressible relief, she smiles shyly and climbs from Paul onto him for a hug. She very nearly strangles Alex in the process. Children are, as ever, a highly mixed blessing.

Behind him, Carly rummages through his kitchen cupboards as she fixes them a dinner of Icelandic hot dogs and salad.

"You are amazing and I will totally cook you dinner tomorrow," Alex says to her as he gently pries the baby's fingers off his throat.

"You're fucking right I am," Carly says. "And yes you are. I'm being nice to you tonight, I'm not being your housewife. Where the fuck is your salt?"

"Cupboard over the stove," Alex says in the same sing-song voice he's been using to speak to

Claudia.

Alex's relationship with Carly isn't as intense as his relationship with Liam, but it's nearly as hard to define. He's a bit afraid of her, but he also trusts her deeply. Sure, they're raising their kids together, and Alex fucked her during his and Paul's first, and so far only, foray into threesomes. But she's always been his magical advice-giver of last resort. She's also one of the few people who is absolutely clear and candid with him. He appreciates her more than he has words for and is glad he can express his fondness with friendly bickering. She gets it.

Being cooped up in a small house with Liam, Carly, and the kids in the middle of nowhere is the sort of experience they had once tried to avoid. At this point in their lives, though, it seems perfectly natural. Last year Carly and Liam moved into the house two doors down from him and Paul. Alex had been incredibly dubious about the wisdom of having so little breathing space, but given how entwined their lives are logistically, living close to each other was highly convenient. Besides, as Carly and Paul continually point out, it was either the house two doors down or two neighborhoods over.

The arrangement has, so far, worked out well enough. They're all still on speaking terms, and Alex doesn't find Liam any more irritating than usual. The accessibility of babysitters alone has been a lifesaver; Alex doesn't trust many people with his daughter, but he trusts Liam and Carly.

Alex feels a little terrible for the couple with the house between theirs, though. The stalkers tend to park in their driveway.

"What have you been feeding her?" Alex asks Carly as he bounces Claudia on his knees to make her giggle. She's grown so much.

"Only the finest fucking organic, grass-fed, free-range baby foods available. All made by hand in my copious free time," Carly deadpans.

Paul chuckles. Nobody in their households would be into the whole organic free-range thing even if they did have the time.

Vic, who's now a year and a half old and walking – a new development since Alex saw her last – grabs the edge of the coffee table and strains a little arm forward to try to grab Paul's coffee cup. Paul clucks at her, moves the cup farther out of baby-reach, and scoops Vic up onto the couch with them.

"Do you want boiled sheep heads tomorrow?" Alex asks Carly benignly. "I've got a recipe."

"You're so full of shit." Carly laughs. "Ali, go wake your father up."

"He has a clock," she says from her armchair, looking up from *Julie of the Wolves*.

"Not that works," Carly points out. Alex snorts.

As if on cue Liam staggers out from one of the extra bedrooms. "What? I'm awake."

He sounds like nothing of the sort. The ridiculous candy-cane-striped pajama bottoms and shirtlessness don't help. Still, Alex is glad to see him. He hands Claudia off to Paul so he can stand up to say hello.

"Whoa, you got built," Liam says as Alex hugs him. Then Liam kisses him on the mouth, like he always does, but apparently forgets to stop so that it winds up being not at all chaste.

Alex laughs, splutters and pushes him away. "I missed you too."

"Oh man, sorry, still not awake." Liam scrubs a

hand through the absolute disaster of his hair.

"Clearly," Carly says. "Please go get dressed so we can eat?"

"Okay." Liam shuffles back to the bedroom. Paul cracks up.

Ali looks up from her book again. "Sorry my dad is bad at shit."

♦

At dinner Liam is significantly more awake, dressed, and, once he eats some food, even manages to scold Ali for her language earlier. He doesn't seem to particularly care about her assessment of his life skills.

He does, however, ask curiously about Alex's diet and what his plans are long-term for his body when Alex avoids the potatoes (too starchy), the carrots (too sugary), and the salad dressing (too everything). From anyone else, Alex would be annoyed, but Liam lacks filters and is interested in the process rather than policing Alex's habits. But Alex still isn't quite sure how to answer him, especially when he really wants potatoes and carrots and salad dressing. It's just not an option while he needs the physique of a Viking warrior.

Alex had bulked up a lot for this role before he'd even left L.A., but now, here, with a grueling workout routine and a grueling filming schedule, his body has changed even more. He feels out of proportion to the rest of the world and his necessary food choices are misery-making. He would rather turn his attention to convincing Claudia that mashed peas, which he also can't eat, are actually super delicious.

He reconsiders when she flings a spoonful of

them into his now shoulder-length hair.

"Dealing with a baby as a Viking is the least glamorous thing I have ever done." Alex reaches across Paul for more napkins.

Carly snorts. "Yeah, keep saying that, big-time movie star."

"Can we not?" Alex says.

"Look, I know you're not mainlining *Variety* out here on the side of a glacier," Carly says. "But you have buzz and Chris Brecker, all-American hunk, as your co-star."

Alex swipes ineffectually at the peas in his hair with a napkin. "Yeah, and there's been buzz for every other movie I've been in too, and that's amounted to cutting room floor, great reviews but no one saw it, and wow at least *Icarus Project* didn't tank as hard as *Jupiter Ascending*."

"Or, you know, Icarus himself," Paul notes.

"You're going to be an action hero heartthrob!" Carly says, pitching her voice up into the register of the younger fans Alex has always been most unsettled by.

"Not counting on it," he says. "Gleefully not counting on it."

"I'm counting on it," Paul interjects.

"Every time I get him on video chat hashtag-SushiGuy here has been talking about the press junket as apparently some sort of frenzy even worse than when I started on *Fourth*," Alex says. #SushiGuy had been the internet's label for Paul back when they first started dating and no one knew who Paul was. Now Paul has devoted fans of his own.

"He's not wrong," Liam says as he tears off another hunk of the dark Icelandic rye bread Alex is proud of himself for making without burning the house down.

"Not you, too."

"What? I was stuck with you all day, every day when you were trying to cope with being everybody's favorite mystery gay. Welcome to round two. This time if you punch a photographer they might even notice."

"I never punched a photographer."

Liam tears off another hunk of bread. "Yeah, but you wanted to."

"Can we talk about *Scism* instead?" Alex pleads. Hearing about Liam's new development project based on one of Victor's old show ideas *again* is way better than talking about Alex's new-and-unlikely-to-be-improved levels of fame.

◆

As happy as Alex is to get caught up with everyone, he's thrilled when the kids have been put to bed, Carly and Liam retreat to their own room, and he finally gets Paul to himself. After long absences it usually takes them weeks to get used to being in each other's space again, but they don't have time for that now. Alex is hungry for every moment they have together.

They put Claudia to bed in her travel crib, pushed against the wall under the window in Alex's room. Vic and Ali are in the bedroom down the hall. Claudia will join them tomorrow night, but for now Alex wants his baby sleeping in the same room as him.

Once Claudia's asleep, he drags Paul into the bathroom and pulls the door mostly – but not entirely – closed behind them. If the baby wakes up, they need to be able to hear her.

Paul, as exhausted as he looks, is happy to have Alex turn on the tap and steer him under the water. After the chatter with everyone all evening, Alex finds it blissful not to have to say anything.

Paul closes his eyes and tips his head back under the pathetic water pressure. "I hate European showers."

"I dunno, this one is looking pretty good to me right now." Alex leans against the shower wall taking in the visual of Paul with his head thrown back, eyes closed, and water running down his skin. Paul doesn't work out in the obsessive and unhealthy way he did when they first got together, but he's still fit and gorgeous and so much saner than he used to be.

Alex runs his palm down Paul's chest, over his abs, and down to his thighs. The touch isn't much about sex. Paul is here and real. When Alex is with him, he feels real too. Paul's always been the center around which he revolves. Six years of marriage and the last two months apart haven't made that any less true.

Paul wipes water out of his eyes and smiles. "Here, you get in, too." He moves aside so Alex can take a turn in the spray. He frowns at the patchwork of scrapes and bruises that cover Alex's body. "What did you do to yourself?"

"Vikings. Stunts. Falling off glaciers." Alex doesn't want the realities of his current job to be an issue, but this is the sort of thing Paul has always fixated on.

"Please tell me you didn't fall off a glacier."

"Nope," Alex reaches for the shampoo. "Too much to look forward to."

2

Alex is glad to have his family in Iceland with him, but knowing he has people to go home to makes work the next day seem so much longer. He passes the time between takes chatting with his castmates and the crew about what he should do with everyone while they're here.

Unfortunately, talking with people about good hiking trails for four adults, a second grader, and two babies who will be in backpacks means making conversation with his co-star Chris. Who is actually an action-hero kind of movie star and not just a guy who got famous because he was on TV.

Chris is fine as an actor. He and Alex have great chemistry on camera. And while Chris isn't a complete tool, he drives Alex up the wall. And not in the entertaining way Liam did back when they barely knew each other.

No, the problem with Chris is that he has a secret girlfriend. Which is the sort of dumbass Hollywood bullshit that makes Alex want to scream. Liam being in the closet about being bi while Alex was very, very out was uncomfortable. Chris being in the closet about being straight or in a relationship or whatever it is he's in the closet about is super disgusting.

As far as Alex is aware, no one's going to threaten Chris because he likes to fuck women. And him implying by omission that he's single or into guys or *whatever* to increase how interesting people find him is just gross. Today, Alex has to deal with a Chris who is cranky that, thanks to those choices, his girlfriend can't come visit him in Iceland too.

"No one cares what we do here. No one knows what we do here. There are more sheep here than people," Alex points out. It's the best thing about Iceland. That, and climbing glaciers.

"It's just easier. More people want to fuck me, bigger box office draw," Chris explains in response to Alex's continued bafflement.

And that's another thing that irritates Alex. Just because he's confused doesn't mean he wants an explanation. Yet, somehow, he still needs to ask. "Do people not want to fuck you if you have a girlfriend?"

♦

"Aren't you sad Alex still has to work, like, twelve-plus hour days while you're here?" Liam asks. It's late afternoon, and the sun has already dropped below the hills behind the house. Paul is sitting at the kitchen table, going through his email. He's technically on vacation. But he and Olivia, his partner in all things business and creative, are getting their new show *Plague*, about CDC staffers in Atlanta, up and running. He can't leave her high and dry.

Besides, it's not hard to deal with a few emails while enjoying everyone else. Ali is playing with Claudia. Vic is merrily raiding a basket of board books. Liam's on the floor with a book, sitting against the couch where Carly is stretched out, flipping through an Icelandic fashion magazine she stole from the plane.

Paul rests his chin on his hand and nearly loses his train of thought staring out the window at the stunning landscape outside. "It's okay. I have you guys," he finally says in answer to Liam's question.

"What do you mean?" Liam asks, leaning his head back. Without looking up from her magazine, Carly reaches down and runs a hand through his hair.

"Having other people around stops me from being a depressive workaholic and a bad partner and father."

"That's cool," Liam says cautiously. "But I mean like, you flew all this way and hardly get to see him. That's gotta suck."

"It's not like he can help it. I'm fine," Paul says.

"Whoa." Carly looks up from her magazine. Liam makes a sad noise when she stops petting his hair. "When either of you say you're fine, you are never actually fine."

Paul spreads his hands. "I'm here and not dysfunctional and not getting upset about Alex's work schedule that I can't change. I am, really and truly, fine."

"Mom's right. No one's fine," Ali interjects.

"You're seven. When did you get so jaded?" Paul asks her.

"Apocalypse movies are in right now. Don't blame me for the state of the culture."

Carly cackles.

"Does anybody want drinks?" Liam says.

"It's not even five o'clock," Paul points out, although Carly is nodding. They haven't even eaten dinner yet.

◆

They do at least eat dinner first. While Paul and Carly clean up, Liam empties Alex's cupboards of all of his glasses – he says he's looking for the best ones, whatever that means. With Ali's assistance he spreads them out on the peninsula that separates the kitchen from the living room. He happily mixes drinks that are all bright shades of green and blue thanks to epic amounts of Midori and Brennivín, the Icelandic liquor they got from the weird government booze depot on the way in. Ali is fascinated by the virgin cocktail Liam shows her how to make with Sprite and some of Alex's green juice that probably involves spinach, not that Ali needs to know that.

None of them drink much, but the mood is fun and relaxed once Paul finally puts his laptop in the bedroom and stops checking his phone.

After Claudia and Vic are asleep, Paul wonders if he should try to end the party, low-key as it is. Alex isn't going to want to come home to a complete disaster of a kitchen, especially given that he's probably going to also want to eat dinner. At least they have leftovers for him.

Liam paces around the room, talking animatedly about the Wikipedia hole about Vikings he fell into earlier that day. He's waving his hands enough to make Paul fear for the drink he's holding and also for Alex's floor. But at least a Liam who's hyper and pacing isn't a Liam who's making them endless drinks no one's really consuming.

"Vacation is wonderful," Carly purrs from the armchair she's curled into.

Liam stops his pacing just long enough to kiss her. Paul's mildly relieved yet surprised when Liam walks right by him with nothing more than a wink.

♦

"Why are you all trashed at nine o'clock?" Alex asks as soon as he gets in the door. He drops his bag on the floor and unwraps himself from the layers required to drive in Iceland without freezing to the seat.

"We're not trashed." Liam is indignant.

"Really? Because nothing that isn't alcoholic comes in blue, and that is a lot of blue." Alex points at a stray drink on the coffee table. "Also, the open bottles and all my glassware."

"I helped Dad with the glasses." Ali pipes up from where she's sitting cross-legged on the floor, very carefully measuring out club soda into her own cup.

"Somehow, I'm not surprised. Where are the babies?"

Paul waggles the baby monitor at him. "The babies are sleeping, and we are not actually drunk."

"Okaaaaay," Alex says cautiously. "Have any of you eaten anything today?" He's annoyed. He and Paul were finally going to get to fuck tonight. If everyone is being chummy with booze in the living room, that seems unlikely to happen unless he decides to be a brat about it. Which he may, because really.

"Yes. With the kids." Carly answers his question. "Four hours ago. Now we are drinking and you still owe us boiled sheep heads."

"Can you make fermented shark?" Ali asks. "I read about it on the internet."

Paul asks him how his day on set was, probably to steer the conversation away from sheep, sharks, and the eating thereof.

Alex relates the conversation with Chris about Chris's secret girlfriend. He's pleased that everyone else thinks his co-star is ridiculous and awful too.

"Wow," Liam says. "He's even more of a douche than I was."

"Yup," Alex says.

"You're not going to tell me I'm not a douche?"

"Nope."

"I'm making you a drink." Liam bounces up from the couch to do just that.

Alex takes the glass dubiously when Liam hands it to him, not sure if he actually wants it. Also, he should probably eat dinner himself before he starts in on blue cocktails made with Brennivín.

"Do you guys want seconds?" Liam asks Carly and Paul. They both nod.

"You all know this shit is kind of hallucinogenic, right?" Alex puts in.

"Ohhhhh." Liam looks off to the side as if taking inventory of his current functioning levels.

"Okay, I'm letting you hang onto this," Alex says. "I am getting food."

He passes the glass back to Liam, but Carly immediately reaches over and takes the glass out of her husband's hand.

◆

Alex eats curled up next to Paul on the couch, their shoulders pressed together. Alex doesn't even care when Paul's laughter makes his arm jiggle. If he has to endure everyone else, at least Paul is happy.

The conversation starts to drift, away from Iceland and the kids and the activities they have planned, to their lives back in L.A. At first, Alex is content to get caught up with everyone's doings while he's been gone. But as the stories go on the conversation becomes less about filling Alex in and more about Paul, Liam and Carly chatting amongst themselves. Alex feels left out.

His sense of exclusion is hardly something he can complain about when he's the one who agreed to move to Iceland for four months. He doesn't really mind being off the hook for their weekly family meetings to discuss schedules, the kids, agreements, and anything else that needs discussing. But still, he's grateful when Vic wakes up and starts hollering, giving him an excuse to leave the cozy little family circle that apparently doesn't need him to function. He takes a sleepily protesting Ali with him, because jetlag is not an excuse for ignoring bedtimes.

Ali busies herself in the bathroom getting washed up and her pjs on while Alex confronts the bundle of angry eighteen-month-old. Claudia, who's been woken up by the noise, is now also crying.

Alex cannot for the life of him figure out what is pissing Vic off so much or what to do about it. He just knows he probably should not be this relieved to be dealing with two distraught babies, except that he has missed these kids. Small children may not be particularly intelligible, but they are at least direct and honest about their emotions. In light of the life Alex lives in L.A., it's refreshing.

Vic finally calms down when he picks her up out of the crib and starts walking her around the room. Within minutes, she's snuffling quietly with her face buried in his shoulder. When he tries to put her back down, though, she shrieks and kicks at the bars and yells "No!" at the top of her tiny-yet-effective lungs.

Claudia, who had started to drop off in the meantime, starts crying again.

"So, not the crib?" Alex asks.

"No!"

"Okay then. You know you're gonna have to go in the crib eventually."

"No!"

"Because as much as I'd love to walk you around all night, you've got to sleep *somewhere*."

"No!"

Someday, Alex is going to tell Vic the story of his very strange life and the ultimately terrible advice his best friend Gemma gave him the night he came home with the offer from Victor to be a star: *You can't say no.* And, if he raises her right, Vic is going to find it fucking hilarious.

♦

In the morning, Paul wakes to find Alex smiling at him. The sun is bright and warm through the uncovered windows, a strange luxury that comes with the isolation not just of this house but of this country. Paul smiles back and says nothing. Alex has always been the one who doesn't need words, but right now talking feels unnecessary for him, too.

"Hungover?" Alex eventually asks.

"Hardly. Sleep. Sun. You. I'm all right."

Alex smiles, and Paul shifts closer to him. With Alex's body so different, they don't quite fit together in the way he remembers.

"What about you?" Paul asks.

"I barely drank. And, aside from our friends' constant presence in my house which is interfering with my plans for Icelandic hibernation? I've got you. I'm good."

"Well," Paul says with a grin he knows is ridiculous. "No one's right here right now except us."

"There are other people in the house." Alex objects.

"Except our rooms don't share a wall and it has officially been too long since I touched you."

Alex smiles so broadly his eyes crinkle up. "Okay then."

He seems happy to have Paul roll on top of him, smiling into the kiss and relaxing back into the mattress. Paul considers making a joke about having to do all the work, but now is not the time for charming snark about the routine of married sex.

Paul licks a stripe down Alex's chest and nips at Alex's thigh instead.

"Marking. Good? Bad?" he asks. He wants to be absolutely clear on what he's allowed to do before Alex stops him in the middle of anything.

"Viking warrior. You've seen what I've done to myself. Makeup doesn't care."

But when Paul shoves Alex's legs up so he can lick over his hole, he whines and pushes him away.

"Alex?" Paul is confused. Normally, he loves this.

Alex doesn't say anything. Instead, he gets up on his knees and shoves Paul back onto the pillows. Paul goes, fascinated by the switch and by the way Alex is staring at him as if entranced.

When Alex folds himself, as best he can, between Paul's knees Paul thinks he's going to get a blowjob, which he is totally on board for. But then Alex presses his fingertips into Paul's thighs, and his own face between Paul's cheeks.

Paul can't quite help gasping. He moans when Alex starts rimming him. He cranes his head up as best he can, because he wants to watch, and finds Alex staring at him, his eyes dark and intense.

Alex almost never does this. The unusualness of it is nearly as shocking as the sensation. He's determined, though, and kneads his calloused palms into Paul's thighs. When Paul shoves his hands into his hair, he whimpers softly.

The spell doesn't break when Paul comes. Alex keeps licking and kissing over what is now far-too-sensitive skin until Paul flips them and, grinning, goes down on him in return.

The sun flooding the bedroom is hot on Paul's bare skin. The soft rhythmic creak of the bed as Alex arches under his mouth is soothing. Everything is bright: The white bedding, the snowfield outside the window, and Alex's pale skin dotted with scratches and bruises.

♦

When Alex and Paul emerge from their bedroom, Carly and Liam look them over, look at each other, and look away in perfect synchronicity.

As amusing as that is, Alex narrows his eyes. "What?" he demands.

Liam grins. "Glad you guys had a good morning."

"You've earned it," Carly puts in.

"Your room isn't next to ours," Alex hisses, bending down to scoop Claudia up out of her playpen. The babies may have no idea what the adults are talking about but Ali is sitting at the table and totally doesn't need to hear this.

Claudia, for her part, chatters happily and digs

her tiny fingers into his sweater. Alex is glad he opted for the ponytail today. Little hands pulling long hair hurts.

"Nooooo, but the bathroom is," Liam says.

"Don't be embarrassed," Carly grins. "Liam had a good morning too."

Alex closes his eyes and groans.

♦

The seven of them eat breakfast together. Liam and Paul can hardly look at each other through the meal without laughing. They're clearly having fun, so Alex lets them at it and doesn't snark. It's definitely a vast improvement over the period when Paul was jealous of Liam, which was followed by the oddly unrelated period when Liam was afraid of Paul.

They leave the dishes in the sink for later and pile into the minivan to drive to a trail. It takes fifteen minutes to coax a reluctant Vic into her car seat while Ali provides entirely unhelpful commentary, but Alex is still delighted the moment they get on the road. He loves living in Iceland, but he's excited to vacation in it too. His filming schedule hasn't left him much off-duty time to explore.

There's so much to see, and all of it is fascinating. California has mountains, but not like this. They're huge, covered in snow except for a few patches of brown and gray on their sides as they slope to the sea. With the drive along a winding road, the cold gray sea stretching behind them to the horizon, Alex feels like they're on the edge of the world.

He parks alongside a few other cars at the

trailhead. It takes almost as long to get everyone out as it did to get them all in. A small part of Alex wishes he was on his own, so that he could do a more rigorous hike. It's impossible, though, not just with the children, but with Liam, Carly, and Paul. Even so, he's thrilled to be with his strange family in this strange landscape.

No one expects him to talk. As they walk Paul and Ali keep up a chatter about how far Húsavik, the town Alex is based near, seems from everything with its one road, tiny cluster of buildings right on the water, and epic mountains. Paul has Claudia in a baby backpack, Liam has Vic, and Alex is keenly aware of Carly close on his heels and also, he suspects, wanting to be alone with this place. They're both something like witches sometimes.

"So, if you didn't have your doting husband and your adorable baby," Carly asks quietly. "Would we ever get you back from Iceland?"

"Nope." Alex doesn't look at her, peering instead up the path ahead where their destination, Lake Botnsvatn, has just come into view. He takes off at a run, Carly leaping into her own sprint toward it a moment later.

As they dash ahead, he can hear Ali ask Paul why he and Carly are such jerks.

◆

They eat dinner together at the restaurant and bar in Húsavik. The place is crowded, because it's Saturday night and it's the only option in town, but no one pays any attention to them or even tries to get pictures. Ali is clearly having the time of her life acting like a tiny adult even without anyone pointing a camera at her. Like Liam, she mostly loves the paparazzi. Her ego is charming, though Alex is mildly terrified by the idea of how gregarious Claudia might be at age seven. She and Vic may not be much in the way of conversationalists, but that also means Alex doesn't have to worry about them interacting with the outside world just yet.

The meal goes on for hours. Dinner in Iceland, Alex has discovered, pleasantly lacks the aggressive efficiency of everywhere he's been in America. Considering they have two babies to tend to, it's a particularly nice pace.

Eventually, the conversation turns to *Scism* again. Alex is happy to listen to Liam talk about dead Victor's show, and happier still that he doesn't have to be a part of it. Because it seems like everyone else they know – except Olivia and Paul – is.

Jackson's already attached as a writer, which is a pleasant surprise. Alex got to know Victor's personal assistant pretty well in the wake of the man's death. They've kept up with each other in the time since, and Alex knew that Jackson, like every other assistant in Hollywood, was pounding out pages. In Jackson's case, they were actually good. Which, Alex supposes, helps explain why Victor hired him in the first place. He can't help but wonder what opportunities might have come to Jackson earlier than this if Victor had lived.

Gemma, Alex's best friend since they were both high school kids who met on the internet, is involved too, in production. She'd been the one to get Liam on board, in fact. She hadn't reached out to Alex about working on the project, but then, Alex doesn't do development and has been occupied with *Saga.*

It's a good team, as far as Alex can tell. The one issue is Liam's ongoing feud with Minette Lewis. Minette is Gemma's boss and mentor who's overseeing the entire project for the network, and Liam can't stand her. Which, as far as Alex can tell, has everything to do with Liam and nothing at all to do with Minette.

Alex has been getting annoyed emails from Liam detailing all the ways Minette isn't respecting Victor's vision or legacy or *something* for months now. Which, given Alex's own complicated feelings about the man and his body of work, he can only barely sympathize with. Victor needs a restraining influence, even – and perhaps especially – now he's dead.

Liam isn't the only one he's heard from about this process, either. Gemma has been emailing just as often, usually from the middle of meetings, complaining about Liam and Minette's antagonism and the almost-but-not-quite shouting matches that have erupted between them more than once. While Alex finds the situation amusing from a distance, he's glad not to have to deal with the drama in person.

"I'm still surprised you want to move to development at all," Alex says. Liam loves to be loved, and there sure as hell isn't any love in there. "I can get why you want to work on one of Victor's projects, but why like this?"

"I want *Scism* to happen," Liam says. "And I do want to start getting back into work, but I don't feel ready to be in front of the camera yet. If I stay on the development side, I can make sure the best hands get involved and that it's the show Victor wanted it to be. Or, well…the show Victor could have gotten away with." Liam grins and turns to Paul. "Are you sure you don't want to be in on it?"

"Victor's fantasy Catholic church political drama pilot is completely not my thing. And not something I want to deal with the consequences of," Paul says for the thousandth time. "Claudia, no, no, no forks for you yet," he adds, leaning over to offer her a spoon in exchange for the utensil she just grabbed from Carly's place setting.

Claudia drops the fork, grabs the spoon, gives Paul a gummy grin, and starts gnawing on the handle.

Liam doesn't seem to notice the interruption. They've all long since gotten used to conversations being punctuated by baby drama. And babies at least are cuter than cell phones going off because of production crises. Or anyone being dead.

"I was there when he wrote it," Liam goes on. "And I was the one who told him he couldn't pitch it. Time wasn't right. But it is now. Better, at least."

"How old even is that thing?" Alex asks because it's better than asking how the time could ever be right. Whatever they do with *Scism*, it's going to piss people off.

"So, remember a few years back, when the Pope announced that maybe gays weren't evil and could maybe be part of the Church after all?" Liam asks.

"Um. Sort of," Alex says, because that's ringing a vague bell, but he doesn't exactly stay current on the doings of the Roman Catholic Church.

"Well, okay, that's not *precisely* what he said. But that was the gist. Which pissed off a whole lot of people, so it got retracted the next day. It was all fucked up. Victor was really, really upset, and I think started fighting with fans about it on Twitter. I don't even know why. But more than anything he wanted to write a show about it, what might happen if part of the Church decided to be, you know, more enlightened and broke off from the rest of it. So we stayed up one night talking about it, and our very different Catholic childhoods, and like *everything* while he wrote a bible. A show bible," he adds. "Not the religious kind."

"Normally, I don't think that's a clarification you'd need," Alex says dryly.

"Victor was furious, but it was such a good time. So that's the thing I want to do." Liam's voice is tender and pained.

"Then why did you tell him not to pitch it way back when?" Alex asks. There's a lot about Victor and Liam's relationship Alex still doesn't understand, and he's fascinated by a Liam who could stand up to Victor about his work.

"A couple of reasons. One, it was half-baked because he was angry. It was brilliant, but…. Two, I didn't want to deal with the fallout."

"And you do now?"

Liam shrugs. For a few moments, everyone around the table is quiet.

Then Liam pushes back from the table. "I'm going to go get some fresh air."

"Do you want company?" Alex asks. Liam still looks pensive and a little sad.

Liam waves him off. "Nah, I'm fine."

Having learned to take Liam at his word, Alex turns his attention to Claudia, who is now trying to cram her entire bib into her mouth.

"What happened to Lee?" he asks after about fifteen minutes, craning his neck to look around the restaurant. It's not a huge space. Liam didn't take his coat with him. If he's still outside, he's in for some misery at the very least.

Carly tips her head toward the side of the room, a grin on her face.

Alex follows her gaze. Liam, far from catching his death in the Icelandic night, is at the bar leaning forward to talk animatedly with the bartender.

Alex sighs, exasperated.

"What?" Carly says. "He's having fun."

"He's flirting with the bartender," Alex protests, his voice low for the sake of Ali, who looks around to see what everyone is talking about. Ali knows, in a seven-year-old way, that her parents are polyamorous; she certainly knows that each of them date other people. But that doesn't mean that Alex wants to deal with a lot of questions about that right now.

"The bartender's hot," Carly observes mildly at normal volume.

"But I'm friends with all the bartenders," Alex moans. "This is the only bar in town."

Normally Alex doesn't mind the shortness of the days. He spends most of the scant daylight hours outside on set where he gets to see the sun for at least a few hours. But with his family here he hates getting up for work in the dark while Paul drowses in their bed and the kids sleep soundly in their room down the hall. Soon his family will be gone again, and Alex finds it harder every day to leave the house. He wishes everyone could just stay until the film is done.

One morning he takes Liam to set with him to visit. On the way, Liam grabs Alex's phone out of the cupholder between them, unlocks it and starts punching keys.

"What are you doing?" Alex asks, not particularly fazed by the lack of regard for his privacy. It is, after all, Liam.

"Downloading an app for you. We've been using it to schedule things for us and the kids, it's been super helpful. It's even got a messaging function!"

"Was there something inadequate about the calendar that's already on my phone? Or texting?" Alex is confused.

"Nah, those are fine and whatever. But this is just easier. It probably won't affect you 'til you get back home, but this way you can like keep an eye on things in the meantime."

"Ooookay," Alex says dubiously.

When he finally parks at the set lot, he picks up his phone. To his mingled horror and dismay, the app Liam installed isn't *just* a scheduling app.

"This is a polyamory app," Alex says, his voice flat.

Liam jiggles his legs. "Yeah."

"For polyamorous people."

"Yeah."

"To manage their schedules and dates and appointments for all their relationships."

"Yeah?"

"We're not polyamorous!" Alex exclaims.

Liam frowns, as if Alex is being completely unreasonable. "But we all have relationships with each other, and schedules to keep and dates and appointments and stuff?"

"Augh!" Alex pulls his hat more firmly down around his ears and reaches for the door handle. It is far too early to explain to Liam why this is appalling.

♦

The next day he takes Ali to set with him, to her delight and the amusement of his colleagues. To his relief, the drive to work does not net him another new phone app. Alex feels immensely proud and fond of how much everyone dotes on her. She's thrilled at the entire experience, but sulks to Alex during lunch in the big heated catering tent about how Liam won't let her be in movies and could he do something about that.

"Sure, they need baby Vikings here all the time," Alex tells her. "Want to come in with me at four in the morning every day?"

Ali narrows her eyes suspiciously at him, then shakes her head. "No. And I'm not a baby."

Alex is relieved to dodge the need to explain,

yet again, the family policy of no child stars, current or former, other than Liam. The topic will surely come to a far less agreeable head at some point.

Another night Carly and Liam go into town for a date, which means Alex and Paul get to be totally on deck for the kids.

"I can't believe I missed seeing Vic take her first steps," Alex opines. He's glad walking isn't an issue with Claudia yet, but still, watching Vic toddle around the living room and get into everything is unexpectedly melancholy.

Paul hums from where he's sitting on the floor building block towers that Claudia is delightedly knocking over. "If it helps, I wasn't in the room for that either. There's lots of ways to miss things. Unfortunately."

Alex knows he should find that reassuring. Instead, as he and Paul put the kids to bed, he keeps thinking about all the things he's going to keep missing once everyone goes back to L.A.

Once the kids are asleep, Paul grabs Alex's hand and pulls him into their bedroom.

Getting some time to finally be alone and not be aware of Carly and Liam somewhere else in the house is a relief. They fuck for a long time. It's intense, Paul's gray eyes focused on Alex's face and his hands tight in his hair. The wind moans around the corners of the house while the lamplight spills warm and golden across their skin.

After, curled around each other in bed – Paul seems to be as unwilling as Alex is to stop touching – they talk softly with their foreheads pressed together. It's the first time on this trip Alex has felt completely connected with Paul, and it's bliss. They may call and video chat often when Alex is gone, but that only accentuates the space between them. It's so good to be in the same room and not have to worry about Paul's next meeting or Alex's next call or emotions lost in the translation of technology, and just talk. About the kids, their work, the books Alex is reading, and the vast Icelandic landscape that makes it feel like they're the only two people in the world.

Which, tragically, they are not. Alex wakes up when the front door slams. He hears laughter and shushing, and the sound of shoes dropping off in the hall. He's tempted to holler about how Carly and Liam are being shitty roommates, but he'd be at least partially joking and Liam wouldn't get it. Then he'd have to get up and talk about it, and all of it might wake the kids. He whines and snuggles close to Paul who is too dead to the world to even realize anything is going on.

◆

It turns out that Carly and Liam are not the worst roommates in the world because they sound like a herd of elephants when they come home at some ungodly hour. Rather, they are the worst roommates in the world because they didn't come home alone.

Alex isn't pissed, exactly. But he is not prepared to see the bartender from the other night emerging from Carly and Liam's room while he's standing in his kitchen making coffee before he has to go to set.

"Oh my god, Bjarki," Alex says, way too loudly for the hour. There is no way he can reasonably be expected to process any of this.

"Hey, Alex."

Liam comes out after Bjarki, shirtless though,

thank god, wearing pajama bottoms. Before Alex can even grouse at Liam about the mess he could have made in light of the fact Bjarki works at *the only bar in town*, Paul comes stumbling out of his and Alex's room, rubbing a hand over his eyes. He's at least thrown on a pair of boxers and a T-shirt, although the latter is inside out.

"Are you okay?" he asks Alex, a worried, sleepy frown on his face.

"Yeah, I'm fine, why?"

"You said there was a Bja – oh." Paul stops in the doorway, taking in the situation.

Apparently whatever Paul thought a Bjarki was, he did not think it was a person. Especially not a person who is now standing in their kitchen, wearing whatever he'd had on last night, having presumably just had sex with Liam and Carly.

"Paul, meet Bjarki. Bjarki, Paul." Alex's life is surreal.

Paul looks like he's struggling to take any of this in, so Alex hisses *bartender* at him in hopes of providing sufficient clarity in limited words. That at least seems to make it click, though Paul clearly still doesn't know what to do about it.

They're saved only by Liam, whose fault this all remains in the first place. Somehow, thanks to his preternatural ability to be charming in any and all circumstances, the whole thing turns into reasonably cheerful and unawkward small talk.

"It's going to be weird every time I go to your bar now," Alex complains to Bjarki while Liam makes orange juice for them all.

"It'll be fine," Bjarki says easily. "You think this is the weirdest thing that's happened here?"

Alex wonders what other strange stories he has

about tourists and film crews who have come through the town, and decides he doesn't want to know.

"I can only hope," he says. Then he points at Liam. "By the way, I don't even know how to make pancakes."

Liam's eyes go huge.

♦

The conversation about Bjarki sleeping over has to wait until that night, once Alex is back from work, Vic and Claudia are asleep and everyone's sure Ali isn't going to come barging out into the living room again looking for a book or a stuffed animal or a snack.

"You haven't dated anyone since Victor died but you totally fucked the Icelandic bartender?" Alex asks disbelievingly, once they're all sitting around the living room. He's not angry, not exactly, but he's baffled and annoyed.

"Are you upset it wasn't you?" Liam asks.

Alex stares. He's not, that's light years from the point, and only Liam would have jumped to that conclusion. "You think my feelings are hurt because you fucked somebody who wasn't me? You've been fucking people who aren't me for ten years." Out of the corner of his eye, Alex can see Paul and Carly exchanging judgmental looks, probably about the ongoing bizarreness of his and Liam's relationship. Like Carly and Paul's relationship is any more normal or sensical.

"Arrangements change and relationships evolve," Liam says. "Also, rules can be different from what they normally are when we're on vacation."

"No they can't!" Alex does not like where this is going. He does not want to have a conversation about whether he and Liam should sleep together. Now or ever.

"Yes they can. We can talk about it," Liam says as if anything that is happening is reasonable.

"I thought we agreed we weren't going to have unscheduled family meetings," Alex says, changing tack.

"Well, we unscheduledly fucked your bartender," Carly says. "So now here we are."

"Okay, yes, see, *that* is the thing we should have talked about," Alex points out, grateful for the rescue. "Because you do not fuck random people in my and Paul's house at home. I didn't know we had to discuss that about houses not at home."

"But this is like a hotel?" Liam says. "Because you don't really live here? And you didn't even decorate this house? And the studio hired housekeeping for you and everything?"

"You know," Carly says with a thoughtful frown. "That seemed way more logical last night when I'd been drinking."

"Aren't you going to have an opinion?" Alex turns to Paul.

"You seem to be doing fine on your own," Paul says. He seems more amused than anything else. "But, yes, definitely with Alex on this one," he says when Alex glares at him.

Alex turns back to Liam. "New rule, okay? Because apparently we need to have this rule. No fucking third parties in shared living spaces without warning or discussion beforehand."

Liam looks over at Carly sheepishly then back at Alex. "Yeah. Okay. Sorry."

♦

Paul expects a rant from Alex when they finally go to bed, but what he gets instead is Alex kissing him as soon as the door is shut. Alex grins fiercely as they shove each other out of their clothes, and Paul can't but help smile back. If Alex wants to fuck instead of complain about Liam, he is happy to oblige, especially when Alex pulls his jeans down roughly and sinks his mouth over his cock.

Once they both come, Alex only bothers to clean them up with the corner of the sheet before rolling onto Paul's chest. Paul expects that he'll fall asleep quickly, but his breathing stays keyed up and he keeps fidgeting.

Paul cards his fingers through Alex's hair and waits for him to speak.

"Did you think I was going to say I was mad it wasn't us?" Alex asks eventually.

Paul doesn't need to ask what he means. "A little bit, yeah."

Alex huffs. "I don't know why any of that had to happen. Not them hooking up with random people, because it's them and that's whatever. I just mean that big thing about it?"

"Nobody was making a big thing about it except you," Paul points out gently. Alex overreacts to things and tends to see domestic process as far more dramatic than it actually is. Alex also isn't using a lot of proper nouns, but Paul gets the gist. "Liam was just trying to have a conversation with you."

"With anyone else that conversation would have taken ninety seconds. With him it's like Robert's Rules of Order." Alex grumbles.

"How the fuck do you know about Robert's Rules of Order?" Paul asks curiously.

Alex lifts his head to stare at him. His eyes are wide in the dim light of the room. "I worked on *The Fourth Estate*. Which you wrote."

"Yeah, not that episode."

Alex buries his face in Paul's chest again. Paul rubs a hand up and down his back. He smiles into the dark when he feels Alex let out a sigh and finally relax against him.

"Hey, so can I talk to you about a thing?" Paul asks after a few quiet minutes have passed.

Alex moans softly. "No more family meetings."

"Not a family meeting," Paul says soothingly. "Just me. Just us."

"Okaaaaay."

"We've talked about finding somebody to sleep with before," Paul starts.

Alex squints at him. "That was never a serious conversation."

"Because you weren't interested in it being an actual thing we might actually do."

"People aren't commodities."

"I agree," Paul says. "And I apologize for the crassness of my phrasing – then and now, but you know what I mean, yes?"

"Yes," Alex says grudgingly.

"Okay. So if you still aren't interested, it doesn't need to be a serious conversation now either. I'm fine either way. But you're younger than me and have had way fewer adventures. You deserve adventures. I don't want you to miss out on them because you're irritated at Liam."

"So you're going to educate me in the ways of threesomes?" Alex sounds amused. "Because we already did that once. Or is this just your excuse?" He pokes Paul fondly in the chest. "Because the first time you met me and, as far as I know, fell for me, I was making out with another guy. So like, clearly, this is a thing for you."

Paul sputters. "No! I mean. Not entirely. Like, okay. A little, sure. But after I broke up with Carly, like, I had a…really random threesome and it was completely amazing. Like, there were dicks *everywhere*."

Alex cracks up and has to muffle his laughter in his pillow so his cackles don't wake the other occupants of the house. "This is how you sell this idea to me," he says when he can finally stop laughing. "We have been together for a decade. *But there were dicks everywhere*."

Paul swats at him lazily. "I'm just saying, no matter how often you make the point that the rest of us are on vacation and you are not, Liam isn't wrong that vacation rules can be different. If that was a thing you wanted to do, doing it here is probably a better choice than doing it back home. And I, as a voice of reason and terrible ideas, would be entirely remiss if I didn't point that out to you."

Alex makes an inarticulate noise into his pillow.

"Also," Paul says, making his voice softer, gentler, as he brushes a thumb along Alex's ear. "I know none of this has been easy for you. Being away from home, and now having all of us in your space. You've been a little off. I can't fix any of that, but I can offer opportunities if you're interested."

"And if I'm totally uninterested?"

Paul shrugs. "We keep each other plenty busy. But I'm just saying, if you want to point out hot Icelandic dudes to me, you know, feel free."

"Can I think about it and also point out hot Icelandic dudes to you without intent?"

"Whatever you want, Alex," Paul says. "It's always been whatever you want."

♦

To Alex's relief no one fucks another bartender, and the rest of the family vacation passes much more like, well, a family vacation. Or at least the way he'd always imagined a family vacation would be. He's never actually been on one. As a kid, there had never been the money. Also his sister had spent a lot of time in juvie. Since then, he's never had the opportunity. Or, really, a functional family with all members present and accounted for.

He's happy to retreat into what passes for domesticity with his friends and his husband and their kids here at the edge of the world. He enjoys dinners with everyone, playing with the girls, and taking hikes with various combinations of people on clear nights when the moon is so bright they can see by it. He and Paul go into town for dinner and groceries, holding hands all the way down the street without worrying about their picture ending up on *TMZ*. Alex doesn't even need his hat here, except for the cold. No one recognizes him or cares on the rare occasions they do. It's the closest thing to normal he's ever felt.

He and Paul are both shamefully grateful, even more than usual, for Carly and Liam's presence that allows them to feel like something other than parents at every second of every day. They fuck every chance they get when they're not on kid-duty. Alex doesn't even feel embarrassed showing up for hair and makeup with his skin dotted with scratches and bruises from Paul's mouth and hands.

♦

The aurora finally appears a couple of days before everyone except Alex is scheduled to return to Los Angeles. Liam grabs Alex's hand and drags him out the door to go see it.

They walk hand-in-hand along the short trail that loops from the house down to the road and back. Liam likes the contact and out here, away from the rest of the world. Alex finds it comforting too. Iceland still feels impossible sometimes – not just the circumstances of being here, and the things Alex gets to do here, but the sheer size and beauty of it. The stars are bright enough that Alex can see the path in front of them, the expression on Liam's face, and even the contours of the landscape as it stretches out into darkness all around them.

The northern lights take up half the sky, a dizzyingly shifting curtain of greens and purples. For the first fifteen minutes Liam is completely silent, which Alex assumes is just about him being overwhelmed with space and color and whatever else is going on sensorially for him. Gradually, he becomes aware that while he may also be doing that, Liam is giving Alex the space to talk if he wants.

Alex squeezes his hand in silent thanks. Liam smiles. Which makes Alex ask, in an attempt to return the kindness, "So tell me. Why Bjarki?" He doesn't necessarily want any more details about Liam's sexual conquests, but talking about his relationships, no matter how temporary, has always been important for Liam. It's a subject Alex is still learning to be generous about.

"He's hot."

"Insufficient answer," Alex says. "I mean, this is the first person you've been with since Victor died…right?"

Liam nods. "Right."

"So why him? Why now?"

"For one, we're a long way from home. It feels easier to do something like that here."

Alex thinks, but does not mention, that that is the exact same logic Paul used to offer him a threesome while in Iceland.

Liam continues. "Two, it's been years since Carly and I did something like that together, and we wanted to finally reconnect in that way. Three, a friendly night with a bartender is an adventure with pretty much no stakes. And four, seriously, he's really hot."

"You know I thought it was low stakes when I started fucking you in D.C.," Alex says carefully. They don't talk about that period of time much. There's no need to; he and Liam have been sure and certain of their place in each other's lives almost as long as he and Paul have. But it seems a valid point to raise. Relationships rarely end in the place one expects them to. Even if they do start in Iceland.

"I know."

"I was kind of wildly wrong."

"I know that too," Liam says. "But Carly and I probably won't ever see Bjarki again. Risk of prolonged attachment removed. Making dubious choices on vacation is one thing, but you still have to be smart about them."

"Paul and I talked about having a threesome," Alex says. "Not with you, I mean," he adds, because he wants to be very specific.

"What inspired that?" Liam asks.

"Apparently Paul thought finding my bartender in the kitchen was inspirational. Also, Iceland, and he agrees with you that vacation rules can be different."

"What did you decide?" Liam bounces on his toes as they walk, fairly bursting at the seams with curiosity.

Alex smiles at his enthusiasm and is relieved he's not volunteering himself. At least not yet. "We probably won't do it now. We probably won't do it here at all. But maybe someday. I get why everyone's into the idea, in the abstract, with whoever. But I look at Paul and anything like that just feels unnecessary."

"It doesn't have to be a necessary thing," Liam points out. "It can just be fun. Or good. Or something you want."

"I know. I just…everyone seems to think that this is totally a normal thing to do. Or at least a normal thing to do when you're famous and a movie star or whatever. And the fact that I *haven't*, makes me feel, I dunno. Like the hick kid from Indiana who still doesn't know what fork to use."

"Threesomes aren't about sophistication," Liam says. "Believe me. Not an indicator."

Alex laughs. "Still. Like. I've never had a boyfriend except Paul."

Liam makes an indignant noise.

"…And you, I guess, or whatever it was we were. The sex I had before Paul, and after Paul, was really kind of faily. Present company excluded!" Alex adds, when Liam makes another noise of protestation. "Okay, present company and Carly."

Liam laughs.

"And maybe that's something I'd want to

change at some point?" Alex says. "Maybe? I guess? But I just don't think it's going to be something we're going to do much. Or ever, maybe. Even if we could. On some level I wish we could. It would make some things so much easier."

"Including the fucked-up thing where you have class angst about your sexual history?"

"Says the rich boy from Brooklyn who's been fucking anyone he's wanted to since he was sixteen."

"That's fair, but my point still stands," Liam says. "I'm glad you're thinking about it. In whatever way is going to be good for you. Even though I'm sad I'm probably not on the list of people you two might fuck."

"Liam!"

"I'm not saying I don't get it, but I still get to have feelings!"

"*Ugh*. Just. Shh and watch the sky."

◆

The morning everyone's due to fly out, Alex wakes up before the alarm and lies there staring at Paul and at Claudia, whose crib they moved into their room for this last night. It's another two months before he gets to be home again, and he knows he can deal with the separation, but goodbyes are always so hard.

Alex makes them all breakfast, with Ali assisting, while the other adults run around getting their last-minute things together.

"Next time you do a project," Ali says, seriously stirring a bowl of eggs with a fork. "Can you go someplace we can see you more than once a year?"

"You'll see me more than once this year," Alex

points out, though he does feel guilty and also miserable.

"It doesn't feel like it. Also you should pick a movie where I can go with you and be something other than a dirty baby Viking."

"Yeah, I'll talk to my agent about that."

"If I get an agent too can she negotiate with yours?" Ali fires back.

Alex cracks up.

At the airport, Liam, Carly, Vic, and Ali wait a little apart from him, Paul, and Claudia. Alex is grateful for the space.

"It completely sucks that you're going to be in New York for upfronts when I get home," Alex says, holding Claudia on his hip and tugging her hat down around her ears.

"What's three days after two months?" Paul asks.

"Three days too long. Let me know when you land," Alex says. The staticky PA that counts for a boarding announcement crackles on.

Paul nods. "Call me tomorrow when you get off work."

"You'll be asleep."

"I don't care." He holds an arm out and Alex, reluctantly, passes Claudia to him. Paul digs his free hand into the back of Alex's hair and kisses him, before he presses their foreheads together.

4

An hour and a half into a meeting in one of the studio's conference rooms, Gemma runs a hand through her hair. She has to restrain herself from grabbing it and screaming in frustration.

Back when Liam first started making noise about *Scism*, Gemma was the one who lured him in to the studio. Since then, she's been the point person trying to coordinate all the moving parts necessary to move *Scism* into production and broadcast. However, the history of vague friendship and personal connections between them that made that possible – and seem like a good idea at the time – is now having the exact opposite impact.

Gemma doesn't get to say yes or no to pilot production or make decisions about money or casting. She's not nearly that high up in the ranks. She's more of a fixer, coaxing all sides towards something that could work and making recommendations.

And she would have recommended calling this whole thing off weeks ago if the project had come from anyone else. But *Scism* is – was – the last project of the legendary Victor Salcido Santillan. Liam is as interested in preserving that legacy as every network is in having one last hit from a now-dead cash cow. No one wants to give up. Jackson, who could conceivably be a voice of reason but is holding onto the project for dear life because that's what writers do, isn't helping matters at all.

At the head of the table sits Minette Lewis. She's

listening to Liam with an expression that does not hide her rapidly dwindling patience for this project or indeed anything involving Liam Campbell and his dead boyfriend's last work. Gemma is sure that if it were up to Minette this whole clusterfuck would have been killed two meetings ago. The network wants this to happen, but they've all been trying to make this work for months and they're running out of not just patience, but chances. And if they do, Victor's last story, and maybe their jobs, are done for.

"All right." Minette cuts Liam off and folds her hands on the table; her pale lavender polish contrasts with the dark copper of her skin. Between her prim demeanor and the edge in her voice, Liam actually seems to be listening. "I recognize that this project was always going to be a challenge and that, if Victor were still alive, we'd probably have passed by now and asked what else he had. Alas, he's dead, and we're sort of into that. So that's in your favor. But it, you, us, this *thing* – is a mess. At this point we have one script that's alternate history, another that's vaguely sci-fi futuristic, and yet another that's so fictionalized no one could possibly think it was the Vatican at all or, for that matter, figure out what the fuck it's about. And none of them are good. I mean, they're fine, Jackson, you're great and you wrote what we told you to write beautifully, but none of them work."

"The sci-fi-y one had some good stuff," Liam says defensively, shuffling through his copy of it.

"It had the totally-not-Vatican dealing with the implications of life on other planets," Gemma points out. "We are not interested in doing a reboot of *Contact* and do I need remind you what a mess the *His Dark Materials* movie was?"

Gemma's job is to play good cop to Minette's bad cop. And that means playing out her part in the plan that she and Minette came up with last night.

"The problem," Gemma says, "is that you're trying to do *Vatican*-lite. And the scripts aren't working because they're so watered down none of us give a shit about them. I don't give a shit about them. Victor definitely wouldn't give a shit about them. And Liam, for all your protests, I don't think you give a shit about them either."

"This isn't an act of kindness, and the business is not your friend," Minette says. "Right now, I'm not even sure the business is my friend, but you need to stop giving us good enough because it isn't."

"In any other situation, this would be a thanks-but-no-thanks meeting," Gemma says to Liam softly.

"What do you need me to do?" Liam asks. He's clearly both annoyed and desperate. It's not a good look, and Gemma knows it's the sort of thing that makes Minette want to strangle people in general and most especially Liam in particular.

"We need you to let Jackson write an angry, fucked-up show that's going to offend everyone," Minette says. "And then we fish or cut bait."

♦

After the meeting, Gemma goes to lunch with Minette at their favorite place. They can usually find parking there, which is a huge plus, and the tacos are amazing.

"I know he's your friend, but he is the most stubborn, intolerable...." Minette trails off as they get their food from the counter and settle into a too-tiny table in the corner.

Gemma doesn't need to ask who she's talking about. "I don't disagree."

"You know, being trans? Super fine. I mean, we all live in this culture, which can be a nightmare, but I'm fine. This life is not angsty for me. Being straight though? Ugggggggh. Why do I have to be attracted to men? Boys like him mess me up." Minette takes a deep breath and visibly forces herself to stop tugging on the finger coils by her left ear. "Sorry, but he is working my last nerve and being attractive while he does it. I can't with any of it."

Gemma chuckles because she understands far too well. "I was living with Alex while having a crush on Liam in the first season of *Fourth*. Believe me, no apology needed."

"And one more thing, if we ever wind up with another dead boyfriend project – his or anybody else's – I'm promoting you so I never have to go to the meetings. Of all the stupid fucking reasons to have to be nice to someone."

"It really fucked him up," Gemma says. The statement doesn't negate Minette's very legitimate complaints, but she feels like she has to say something. There's Liam who is annoying and then there's Liam who is struggling. She was only on the periphery for that, but even she knows how much Victor's death had upset everyone who had been close to him. "I mean, people dying is sad."

Minette ignores her. "Victor wasn't even nice! I realize I didn't know him, but I am accurately describing a consensus opinion here."

"I don't think Liam would disagree with you," Gemma says.

"And yet here we are." Minette gestures with her drink.

"Yep."

"Are they going to get it right this time?" Minette asks.

"Would you mind so much if they didn't?" Some days, like today, Gemma's not even sure which side she would come down on.

"I'm a hero if we can make this thing work," Minette says. "And if we can't, and they con some other network into it? My career could take far better turns."

"Do you think that could actually happen?" Gemma asks. She figures if Liam and Jackson can't make this work here, they sure aren't going to make it work anywhere else.

"Depends how much it's worth to whoever's next on their list to fuck us up."

Gemma moans. If she and Minette and who they represent say no, it'll increase *Scism's* value, but Liam's too naive to realize that. Gemma hopes she isn't going to have to be the one to explain it to him.

"Mmmmhmmm." Minette hums in agreement.

"To answer your question, I think they'll make it work," Gemma says. "The question is whether we'll have shoved them out a window first."

"How have you not done that already? Years ago?" Minette asks.

"Liam really is very sweet. At least, usually, and when he's not coping with his dead boyfriend's project. Just be glad you don't have Alex involved in this mess. You think Liam's insufferable because he's in love with Victor. Alex *hated* Victor and was eight hundred times worse."

"And yet you still want to attach him to this."

Gemma takes a sip of water. Getting Alex involved in this project would be a career coup of her very own. If she can just get it to work. And if she can stay on speaking terms with him long enough to make it happen.

"He's J. Alex Cook," she finally says. "Liam adores him. Audiences like to watch him. And, whether he knows it or not, he owes me."

"Why?" Minette leans forward, curious.

"Because Alex would have never moved to L.A. without me."

Minette tips her head to the side slightly. "Tell me more."

"I got us our – his – first apartment. I taught him how to use a fucking bank account. I rented his also-successful husband's house when they wanted to move in together and math was hard. And because when you become famous, and you leave your friends behind, that's what you do. You owe people." Gemma doesn't hold a grudge. Not exactly. Her feelings are too fraught and the wounds of Alex's cruelty, if only by omission, are too deep. She doesn't have a grudge. She has rage.

"But you're still friends," Minette asked, her eyes narrowing with caution.

"Sure," she says. "Want to see how much?" Gemma is aware she probably sounds like she's offering the worst sort of Hollywood dare to Minette. But she has no intention of popping out her phone, calling up Alex and handing the phone over to her dining companion. That would be L.A. newbie bragging and Gemma is lightyears beyond that sort of thing as she finally settles into her niche in this company town's ecosystem.

"Do I?"

"He's having a welcome back barbecue next month, assuming he escapes Iceland without falling off a cliff," Gemma says. "Want to be my plus-one?"

◆

Paul's had many offices over the years, from the cramped desk shoved in the corner of a cube farm as Victor's writing assistant to his current digs: an office all to himself in the suite his production company rents. The *Fourth Estate* offices are long gone, as are the *Winsome, AZ* ones. He's not sure this latest move is his favorite. The elevator in this building doesn't always work, the fluorescent lights are as bright and terrible as fluorescent lights always are, and the walls are a disconcerting shade of what Olivia, his partner in writing and all things business, declared as "eggnog gone bad." But there's phone lines and internet and a whiteboard, so Paul really has everything he needs to do the work of writing their next show.

However, right now, Paul really doesn't want to be here working on script ideas with Olivia. Sarah, his sister and Claudia's biological mother, is visiting and he just wants to get home and hang out with everyone. Alex being in Iceland for so long has been the perfect opportunity to have Sarah visit, both to lend a hand with the kids and to bond more with the girls.

Ever since Claudia's birth Paul's been much better at work-life balance. Some of that has come from necessity; he quickly discovered that it's impossible to work 20-hour days with a colicky infant… or any infant at all. But Paul also feels more settled. He loves his job, his husband, and his daughter. And the support systems they've built with Carly and Liam have kept him on an even keel and away from the workaholic tendencies being alone and insecure brings out in him.

When Paul first suggested they co-parent their kids in the mess after Victor died, before Vic was born, and before Alex and Paul had even agreed to have a baby, he had been desperate. But the arrangement works and has given them all a chance to have adult social lives and jobs and occasional nights off from childcare. They're building an actual family that's something more than when they were two couples contemplating how and whether children fit into their lives at all. It's pretty fucking awesome.

In fact, in order to protect their arrangement – and themselves – they're considering making it legal. Thanks to the miracles of progressive California family law, children have been granted the legal right to more than two parents in situations that are similar, if not identical, to their own. There's no real reason their situation should be excluded; it's just going to take lawyers and time to figure out.

Paul tries his best to put aside thoughts of Alex and his kids and focus on the blank Word document open on his laptop in front of him. He fails. Instead, he zones out with thoughts of what Alex is doing in Iceland right now – sleeping, probably – until Olivia throws a whiteboard marker at him. Again.

"Oi," she says. "Pay attention."

"Do I have to?"

Olivia chucks another marker at him. "We can brainstorm for our next big hit or we can go over the plan for upfronts again."

"Oh God, I don't even want to think about that." This will be the first time Paul is going to upfronts since *Winsome* ended two years ago, and the first time Olivia will be going with him as co-creator for *Plague*. "No one's going to want to talk to us anyway. We're not the talent," Paul points out, in an effort to calm his own anxiety.

"Reassuring," Olivia deadpans.

"Our people are great. You just have to trust them," Paul says. "They know what to do."

"Thank God for that," Olivia says. "'Cause you're the one who thought combat dolphins were a good idea."

"Combat dolphins were an *amazing* idea."

"They really weren't, they're still really not, and I'm going to be grateful forever that's not the thing we have to sell in New York."

"I can't believe I'm going to be in New York for this shit when Alex comes back from Iceland." It's the worst part of the whole miserable thing.

"Yes, you've mentioned. Eight times already today."

"I'm restraining myself," Paul replies.

"I can tell."

♦

Paul wishes Alex was with him when he pulls onto their street.

At least Alex being gone does not, as in years past, mean Paul has to go home and be alone. Once he feeds an insistent, if rather old and creaky, Todd he cuts through their neighbor's backyard to Carly and Liam's house.

There he finds Carly on the back deck on a lounge chair with a gurgling Claudia crawling up her chest trying to dig her hands into her hair. Vic is clomping around the deck in a pair of Liam's shoes and giggling whenever she trips. Sarah is at the patio table next to Ali, who's frowning over her math homework.

Paul climbs the steps up to the deck. Vic notices him first and toddles over to him, waving her arms to be picked up.

He makes sure the gate at the top of the steps is locked behind him before he obliges, making sure Liam's shoes stay on the deck. Holding the toddler on one hip, he gives Sarah a one-armed hug hello and leans down to kiss Carly on the cheek.

"How were the munchkins today?" he asks.

"No complaints here," Carly says, setting Claudia down on the deck and levering herself to sit upright. "Although I won't mind handing them over to you and getting work done tonight. This one's given up afternoon naps." She taps Vic's bare foot.

Vic tucks her head against Paul's shoulder and laughs. Her curly dark hair, so much like Liam's, catches in Paul's beard.

"I'd noticed that. At least it's not just when she's at our place."

"Yeah, not so much."

"Where's Liam?" Paul asks, looking around.

"Visiting Victor," Carly says.

Paul nods. Sometimes when Carly says that it takes him a moment to remember that she means Liam is at Victor's grave, not Victor's house for an overnight. That mistake happens less frequently these days, but Paul isn't sure it will ever stop entirely.

◆

Liam turns his Prius onto the 101 and frowns at the traffic, not because it's any worse than usual, but because it's always terrible. He spends more time than is strictly reasonable being pissed off at Victor for being buried in a part of town he never used to have to go to except to meet with his financial advisor.

Now he tries to visit about once a month. He parks and walks across the plaza in front of the Cathedral of Our Lady of the Angels with its constellations cut into the concrete. He and Victor used to spend hours discussing those stars as everything from industry metaphor to snide enticement to the non-religious. Victor had found it particularly brilliant that they were underfoot.

The descent down into the mausoleum, from bright daylight to sudden dark to pleasant LED illumination had been unnerving when Liam first started coming here. But now the trek down the three flights of stairs are a routine like any other. The rituals Victor enforced on him in life had always, at least a little bit, been about discomfort and pushing Liam's limits. There's no reason to expect him to be any different in death.

Liam still wishes it were a little darker down here.

He passes Gregory Peck – he loves pointing him out whenever anyone comes with him – and rounds a corner to the hallway where Victor is. Some of the niches have flowers in front of them, but Liam never brings any for Victor. It would only piss him off; most people buy cheap flowers for the dead. They're ugly, and they ruin the lines. Or at least so Victor used to tell him.

Victor's niche is in a little alcove, tucked away

and out of sight from the corridor. Liam always wonders if Victor chose this spot on purpose, because it means Liam can be here, at his feet, and not be observed by casual passers-by. He sits, as he always does, with his back to the stone carved with Victor's name and the dates of his birth and death.

In a quiet voice that won't carry too far he tells Victor about the meeting, about the one-last-chance *Scism* is getting.

"I finally told them they could write angry and fucked up," Liam tells him quietly. "It's going to piss people off." He tips his head up gently so that he can feel the cold stone pressing at the back of his skull. "I figured you'd be okay with that. You never minded pissing people off yourself. But then, I was never sure why it was so much easier for me to love you than it was for anybody else."

5

Despite how ready he is to be home, by Alex's last day of filming he's melancholy at the prospect of leaving. Iceland has been a glorious adventure and is a beautiful country. In thirty-six hours he's going to be back in L.A. After so long away, that feels hard to believe.

There's a party that night at the bar in town with all the cast and crew. Alex stays as late as possible, hugging people and laughing and exchanging contact information as if he's a normal guy who can have friends just like anyone else. He knows none of these people will contact him first. It's all on him, and while that should make it easier, in his head it makes it harder.

Even though he feels awkward about it at first, he makes sure to hang out at the bar with Bjarki for part of the night. They've been friendly while Alex has been here, and he'll miss him. Both despite and because Bjarki was, absurdly, in his kitchen at five in the morning after having had a threesome with Carly and Liam.

The sky is just starting to fade from black to gray by the time Alex drives back to his house to pick up his bags. He'd meant to get a few hours of sleep before leaving for his flight, but the house feels far too empty and lonely now to want to stay longer than necessary. He can doze at the airport.

From his front door Alex takes one last picture of the mountains and the sea, glimmering with deep blues and an unearthly purple in the predawn light. He sends it to Paul, Liam, and his mother, along with a text: *Goodbye to the end of the world.* His text to Carly is a bit more prosaic; she's never really had time for his melodrama.

◆

A homecoming without Paul is, as far as Alex is concerned, not a homecoming. Alex could very well have flown into New York and met him there at upfronts. But he wants to see his kids, and has no desire to be out in public with Paul for the hell that is that industry dog and pony show. He also had no desire to sit alone in a hotel room for three days while Paul works and the girls are back in L.A. There's no good solution to the problem, and Alex considers the whole mess to be another bucket of reasons to be irritated at their jobs they mostly love and are definitely good at.

Still, walking into an empty house – he'll pick up Claudia from Liam and Carly's as soon as he drops off his bags – makes him wonder if he shouldn't have opted for New York after all. At least Todd is here, winding around Alex's ankles and demanding attention while Alex lugs his suitcase upstairs.

On Alex's pillow is a note. *I adore you*, it says, with Paul's name scrawled underneath.

◆

The next day for Alex is one of catching up on messages from his manager Margaret, his agent Vanessa, and other important people he should get back in touch with. He doesn't have to be anywhere but at Paul's desk in his basement office with Claudia in the playpen next to him. Still, the effort of filling in his schedule and composing cogent replies to emails is draining.

At six, carrying Claudia, he walks over to Liam and Carly's house to pick up Vic and Ali. He's exhausted, but he's missed his other kids desperately. And Carly and Liam definitely deserve a break.

Liam, to Alex's complete unsurprise, takes Claudia from him, kisses him hello, and invites him to stay for dinner. "And the whole night if you want. I mean, we have a guest room," he says.

"Thanks and all, but that would defeat the purpose of me having the girls tonight. Besides, I am aware of your guest room," Alex says drily. "I have slept in your guest room."

"Not in *ages*," Liam says sadly.

"Because I was in Iceland. What even is this? Are you pining?" Alex asks. "I'm right here."

"You were gone a long time," Liam points out. "And you're going back to your place now."

Liam's sad eyes mean he's definitely pining. Alex isn't sure how he manages to do that. The ways Liam loves are deep and multifaceted. Alex is fine with that but he's still far from understanding it. Why should Liam care if he's asleep under this roof or his own down the street?

"I spent all that time in Iceland alone in a house," Alex says. "I love you and I'm happy with the kids but I cannot cope with people yet. Or maybe ever." Alex double-checks to make sure there are enough of Vic's pacifiers in the bag Liam gives him to keep her for the night. There are some at home, too, but her ability to lose them is legion, and there is only one kind she will consent to use.

"Alex," Ali says from where she's sitting on the

stairs, waiting with an air of immense patience while the babies are readied for transit.

"Yeah?"

"How old will I be when I stop being a kid you like and start being a people you don't like?"

Alex wishes Hollywood didn't produce such astute children. But neither that, nor his introversion, is Ali's fault. "I'm always going to like you," he says firmly.

"How do you know?" Ali asks. "You've never had a kid before."

"When did she get so terrifying?" Alex asks Liam not quietly enough.

"While you were in Iceland," Ali says.

♦

The next afternoon at his and Paul's house Alex is trying to convince Claudia to take her nap. Vic, in her own crib in the same room, seems ready to sleep but fusses every time Claudia does, which isn't making things easier. And then Alex's phone rings, which upsets the whole process. He needs to remember to start silencing it when he's trying to get the girls to sleep. L.A. crises are important, but naptime is a vital necessity.

He gives up on trying to settle Claudia and picks her up, holding her on one hip and using his other hand to clumsily answer the phone. Behind him, Vic grumbles with discontent.

"Hello, stranger," Gemma says when Alex answers.

"Hey."

"How was Iceland?"

"Cold." To be honest, Alex is more interested in Claudia, who is now fussing more loudly, than in putting together words for an adult conversation.

"Do email and video chats not work there?"

"What?"

Gemma sighs. "Never mind. I have a favor to call in."

"Ah?" Alex asks vaguely. Claudia is now lunging for the lamp on the dresser, in an apparent bid to gnaw on the lampshade.

"Yes. You know Minette Lewis?"

"We've met," Alex says. "Liam complains about her belief or lack thereof in Victor's work. Constantly."

Gemma gives a short sigh. "I want you to let me bring her to your welcome home barbecue."

Alex still isn't entirely on board with the welcome home barbecue idea in general, but he suspects it's not really up to him. Random guests he doesn't know very well, and whom Liam does not play well with, do not make him more enthused.

"Okayyy," Alex says slowly. "Why?"

"Because this thing between her and Liam is making my life unbearable."

"Define 'thing,'" Alex says cautiously. He's not sure he wants to know.

Gemma hesitates. "They're on the same side but think they're not. And every time either of them gets me alone, they're talking about the other. It's a giant case of them both protesting too much. I just want this show to work well enough I don't have to think about it, or them, all the time."

"So you want to throw them together for an afternoon of cooked meat, beer, and babies."

"I think Liam would relax around her if they met somewhere that wasn't around a conference table. And I think it would help if she saw the side of him we all actually like."

Alex makes an unkind noise. "Why wouldn't introducing Minette to our dysfunctional group of family and friends make the situation worse?"

"None of us are as bad – or unique – as you think. We never have been. And Minette likes me," Gemma says. "I need her to like Liam, or at least have a screaming match with him and get it all over and done with. Which isn't going to happen if they never see each other outside of a meeting room. Now, Alex, God of Chaos, make up, just a little, for not calling or writing for the last four months and let me bring your ex-boyfriend's arch rival to your welcome-home cookout."

♦

The day Paul is scheduled to get home from New York, Alex has to face one of his greatest rounds of fame horror yet. He's done photoshoots before and knows the drill. That's nothing new. But he's never done a photoshoot like this.

It's for *GQ* and for a feature all about him. This is totally different than being part of an Emmys preview or a focus piece on *Fourth*. And while people have done solo profiles about Alex before, they've never been in a publication this big or with an angle like this.

This time, the whole piece is predicated on the idea of him having become a big-budget movie star. The prospect feels remote even as it is what's happening in his life.

Most ridiculously, there's a videographer documenting the photoshoot process for some sort of web special. Alex doesn't know when stuff like this became the done thing, but everyone has assured him this is normal. Normal, he thinks bitterly, is a moving target. In this situation, with a camera always rolling, even when Alex is off he'll be on. He can't decide how much he should be performing versus how much he should let this all be as intrusive as it seems. The whole thing is giving him a headache.

At least having the videographer there lets him get the interview portion out of the way at the same time as the photoshoot, which he hopes will let him keep being a person instead of a doll. It doesn't work. The questions – about his diet, his workout routine, the physical work of the movie – are all about his body in a way he has rarely engaged with in his own head and never engaged with in public. If Alex has been a sex symbol, he's never been the pinup-model sort. Alex knows he's attractive to the public generally, but he's never been a part of the mainstream, heterosexual fitness cult. Until now. Because of a body he doesn't even think of as his own. He wants to go back to his smaller, lither self as soon as he damn can.

Which means he is, absurdly, chatting on the record with the interviewer about yoga and the ballet that's going to replace the weight training sessions he was doing before he left L.A. Paul walks in while they're in the middle of that. Judging by the T-shirt, jeans and a look that suggests he hasn't slept in a couple days, he's come straight to the shoot from the plane.

This was always the plan, but Alex is unexpectedly overwhelmed. He hasn't seen Paul in months. For a moment – just a moment – Alex loses the thread of the answer he was giving.

Paul smiles at him, his eyes so warm and

intense they take Alex's breath away. Paul's gaze sweeps over him like he's so glad Alex is there and like he can't stand not to put his hands on Alex right the fuck now. All Alex wants is to run to him.

But this is work, and Alex can't. Also the fucking video camera is still rolling and they are very careful about what and how they are together in public. Paul's arrival also means the journalist starts asking prying questions about their family. Alex is grateful when Paul shuts the guy down efficiently and effectively. He's never needed Paul to protect him in public, and this isn't even that, but Alex's ability to cope with intrusive questions is lower than normal. Knowing he has someone who can do the hard work with him feels good.

The photographer waves a hand at Paul. "Hey, do you want to get him in here too?" he asks.

Alex looks over his shoulder at Paul and tries not to be too eager when he shrugs. They're essentially done. The magazine won't use anything this unscheduled anyway, especially not that features Paul wearing nothing that can even be called airplane chic.

"Sure," Alex says.

They banter with each other and with the journalist and the photographer. They're used to performing this back-and-forth from the various carpets they've done together, but they're rarely this overtly flirty. Normally Alex has more self-control, but if he can't drag Paul off to fuck at least he can do this. As is his habit whenever possible, Alex tucks himself closer and closer against Paul as they talk. When Paul puts an arm around him, he feels as good and safe as he has in months.

Everything gets so casual that Alex eventually

gives in and wraps his arms around Paul's neck. This way he can just lean into him and disappear as best he can. It takes him a moment to realize the sound of the camera shutter – virtual, since it's all digital, but photographers and models still like it for timing purposes – isn't in his head from shooting all day. The photographer is still taking pictures.

Alex rocks side to side with Paul and slowly pivots them until he's facing the camera. Then he peers over Paul's shoulder and shows the photographer all his wrath.

The man startles slightly and lowers the camera, but not before taking the shot.

Alex grins to himself. That, and what he hopes, in spite of it all, are sweet pictures, are really all he needs.

◆

Dinner that night is at Carly and Liam's. Alex would prefer to go back to his and Paul's house and climb straight into bed with his husband, but with family obligations it's not to be. Still, dinner with four adults makes managing three kids easier. It's even pleasant after the meal is over and the kitchen's been cleaned. Everyone goes out to the back deck, and Alex can curl up next to Paul on the swing and be quiet while the kids play and conversation drifts around him.

He lifts his head, though, when Liam casually mentions that he talked to their joint next-door neighbor about wanting to be the first to know if and when they put their house on the market.

"What the hell?" Alex demands. He's not sure how amused – or horrified – he should be.

"I was just asking," Liam says.

"Yes, but why?" Alex asks. "Also I thought we had rules. No traumatizing the neighbors."

"They weren't traumatized," Liam says.

"You don't know that," Alex protests. "You were either inappropriately proactive or extremely weird and, you know, *you*."

"Oh," Liam says, considering. "Just inappropriately proactive. I promise. We were talking about real estate in New York versus in California and the challenges of raising kids on the opposite coast from your family. What?" Liam says at the look Alex is giving him. "Their grandkids live in Massachusetts."

"Okayyy," Alex says slowly. He didn't know their neighbors even had grandchildren. And while he might not know enough about the people who live between them, Liam definitely knows too much.

"Anyway," Liam. "Paul and I were talking –"

"Thanks, bring me into this," Paul mutters when Alex turns his head to look dubiously at Paul as well.

"– And we thought it might be awesome to buy the house between us. If it ever came available."

"For joint production offices," Paul puts in hastily. Alex is relieved. At least someone here knows that clarification is necessary. "Since Liam's doing development now, and Olivia and I can always use the space."

"I've got dibs on the third floor," Carly says from her lounger. "Studio space!"

"Wait wait wait," Alex says. "Wanting space for work is one thing, but why are you going all *Sister Wives* on me?" He's not angry, just perpetually baffled by everyone else's choices.

"Is that show even still on? Liam asks.

"Does it matter?"

"No, probably not. But the house is a valid issue."

"Oh my God, Liam," Alex says again. He flops back against Paul and wriggles his shoulders until Paul gets the hint and wraps his arms around him.

"It's just a thing we've been talking about," Liam says.

Alex tips his head back on Paul's shoulder and gives him an exasperated upside-down look. Paul gives him a smile of commiseration and turns his head so he can kiss Alex's temple.

"You know, Liam, I married Paul. Not you and Carly," Alex says.

"But –"

"That was not a statement about marriage or poly or *anything*. That was a statement of, apparently I can never leave you alone again. Now tell me more about your terrible idea for turning our neighbors' house into your incestuous emporium of creativity."

◆

Once they're home and get Claudia settled down to sleep, Alex drags himself into their room and flops face-first into his pillow.

"Are you okay?" Paul sits down on the bed next to him.

Alex raises his head to squint at him and brushes his hair out of his eyes.

"I'm tired. I'm horny. I'm so glad to be home. I'm so glad *you're* home. But mostly, I would like to not talk about anything involving our friends who we are way too close to or about the neighbor's house that is not actually for sale. So you should stop worrying at it. Any of it. And shhhhhh."

"Shhhhh?" Paul wants to point out that Alex is being overly dramatic about family matters but suspects this is not the time.

"Just be quiet with me. I haven't had this in months."

"Had what?"

Alex rolls his eyes. "You. Us. Our baby. Our house and the creepy canyon winds. Let me enjoy it."

Paul scoots closer and Alex can see him smile in the dark. "It's like you never left."

Glad as Alex says he is for the quiet, he can't seem to lie still himself. He shifts restlessly again and again until Paul drowsily asks him if he's okay.

Alex sighs and rolls his head over to look at him. "Re-entry is hard. It turns out doing re-entry when I have to deal with Carly and Liam and the kids, too, is *really* hard. Also I hate meetings. And interviews. And I know you keep saying a welcome-home party is a good idea but I really don't want to go. I can't believe you talked me into that."

"It is a good idea." Paul keeps his voice quiet. "I know you're happy doing your introvert thing, and I know family can be hard for you, but you let people drift. And you have so few people in your life you actually like, you shouldn't let them go."

"I know, I know. You've said," Alex huffs. "I also hate photoshoots."

"You looked hot," Paul says.

"Are you coming onto me after I just bitched about photoshoots?"

Paul slides a hand up under Alex's T-shirt. "Yes?"

Alex laughs. "Seriously?"

"It's been two months. I missed you."

"Missed you too." Alex shifts onto his side to kiss Paul.

When Paul rolls them over, though, and grabs the hem of Alex's shirt to pull it off, Alex stops him with a hand to the center of his chest.

Paul sits back, uncertain, but takes it as a good sign when Alex takes the shirt off himself and practically tackles Paul to the mattress.

Whatever Alex has in mind, though, he seems in no rush to actually get to it. After he tosses the rest of their clothes on the floor, Alex spends ages running his hands, then his mouth, all over Paul's body.

Paul jumps when Alex scrapes his teeth over his nipple, which makes Alex grin wickedly while he licks a stripe across Paul's chest to the other. Apparently the streak from Iceland, of Alex preferring to do rather than be done too, is continuing. Which Paul has no complaints about. It's breathtaking to watch him skim his fingertips over Paul's hips and down between his cheeks, and Paul can't help but groan when Alex finally sinks his mouth over him.

He's reminded of the very first time they hooked up. That Alex had been twenty, overwhelmed, and terrified. Alex has grown so much more confident in sex over the last decade and change, but there's a tentativeness to everything he's doing now that Paul finds unhelpfully appealing. Also very strange.

Paul asks about it afterward, when Alex is

sprawled on Paul's chest, his hair loose and messy on his shoulders.

All Alex says, though, is, "Apparently the only thing worse than being the twink, is not being the twink anymore."

6

This party, as far as Alex can tell, is going to be a complete clusterfuck. For reasons he's still unclear on, Gemma is bringing Minette who Liam is constantly at odds with but desperately needs. Darcy and Jackson are not dating each other at the moment, but are both coming – supposedly because of their affection for Alex, but probably just to continue their game of social chicken until they get back together…again.

Raphael, Alex's friend since their days together on *The Fourth Estate*, and Raph's wife Irina are bringing their kids. In theory, that's fine and will give Ali something to do other than try to be a miniature adult. But Alex can't deny that he's somewhat terrified by sophisticated Hollywood children when they move in packs. At least Ellen, one of Victor's directors who now works regularly with Paul, and her wife Claire won't be a source of drama. And Olivia is fine as long as she and Paul don't start talking about the damn combat dolphins again.

Paul doesn't let him hide out on the deck with the grill. Alex finds this tragic, even if he's supposed to be cutting back on his all-meat-all-the-time awesome Viking diet of carnivorous excess.

"Answer the door, you know how to do that," Paul tells him, and steers him back inside after he sneaks out to light the grill anyway.

Playing host at a party thrown in his honor strikes Alex as both exhausting and unfair. He can't help but feel like a 1950s housewife as he grins and ushers people inside to enjoy the event that's not exactly making him glad to be home.

When Gemma shows up with Minette, Alex has no idea what to do. He agreed to her being Gemma's plus-one, but now that she's really here, he's worried about Liam. Maybe he should have warned him. From both Gemma's and Liam's stories, whatever's going to happen with them stands a good chance of being a disaster.

But Alex has spent a lot of his professional life on carpets and schmoozing people. He gives his most charming smile, compliments Minette's dress and Gemma's hair, and steps back to let them in.

Gemma gives him a hug and whispers in his ear. "We're going to talk. Later. Be nice now." She pulls back and smiles broadly.

"What'd I do?" he asks with wide-eyed innocence. He appreciates being warned that he's going to get scolded. And she's definitely earned the right.

Gemma gives him a disparaging, if amused, look and sweeps past him, Minette at her shoulder.

♦

It's not a high-stakes room, but it's also not that easy. While she and Gemma are friends, and Minette's had professional contact with a large number of people here – thankfully not just regarding *Scism* – her presence here is awkward. She has no good reason to be here. Sure, the reconnaissance is interesting, but she could easily give away as much as she's gaining in the endless game of power plays that is life in L.A.

And then Liam arrives with his wife Carly and their two daughters.

Alex greets them at the door too. From over Gemma's shoulder Minette sees Liam kiss Alex hello – on the mouth. She knows that Liam and Carly are poly and that Liam and Alex are friends – *everyone* in Hollywood knows Liam Campbell and J. Alex Cook are friends – but she doesn't know what that's about. The public display of affection or whatever it is doesn't help Minette reconcile the mess Liam is in meetings with the charming media darling he is when he's in front of the camera.

She looks away hastily as Liam comes tromping into the kitchen bouncing his baby on his hip. Minette remembers her name is Victoria and realizes with a start that she must be named after Victor. That's so fucked up Minette doesn't even know where to start judging his choices. No child should be saddled with that man's legacy.

Minette watches Liam as he works the room, saying hello to people with a systematic enthusiasm, although all she gets is a polite nod and not the gregarious embrace everyone else does. Which is completely fair. Minette doesn't know what she'd do with that much physical contact with him.

Liam, Victoria still on his hip, gives Paul a one-armed hug and fist-bumps him. The problem with Liam, she decides, is not that Liam can't be charming or confident when he wants to be. The problem is that he does not always *want* to be. The Liam Campbell who eventually sprawls out on the floor while Victoria and Alex and Paul's baby crawl all over him may not be a suave adult, but he sure looks like an improvement from the guy she's been trapped in so many shitty meetings with.

◆

"Is everybody here?" Alex after Darcy finally arrives. Maybe if he's done with door duty, he can go back to skulking out on the deck with the dead meat.

Paul begins to count on his fingers. "Victor's dead, we all hate Mark..."

Alex stares at him. "Please don't do Liam's list thing."

"You asked!"

Alex turns to Liam, who's drifted over to him. "You need to stop hanging out with Paul."

Liam blinks at him. "Why?"

"Because my husband is now making creepy lists the same way you make them and it's annoying."

"I'm not creepy!" Liam protests.

"Wedding ring from a dead guy," Alex says flatly and walks away. He and Liam have both learned to find humor in the darkness.

Paul will probably just chase him back into the house, again, if he tries to sneak away, so he steers towards Gemma instead. She's pouring herself a drink. Minette, her own beverage already in hand, stands next to her surveying the room with an air of calm self-possession. He is reminded, disconcertingly, of Victor.

"What are you running away from?" Minette asks as if it's perfectly reasonable to assume he might tell her.

"You want a list?" Apparently lists are a theme today.

"I'm not sure. Do I?"

"Well," he says, pursing his lips. "Liam is weird,

and my husband is oblivious to things that are weird, the children are terrifying –"

"The children *are* terrifying," Gemma concurs. "Is Ali still determined to continue the Campbell acting legacy?"

"That slowed down once we made the rule she had to finish her homework every day before she could ask to be in a movie. But yes. And for some reason we're having a welcome-home barbecue for me when I'm not supposed to eat steak and whose idea what that?"

"Whose idea *was* that?" Gemma asks incredulously. "Also why can't you eat steak? You're from Indiana. Aren't you like made of steak?"

"I'm on a diet," Alex says glumly.

"You and everyone else in L.A.," Minette puts in. "I'd tell you not to fall for it, but I know the reality we're living in."

Alex decides he likes Minette. Whatever Liam's issues are with her, she sees the world clearly, and that's worth a lot.

"Seriously. L.A. sucks. We've been on diets since we moved here," Gemma says.

"Except Sunday nights with HBO."

"Except that," Gemma says. For a moment it feels like what life was like when they lived together in a shitty apartment. "But you look great," she says, squeezing his shoulder for affect. "Please don't tell me this is all starvation and protein shakes."

Alex moans softly. "I have to de-Viking."

Minette laughs aloud. Gemma puts a hand over her mouth and starts giggling.

"I hate you." Alex says even though he's smiling.

He feels terrible that it's probably the kindest thing he's said to Gemma in a while, but he has never had any idea how to fix the fallout from the massive divergence in their paths. He used to think that her waiting around for him to do it was desperate. Now, he mostly knows it's an indictment. That she's working with Liam on dead Victor's show just makes the situation even more impossible.

◆

Once dinner is underway, all of the adults, plus Vic and Claudia in their high chairs, are seated around the big table in the dining room. The other children are at a card table in the kitchen, totally happy to be the cool kids and not deal with the boring adults talking about boring adult things.

While Alex is still not thrilled about this entire gathering, at least now that there's food happening he can content himself with being quiet as he listens to other people's conversations. He may not enjoy interacting with people en masse, but they are interesting in the abstract, especially when they're willing to let him be. A couple of seats down from him, Jackson and Liam are discussing the latest redraft of the *Scism* pilot while they give Minette, who's seated across from them, cautious glances.

Alex frowns at his very large salad and his very small piece of barely cooked but exceptionally charred meat. He knows *Scism* is desperately important to Liam. He's still completely relieved Paul has nothing to do with it. It is a great concept, but it's clearly going to be a long and peculiar road that will likely end in controversy and possibly protests outside the studio. People are into protests these days.

Paul and Olivia are riffing on awesome ideas for horrible diseases to inflict on their *Plague* characters when Alex's phone rings. It's the worst habit of modern life that all of them always have their phones no matter where they are. He frowns at an Indianapolis number he doesn't otherwise recognize and pushes the call to voicemail. It's likely a misdial, considering he's still, absurdly, carrying an Indiana number.

It rings again. Alex wonders what the chances are that his mother has a new number versus some catastrophe he can't even imagine. He quashes the urge to stick his head into the kitchen to check to make sure the kids are all okay.

As the phone starts ringing a third time, Alex excuses himself from the table and hits answer.

◆

Paul doesn't think too much about it when Alex goes outside to take a phone call. When twenty minutes pass without him coming back, though, he starts to worry. As much as Alex hasn't wanted to be at this party, he'd surely keep any conversation short unless it was urgent. Considering the group they have assembled here, Paul has a hard time imagining what the issue could be. He lets another five minutes pass, then goes to check on him.

He finds Alex on the lower level of the deck. He's no longer on the phone but is clutching it as he stares out at their pool.

Paul knows that look, knows he should wait for Alex to speak first, but Alex doesn't even seem to be aware of his presence. Paul has the sudden worry that something terrible has happened to Alex's mom. He can't think of what else could be so bad.

"Is everything okay?"

It takes Alex a moment to answer. "Yeah." He doesn't turn to look at Paul.

"Was that your mom?"

"No."

"Are *you* okay?" Working, and living, closely with Liam has taught Paul that sometimes he needs to adjust his questions slightly to get meaningful answers. However, the patience in his voice is learned from years with Alex. He suspects this is going to be one of those conversations where he has to drag information out of him piece by piece.

"I'm not sure." Alex hesitates then says, "That was my sister."

"The one in prison?" As far as Paul knows he only does have the one. Although the thought suddenly occurs to him that Alex might well have a sister Paul doesn't know about. Such a thing would be strange, but then Alex is strange and keeps more secrets than is convenient.

Alex turns and narrows his eyes at him. "She's not in prison anymore."

So he still only has one sister…probably.

"Did she break out?" Paul blurts.

Alex stares at him incredulously. Which is fair. There are lots of perfectly legitimate reasons why Alex's sister is no longer in prison. Alex just looks so freaked out, Paul's brain is going to unreasonable places.

"No." Alex is scornful. "What's wrong with you?"

"Okay, this conversation is not about what's wrong with me." If Paul wants any chance of getting useful answers out of Alex, he's going to have to steer him back around to the original topic of this conversation. "What's going on with your sister?"

Alex sighs. "She paid her debt to society and is currently sleeping on my mother's couch, and why doesn't anyone ever tell me anything?"

"Hey, it's not like I knew." He's trying to keep the tone of the conversation light, but Alex is having none of it.

"Tell me about your sister," Paul says, changing tack.

"I don't like her, and now she's not in prison, and my mom gave her my phone number, and I hung up on her like three times because she's not someone I want in my life. Also, she calls me JJ, which I'd have to put a stop to if I was speaking to her ever again, which I'm not."

Paul stares at him for a minute. "I have no idea what to say to any of that. Which means your choices are to tell me what to say or to come inside and eat more salad."

"Can I just stay out here and not say anything? To anyone? Like ever?"

"Only if you want to explain this to Liam. 'Cause if we're out here much longer you know he's going to come looking for you."

Alex groans. "Fuck my life."

◆

From where Minette is sitting she can see Paul and Alex before they come back into the dining room. Paul has his arm around Alex's waist and murmurs something in his ear before he kisses his cheek, unwraps his arm, and nudges him through the doorway and back to the table.

Alex is pale under his freckles and looks like he's seen a ghost. As he makes his way to his seat Liam, his own face drawn, twists around, grabs Alex's hand, and gives him a wordless, questioning look that's uncomfortably intense.

Alex's expression doesn't change, at least not that Minette can tell, but Liam must see something because his face loosens and he smiles. He presses a kiss to the palm of Alex's hand before he lets it go. He resumes talking with Ellen as if nothing had interrupted him. Alex squeezes Liam's shoulder briefly and slides into his own seat next to Paul.

Minette realizes she's staring and tears her eyes away from Alex. No one else seems to have noticed, or if they have, are too polite to show it. She files that tidbit of information away for later; she doesn't know how to process it right now. Especially when Gemma swears up and down Liam and Alex aren't fucking.

"Yeah, that just happened, and yeah, it's totally normal because they're totally not normal," Darcy DeRosier leans over to mutter in Minette's ear. Darcy is an actress who works frequently with Paul, and Gemma's keen to attach her to *Scism* if the project ever gets that far. Minette knows her by reputation – she's highly talented and has a knack for saying absurd things – but hasn't met her before now.

"Ooookay," Minette says, because some sort of response seems necessary. But Darcy is almost too convoluted for her to follow.

"Yeah," Darcy smiles brightly, as if she completely understands Minette's bafflement. "Pretty much. So, you're working on Dead Victor's show, yeah?"

Minette is starting to get seriously uncomfortable with how everyone refers to Victor as 'Dead Victor.' As if they all have to keep noting that detail so that he'll stay that way.

"At the moment, yes," Minette says. She glances over at Liam, but Liam is absorbed in his conversation with Ellen. He's gesticulating animatedly, and his face, with his bright blue eyes framed by dark lashes, is annoyingly lovely.

"I'm glad there's gonna be one more Victor show. Working with him on *Winsome* was incredible. I mean that show was Paul's baby, but you know, Victor's a legend."

"We definitely hope it's something we can pick up," Minette says diplomatically.

"I know it's still in development hell. But you should know, if you ever do get greenlit, I will *totally* be an evil nun."

"I'm not writing you into the script, Darce," Jackson says from down the table.

"You don't have to!" Darcy says. "I mean like, you should already have an evil nun anyway. Or a misguided nun mentee. I mean. You're setting this in the Vatican. You've got to put in some good parts for the sisterhood."

"I've got it covered," Jackson says. He sounds annoyed, but Minette can see the smile playing at the corner of his mouth.

♦

Alex brightens up a little after everyone leaves. Once the kitchen is decent and they've put Claudia to bed, he and Paul chase each other – quietly – down the hall to their bedroom. Inside, Alex pushes Paul against the door and slides to his knees, undoing Paul's jeans as he goes.

Paul lets his head fall back against the door until Alex sinks his mouth down on him. He's exhausted. Part of him just wants to skip the sex and go to sleep, but as soon as he looks down at Alex he can't think of anything else but this.

He threads his hands into Alex's hair and holds him there. The sound Alex makes when Paul winds the long red strands around his fingers and tugs is pained in the very best way. Paul would smile, but he's too busy being taken apart by Alex's clever hands and skilled mouth.

After Paul comes he grabs Alex by the front of his shirt. He hauls him up into a kiss and shoves his hand down the front of Alex's jeans. It's messy and not particularly coordinated but apparently it doesn't need to be. Alex moans into Paul's mouth as he comes, too.

Cleanup is perfunctory, and Alex doesn't bother to put any clothes back on before he flops onto their bed. "Okay, I love Iceland, but even my awesome house was cold at night and I missed being naked."

"Mmm. I missed you being naked too." Paul crawls up on the bed next to Alex and kisses his shoulder before he rolls onto his side next to him.

Alex laughs softly and closes his eyes. Paul gives them both a few minutes just to bask before he says, "Can we talk about your sister now?"

Alex squints an eye open. "What's there to talk about?"

"She's out of jail and calling you. What's not to talk about?"

"Prison. Jail is just for, like, unpaid parking tickets and stealing street signs."

"That is the most Indiana thing you have ever said to me."

"We could talk about the summer I spent illegally slaughtering chickens so I could buy a car."

"So your sister...." Paul says, after a startled beat, because really, what is he supposed to say to *that*?

"Finally stopped calling back," Alex points out.

"And is she going to continue not calling back?"

"Hey, aren't we working on that 'can't worry about it until it happens' thing?"

Paul narrows his eyes. That's a bit of a cheap shot, but Alex has a point. Kind of. "Okay, but, can we talk about how you didn't know she was getting out of jail?"

"Prison."

It's moments like this Paul doesn't understand how it's Liam who's the autistic one.

"Fine," Alex says when Paul doesn't take the bait. "She wasn't convicted of any crimes against me, so I don't get victim notification. I don't talk to her, so she didn't tell me. And my mother, clearly, didn't want to have this conversation with me, which is fucking rude, considering she gave Delilah my number, but, she did raise me so are you really surprised?"

7

A week after the party, Alex goes rock climbing at one of his favorite spots. The work of getting his ropes prepped comes back to him as if he hadn't taken months off. But that's the only thing that does.

The climb itself is surprisingly frustrating. Alex's newly muscled physique makes the endeavor harder, not easier. Sure, he's stronger in many ways now, but the muscle he's carrying is also heavier, changing how he propels himself up the rock. Everything feels wrong. He misses his old body.

He considers giving up, but he knows he'll be annoyed, at himself and the world, if he can't get to the top. The struggle is annoying and strange, but at least being out of the house and away from other people gives him a chance to think.

Alex begged his mother to do something to stop Delilah from calling. But Laura is either content to let her children sort out their squabbles on their own, or Delilah is ignoring her. Both seem equally likely. He blocked Delilah's number for a couple of days, but the silence made him even more nervous, so he unblocked her. Now all he can do is ignore her calls.

When Paul asks about her, Alex lies and says they talked about something meaningless before changing the subject. He very much does not want to have extensive conversations about his sister. Or any conversations about her at all. He definitely does not want to deal with Paul insisting that Alex talk to her, which he surely will when he finds out Alex has been lying.

But Delilah is only part of the problem. Alex's balance has been thrown off. Usually when he comes back home after a long time away, he hibernates with Paul. This time, with the girls in the equation, that hasn't been an option. Alex loves all three of the kids, but sharing Paul with them – and with Liam and Carly – is sometimes hard.

When they were all in Iceland together, he'd felt left out of the life they all had back in L.A. Now he still feels more like a bystander than a willing and eager participant. With shuttling the kids back and forth and the way-more-than-weekly family dinners together, the lines between his life with Paul, and Liam and Carly's, feels like it's disappearing completely. Alex just scrambles to keep up with the changes.

When he finally gets all the way up the cliff, Alex lets himself sit for a while before he starts the climb back down. His arms and back ache, and sweat is trickling down the back of his neck. But the breeze stirring his hair is pleasant, and the view is everything. In the distance, across the scrubby vegetation and the rocks and canyons, he can see the buildings of downtown LA. Alex fled Indiana more than ten years ago. He got in his car and, with very little in the way of a plan, drove west to look for a better life. He found it here, not just with Paul but in the difficult, demanding city itself. Soon, he'll have to go back to its grind, but he wants just one more minute, here on top of the world without anyone asking anything from him at all.

◆

Going to parent-child yoga classes is possibly the most Hollywood thing Alex has ever done. Which is saying something, considering he's been living here for ages and is now on a hideous plants-only diet.

But if he has to do crap like yoga to get his old body back, it's way more fun to go with Ali. Sure, she's occasionally terrifying when she's trying to engage the media in the same way that her father does, and Alex still feels intimidated by her when she's with a passel of her peers. But when he can hang out with her on her own, she's hilarious and casually judgmental in a way that reminds him of Carly. And of himself. Which is both amusing and surreal, considering how Alex found out Carly was pregnant with her, which is a story he will never share with Ali. Ali may be aware of her parents' polyamory in a seven-year-old way, but she *never* needs to know that Alex and Paul had a threesome with her mother.

"Are you still fighting with your mom?" Ali asks as they walk from Alex's car to the yoga studio.

"I'm not really fighting with her," Alex says.

"I heard you yelling. On the phone."

"Is yelling always fighting?" Alex asks.

Ali gives him a withering look. "It is when it sounds like that."

"My sister sucks," Alex says. Which isn't a kind way to put it, but he's sure as hell not giving Ali details there.

Ali nods sagely. "So does mine. She cries a lot."

"Vic is much nicer than my sister. Don't be mean."

"What'd your sister do?"

Thankfully, they reach the studio. Alex pulls

the door open for her in lieu of answering. "I'll tell you later."

Ali locks her legs and stays where she is. "Really?"

"Totally."

Ali narrows her eyes at him. "Today-later or years-later?"

"You've been learning from your dad."

"Allllleeeex."

"Go on in, class is gonna start. We don't want to be late."

Ali folds her arms over her chest. "But if we're late more people will notice us."

◆

Figuring out how to do small talk with the other yoga parents has not been going well, although he's learning. Marginally. Having the kids to talk about at least provides a topic that's not his job or his personal life, and the general ethical code of Los Angeles prevents people from asking too many intrusive questions. But he knows that eventually, somehow, it's going to become public knowledge that he and Ali go to these classes. Then random fans will decide to get on planes with their own seven-year-olds for an awkward yoga stalking vacation. Even in his own head he sounds paranoid and irrational. But he also knows he's not wrong.

He finally extricates himself from a conversation on the supposed advantages of a thirty-day kale cleanse with a woman who probably doesn't vaccinate her children and manages to make his way over to Ali. She's holding court with a couple of other kids. Before he can tap her on the shoulder and ask if she wants to get smoothies, he overhears what they're talking about.

"You do *not* have four parents," one of the kids, a boy about Ali's age, says. "Nobody does. Unless there's divorce."

"Well, I do. And no one's divorced, and California says I can, so you're wrong," Ali shoots back matter-of-factly.

"No, you have your mom and your dad and your mom and dad's friends who take care of you sometimes."

"Co-parenting," Ali says with a toss of her hair that is pure Carly. "It's like when lots of people cooperate to be parents so no one has to do everything. So all my parents get to be awesome and take care of me. And my sisters. Three of us is a lot of work."

"Ugh," the boy says. "You only have one sister. Stop being pretentious."

"*Excuse* me," Ali says, gearing up for what's obviously going to be an epic seven-year-old takedown.

Alex decides it's time to intervene. Ali's holding her own and surely could continue to all day, but she doesn't have four parents – of whom he is very much one – so they can leave her to fight playground battles on her own.

Alex puts his hand on Ali's shoulder and looks at the kid who has just called her pretentious. "You shouldn't use words you don't know the meaning of."

"And you shouldn't let her think she's special."

"We'll work on that when she actually has some peers who can keep up."

Ali turns and looks at Alex. He can't tell if she's pleased, embarrassed, or completely aghast.

"We should go," she says.

"What?" Alex's heart starts to hammer in his chest because he's just been arguing with a seven-year-old and that's both bad form and not deeply rational. "The fun's just getting started."

"No," Ali says. "It's really not." She turns to the boy. "Would I lie about having four parents when this is one of them?"

Alex stifles a laugh as Ali grabs the hem of his T-shirt and physically drags him out of the studio.

♦

"Mom's gonna be mad at you," Ali says to Alex over smoothies. "And Dad. And probably Other Dad. But Mom's scarier."

"I suppose it's not ethical to bribe you not to tell her, is it?" Alex says. He's well aware that both Liam and Carly, not to mention Paul, are going to be pissed at him. They'll be justified, too. Picking fights with the under-ten yoga set is not a good look. No matter what the provocation was, Alex probably shouldn't have done that. At least not that way. But Ali was sort of named after him, and his odd family circumstances mean she's his to love and protect. He is absolutely going to do that no matter what the costs.

"No," Ali answers. "I mean, I'd definitely negotiate with you. But I think the internet is gonna beat you to it. Xavier's mom was totally tweeting that whole conversation."

"How can you be sure?"

"I follow her."

Alex is suspicious. "I thought you weren't allowed to have a Twitter account."

"It's not one that anyone knows is me," Ali says.

Alex groans and wishes there was vodka in his banana, strawberry, and spirulina smoothie abomination.

"I know why you did it," Ali says after a pause.

"Oh?" Alex wonders if he should be alarmed.

"Yeah. You wanted to protect me. Which is nice in theory, I guess. But I can take care of myself."

"I know you can," Alex says. He just doesn't want her to have to. Even if the worst she ever faces in life is a mouthy seven-year-old in yoga class.

Ali sighs like he's being dense on purpose. "Then *stop it*. Seriously. You're just making life harder for me."

♦

Alex hangs out with Ali for the rest of the afternoon, but he knows he can't avoid the other adults forever. Especially when they're all scheduled to have dinner that night at Carly and Liam's house.

Any faint hope that they somehow missed the social media tempest evaporates as soon as he and Ali walk into the kitchen. All three of them – Carly, Liam, and Paul – turn to look at him from where they're standing around either making dinner or playing with the babies. Paul looks aggrieved. Liam looks worried. Carly looks pissed.

"After dinner," she says as Alex drops his bag by the door and Ali scampers over to help Paul with whatever he's cooking. "We'd like to have a word with you."

"Told you she'd be mad," Ali says placidly, without turning around from watching Paul.

"*Without* the children who can talk," Carly says pointedly to her daughter.

The meal isn't a fun one. Everyone attempts to act normal, but no one is very good at it. Alex has to force himself not to cringe from the tension. He knows he fucked up, but surely not so badly as to merit this level of ominous anticipation. Having to wait for whatever scolding is coming makes everything seem far worse than Alex thinks is strictly appropriate. Chewing feels like an effort while Paul and Liam and Carly chatter about nothing in particular to fill the silence.

Finally, when they finish eating and get the kitchen cleaned up, Liam quietly suggests to Ali that she take her book upstairs to read.

"Ugh," Ali says. "Alex is the one who messed up. How come I get sent to my room for it?"

"You're not being punished," Liam says. "You can go downstairs to the basement, too. Or out to the back deck. Or –"

Ali sighs the way only a seven-year-old can sigh. "I get it, Dad." She grabs her book and stomps up the stairs.

Once she's out of earshot, Alex raises a hand. "I get it, too." He's shooting for levity, but Carly's unimpressed expression tells him he's fallen well short of the mark.

"Living room," she says, pointing with one hand while scooping up Vic and setting her on her hip with her other.

The collective scolding Alex proceeds to get from the three of them is, as far as he is concerned, completely unnecessary. He knows he screwed up. He's willing to admit he screwed up. But listening to his husband and friends go over the point again and again – and again – is more than he wants to endure.

"What do you want me to say?" he finally snaps after Liam's third repetition of the evils of arguing with someone else's child. "I said something stupid. People say stupid shit all the time. The world never ends."

"If you have issues about how we deal with rude people in public we can talk about those and come up with a reasonable plan that perhaps suits you better," Liam says. "But I know you. So could you maybe not take out whatever angst or irritation you have about people in general on people in particular? Especially in front of an audience of strangers?"

"It was a very particular grievance," Alex says shortly. "And I do not want to talk about my issues. Least of all with you." A conversation with Liam about one subject usually ends up covering four or five others. Sometimes that's fun. Sometimes it's irritating. Right now, however, it's dangerous. Alex has avoided discussing Delilah with Carly and Liam so far, but he's pretty sure a discussion about children at this moment will open that can of worms. It would be his own fault, but he does not want to go there.

Liam takes a deep breath, the one Alex knows means he'd like nothing more than to yell despite his finding yelling inappropriate. "Okay, first of all, I am not your enemy here. Secondly, it was my kid you leapt to a noble and completely awful defense of and landed us all in the spotlight of internet outrage, so I'm going to strongly recommend you talk to someone."

"I am fine talking to someone. I am not fine talking to everyone about my every thought and flaw. God, would you all stop ganging up on me?"

Alex directs his glares at Liam and Paul in particular. He can't believe Paul hasn't found the nerve to say *something* in this disaster.

"We're not ganging up on you," Liam says.

Carly tosses her hair, clearly impatient.

Alex wonders gloomily why they couldn't have had Paul talk to him about this mess. Alone. That would have still sucked, but at least it would have prevented him from having to be shamed in front of an audience. Because that's what Liam and Carly are, no matter how little they seem to think they should be.

◆

When they leave Carly and Liam's, Alex stalks ahead of Paul. He's carrying Claudia on his hip, which reduces the dramatic effect of storming off, but the angry set of his shoulders tells Paul everything he needs to know.

He trails after him as Alex gets the front door open one-handed and climbs the stairs. He hovers in the doorway of Claudia's room while Alex gets her into her pajamas and ready for bed. It's a routine that usually relaxes Alex, but once Claudia is in her crib and Alex checks that the baby monitor is on, he brushes past Paul without saying a word.

Paul sighs and follows Alex. His husband's tendency not to talk when he's upset has never been charming, and over the years Paul has stopped expecting it to change. Also, no matter what Carly or Liam may think, it's not *always* Alex being intentionally difficult. Sometimes it is, surely. But sometimes it's just Alex trying and failing to know his own emotions or communicate them effectively. Paul can hardly blame him for that, even if it drives him up a wall.

"Way to be supportive," Alex says when he finally lands in the kitchen. He yanks the refrigerator door open. Paul suspects he doesn't actually want anything to eat and is just searching for a reason not to engage with him.

Paul slides onto a bar stool and waits for Alex to be done with the fridge. He finally emerges with a water bottle, which he plays with rather than sit down himself.

"I'm sorry for the family meeting," Paul says. Surely now is not the time to remind Alex that he really had been in the wrong. Besides, Alex clearly already knows or he wouldn't be so sulky right now.

"The meeting was whatever. But I would like not to be dogpiled by Carly, Liam, *and* you."

"I know," Paul says. "But when things come up that affect the whole family, shouldn't the whole family be involved?"

Alex opens his mouth to protest.

"I'm just saying, I think you're reacting to the method of conflict resolution rather than the actual conflict itself."

"Ugh, you've spent too much time in therapy."

"At your insistence. If you need them to deal with shit differently, that's a conversation we can have."

"As a group? Or just you and me. 'Cause I gotta say, Paul, this whole co-parenting thing? Feels a lot less like a platonic non-marriage of equals and way more like everybody deciding for me what I'm going to do and how I'm going to do it. Which is a fight I am fucking sick of having."

"And I'm asking you what your ideal

alternative is so we can maybe make that happen."

Alex shoves the water bottle onto the island and slumps down next to Paul. "I want to feel like part of this family again. I want to feel like you're not treating me like a child. I want to feel like I have at least one ally against the entire world, even if that world includes our friends."

"You know, everyone is not out to get you. Up to and including our best friends."

"It sure doesn't feel like it. Especially when I just spent the night getting yelled at while you sat there."

"Okay. I get that. And I'm sorry. I could have handled that necessary conversation better. But –" Paul considers his next words carefully. "I think maybe you tried to rush back into life too fast here. Or maybe we rushed you back. Which isn't fair of anyone, including me. But you don't have to be at one hundred percent. Not right away, and not ever, really. If you need to step back a little, be more gradual about getting back into life with everyone, I think you should do that. And if you need to take a break, we can figure out how to do that. I know anyone having time to themselves is at a premium around here."

Alex shakes his head. "A slower re-entry would have been great. But that's not how our lives work, and I just have to deal with that. Honestly? I don't want to be around less. Especially not now. Like, I get that you and them were one big happy family while I was gone. And I'm glad for that. Support networks, avoiding depression, no mental breakdowns – all good things. But, Paul, you're easy to sway and you love to be loved. And I keep feeling like you're choosing Carly and Liam over me because they've been around more, and logistically, that's probably always going to be true."

8

Aside from the welcome home barbecue, Gemma hasn't heard from Alex since he got back to L.A. She doesn't lose too much sleep over that fact; she knows Alex's habits too well by now. Expecting him to take initiative in making contact is an exercise in futility. Being upset at him is, at this point, a waste of energy.

So Gemma's not annoyed that Alex, her former roommate and one-time best friend, hasn't reached out to her. She's just extraordinarily aware of the facts. That doesn't stop her, however, from texting him on the way to her car between meetings.

I'm going to be in your neck of the woods this afternoon for a meeting. Wanna grab coffee?

To her pleased surprise, Alex responds almost immediately: *Yes!*

They arrange a time and place, and Gemma goes into her next meeting feeling somewhat buoyed by life. Sometimes being more generous than she wants to be is the right choice.

The meeting runs late due to some tricky negotiations about featured billing on a show that has just gotten a series order, so she's equally late getting to the coffeeshop. Which is fine, because Alex is apparently running on L.A. standard time too. She orders a drink, texts him to let him know she's there, sits down with her phone to deal with her inbox, and waits.

And waits.

And waits.

An hour after they were supposed to meet,

Gemma finally texts him again. *Hey. Did you die?* It's not something she should joke about, probably, not after Victor, but Alex has a warped sense of humor. And after spending so much time with him and his extended chosen family, so does she.

Oh, crap. Sorry, he replies a good ten minutes later, at which point Gemma is done with her inbox and has moved on to the rest of her social media. *Baby emergency. Raincheck?*

Which in and of itself would be fine. Babies happen. But Gemma talks to Liam a lot, and Liam is very proactive and insistent on sharing his and his family's schedule. Carly and Paul have the kids today. Whatever is going on with Alex right now, it has nothing to do with the kids.

Gemma could, and probably should, explain to him in great detail using small words why he's rude, a dick, and disrespectful of her and her time, but she's so tired of doing that kind of work. Especially with him. Because no matter what she says, nothing ever seems to change.

Sure, she replies curtly, tosses her empty cup in the recycle, and leaves.

♦

Gradually, life returns to normal, or at least as normal as it ever gets for Paul. Which means that on a Tuesday afternoon in mid-June he's in his office at their production company on a gruesome yet fascinating phone meeting with their medical expert for *Plague*. The show may not be a procedural in a traditional sense but Paul, Olivia, and their writers still need an understanding of the world their characters are living in. Once the call is done, he spins his chair back around to find Olivia leaning in the doorway, clearly judging everything.

"Starting Take Your Daughters to Work Day early?" she asks.

"I always bring the babies in," Paul says. Vic and Claudia are on a blanket spread out next to his chair, where Vic appears to be trying to teach Claudia to play pat-a-cake. People love to stop by Paul's office to play with the kids. It's like puppies, only better.

Ali, sitting in the chair on the other side of his desk with a coloring book she's doodling in the margins of, looks up at Olivia imperiously. "It's okay. I take care of them."

"You know this is like a CPS situation waiting to happen," Olivia says.

"I take care of Liam at home, too." Ali says.

Olivia gives Paul a *what-the-fuck* face.

"What? She does," Paul says.

They don't, of course, actually use the seven-year-old to babysit the younger kids, but Ali is immensely proud when it comes to the babies and has always understood that helping out – with Vic and Claudia, with her father, with their complicated and collective lives – needs to be everyone's job. Even hers.

And, on days like this – when Alex and Liam have meetings and Carly's working – Ali ends up hanging out with the little ones in Paul's office so Paul can get some work done. Not that he's actually accomplishing much, but it's better than nothing. Sometimes he even gets to write and send an entire email before Claudia or Vic demand his attention again.

"Still," Olivia says. "I'm judging you."

"It's okay," Ali says calmly. "So am I."

"Excuse me," Paul says to Ali, amused. He's uncertain if she's judging Olivia or him.

"You said I could go network in the cafeteria."

"I said you could walk to the cafeteria, get a snack, and come back, yes," Paul says. He feels as horrified as Olivia looks.

"Well can I go?"

"Sure, do you have your phone?"

Ali sniffs. "I'm not going to get lost."

Paul gives her a stern look.

"Yes, I do," she says with an air of long suffering.

"Okay. Be back in half an hour."

"Yes, Dad." Ali darts out the door, making sure to shut it behind her. Vic toddles after her, and reaches mournfully for the door handle just beyond her reach.

"Oh, so you're 'Dad' now?" Olivia asks, once she's gone.

"Only when she's annoyed at me."

Olivia chuckles and sits down in the chair across from Paul's desk. She makes a face when Paul scoops Claudia out of the playpen, but Paul knows she's fond of the kids. Just judgmental of his life choices, which is pretty fair in most cases.

"I've been thinking about *Scism*," Paul says, leaning over to rummage in a drawer for a snack for Claudia, who's starting to make hungry noises. At least it'll be years yet before she'll be asking to go network in the cafeteria.

"Oh no…in what way?" Olivia asks cautiously.

"Tell me it's a bad idea to get involved."

"You have *Plague* in production, we already have another show in the hopper, and you have, as we just discussed, three children. Whatever idea you're having it's a terrible one."

"Yeah," Paul says. "I know."

"Then why are you asking me about it?"

Paul offers Claudia the little tupperware dish full of Cheerios and prays she doesn't decide to dump them all over the floor this time. "I started working for Victor when I was twenty-three. I wasn't even out to myself. Now, I'm forty, married, have kids, and am a showrunner. Victor made all of that possible. I can't pay him back by being terrified of *Scism*, but it's hard enough as it is to be a present and reliable parent and partner. I feel fucking torn between so many people, and the punchline is some of them aren't even alive."

♦

On a bright day at the end of June, Paul comes home to find Alex waiting for him in the living room.

"Where are the kids?" Paul asks as Alex practically launches himself at him the moment he steps into the room.

"Ali's at dance class, the babies are napping, and nobody is due to come pick anybody up or drop anyone off for another hour." Alex is already digging his hands into Paul's pants. Paul would laugh at him and push him back – it's been a long day, he's exhausted, and Liam especially has been known to arrive early when the kids are involved – but it's Alex and he just can't.

They don't make it to their bedroom or even upstairs. Alex drags Paul to the couch and drops to his knees, nipping and sucking at his stomach and hips as he pulls Paul's jeans down to his ankles.

While Alex is super into being marked up – and

Paul is *really* into marking him – Alex has never shown any inclination to reverse that scenario until recently. Now, though, he seems fascinated by Paul's skin and the things he can do to it. Paul doesn't bruise as easily as Alex – Paul's not sure anyone bruises more easily than Alex – but Alex is still clearly fascinated by the lines he can leave with his nails. He sucks kisses into Paul's thighs until he hisses with the sensation.

Paul runs his fingers over Alex's cheek – clean-shaven, now, but even paler than usual after so long in so little sunlight – and Alex's eyelashes flutter. As focused as he is on making this moment what he wants, he's clearly as deep in his small, submissive space as he's ever been.

When Paul comes Alex doesn't even bother trying to swallow. His breath is ragged and Paul knows that he's about to finish, too. He does, a moment later, panting.

He slumps forward, his forehead resting against Paul's knee, while they both breathe together.

The doorbell rings. Paul swears. He's nowhere near being able to face the world and is sure Alex isn't capable of it either.

"Can you get it?" Alex asks, his voice small.

"You're leaning on me," Paul points out.

"Can't move," Alex chuckles breathlessly, but he does manage to lift his head.

The doorbell rings again, and someone pounds on the door.

"I have a key!" Liam calls, his voice muffled through the door. "Alex, the deal is you answer the door, and I don't use the key!"

"Asshole," Alex mutters. He gives Paul a quick,

dirty kiss then scrambles out of the room and upstairs. Paul has to scrub his own face off with a tissue before he can finally go let their friends in.

Paul and Carly have just started getting things together to make dinner when Alex comes down the stairs, face clean, hair combed, and carrying an obviously just-woken-up Claudia while Vic scoots down behind him.

"You know, we are not doing this co-parenting thing just so you two can fuck all the time. Hey, little girl, Mama's got you," Carly says, holding out her hands for Claudia, who goes eagerly. Paul's glad Ali's not in the room to hear the profanity.

"We can multitask," Alex says. Liam gives him a high five.

◆

Alex is very happy to put worries about embarrassment, interruptions, and the rest of the world aside and focus on making dinner with Paul for seven people in their kitchen. Liam sits at the kitchen table trying to play a card game with Ali, and Carly keeps the babies corralled.

This, right here, he can handle. Given recent crises, Alex is also happy for the relative bliss of mandated family time social media blackouts. Which is why, when his phone rings, he checks it only reluctantly. It's probably just Delilah again.

Except it's Gemma. He really should take this call, because friends are certainly not social media. Alex feels a twinge of guilt for standing her up. At least she hadn't seemed mad. And at least she's probably not calling now about a work emergency – if she were, Liam's phone would be ringing instead.

"Have you seen Twitter?" Gemma asks when he answers.

"Family dinner night. I'm busy trying to not destroy the pasta."

"You probably want to look at Twitter."

"Why, what happened?" he asks warily. There's a note of urgency in her voice that spikes Alex's adrenaline, but she also sounds a bit judgy.

"You should see it yourself."

"Gemma," Alex nearly snaps. He hasn't had to deal with cryptic doom since Victor died and would prefer not to deal with more of it ever again.

"Just grab somebody's phone, please, Alex."

"I could hang up on you," Alex suggests.

"Asshole. I am trying to help you with your nonsensical life. Again. Just do what I'm telling you."

That doesn't reassure Alex, but he digs Paul's phone out of his back pocket where he's standing next to him at the counter slicing bread.

Paul gives him a puzzled look over his shoulder.

Alex shrugs. "Gemma says there's a Twitter emergency."

He unlocks Paul's phone with one hand while still keeping his own pressed to his ear.

Whatever the issue is, apparently Paul is also involved. His phone is lit up with Twitter notifications, all of which seem to have Alex at-mentioned. There's a third handle involved he doesn't recognize.

Alex navigates back to the tweet that started it all. When he finds it, he stares at it in shock and growing horror.

"Do you see it?" Gemma asks briskly.

Alex nods before he remembers she can't see him. "Yeah."

"Alex," she says, her voice softer now. "Is that your sister?"

◆

"Jasper Alexander Cook, would you stop freaking out and sit the fuck down?" Carly finally snaps.

"I'm not freaking out."

"Well, you're pacing very fast and very forcefully, and it's driving me nuts. And I live with Liam."

Alex picks Claudia up from her blanket spread out on the floor and starts maneuvering her into her high chair. She's not particularly happy about the change, and Alex clucks softly at her grumblings.

"What happened?" Paul eventually asks.

"My sister." Alex, sullen, attempts to fish a buckle out from under Claudia's leg.

"Is she coming here?" Liam is obviously alarmed.

"No."

"Is she threatening you?" Carly asks.

"No."

"Is she threatening the kids?" Paul asks.

Alex sighs. Instead of answering he shoves Paul's phone back across the table at him. Paul picks it up, unlocks it, and stares at the screen.

The Twitter handle is @Sindiana096 which makes Paul want to bang his head against the wall in frustration. Alex and his sister share a sense of humor.

The tweet itself is another matter. *If my big brother & my brother-in-law want to have another baby*

I will totally be the baby mama.

"Your sister's a brat," Paul observes mildly.

"It runs in the family," Alex says.

"Can you even be sure it's her?" Paul asks. Behind Alex's shoulder, Liam and Carly exchange concerned looks with each other.

"It's her. It's definitely her. And everyone knows it's her, too," Alex says, waving a hand at Paul's phone. "You don't want another baby, do you?" he asks, his voice a little desperate.

"What?"

"Because we agreed. Just Claudia. Like I expected you to bring it up because kids are awesome and maybe you want to be bio-dad and you like to revisit agreements and whatever but we said just one?" Alex's voice rises to a pitch of franticness that Paul finds endearing and would be amusing if the circumstances weren't this upsetting.

"I don't want another kid," Paul says as soothingly as he can. He's very conscious of Carly and Liam's presence, especially after Alex's anger the last time he thought Paul was siding with them. But he's grateful they're there. Whatever freakout Alex is having, Paul's glad to have backup. He's also very aware of Ali, who is watching the whole thing unfold with narrowed eyes. Vic toddles over to Carly, who catches her up on her lap.

"This family or whatever you all think it is or want it to be is complicated enough," Alex says. In her high chair, Claudia starts to fuss. "Adding my felonious sister to it is the worst idea ever. Especially when I'm apparently the next big movie star and the world is obsessed with me, and what I eat, and who I fuck, and which kids are or are not mine. And even if I did want another kid and another excuse for you all to entangle yourselves in my life, Delilah is a terrible choice for bio-mom. I do not want my daughter to be a criminal addict or have to go to court when my sister sues us for custody in like ten years."

"I have no idea why you are flipping out or why you think any of this is on the table. It makes zero sense," Paul says, although now he's worried. Alex's breathing isn't quite right and this has all the hallmarks of an incipient panic attack. Claudia, catching her father's mood, progresses from fussing to crying.

"Maybe not to you, Mr. Crickets." Alex hums at Claudia, who doesn't seem reassured.

"Are you okay?" Paul asks gently. He offers Claudia her bottle; she takes it eagerly but then flips it upside down and starts gnawing on the bottom of it.

Alex shakes his head.

"What do you want to do right now, other than shift your sister to a different dimension?" At some point they're going to have to bring Carly and Liam into this conversation, but first Paul needs to make sure Alex is taken care of.

Alex doesn't respond right away, staring at Claudia. She looks back at him, still seriously chewing the wrong end of her bottle.

Finally, Alex draws a sharp breath. "I want to know you don't want to have a baby with my sister," he repeats insistently. "All of you." He turns to Carly and Liam.

Carly looks baffled. Liam's brow is furrowed with concern.

"What makes you think we want that?" Carly asks, even as she gives Paul a look that is both sharp and confused. Paul doesn't know much more than she does.

"Just, tell me. Please," Alex says. "I need to hear it out loud."

"I don't want to have a baby with your sister," Liam says earnestly.

"Me neither," Carly says.

Alex nods a little shakily. "Okay. Good. And you?" He turns his gaze to Paul. His expression is accusatory, though God knows why.

This panic has come entirely from Alex's imagination. But, Paul supposes, that's what panic does. "I don't want to have a baby with your sister," he says firmly.

Alex nods again, less shakily this time. "Thank you. All of you. Now. Let's eat, and then can everyone else go home and leave Paul and I and our one and only bio-baby alone?"

◆

Strained meals are apparently becoming a thing for them. And a strain caused by Alex being on the edge of a panic attack isn't any more pleasant than a strain caused by him lashing out at a kid at yoga class. As Alex picks at his salad and doesn't engage in any of the stilted conversation Liam gamely tries to keep going, Paul wonders how much worse this is going to get before it gets better. He's not sure why life after Iceland isn't working for Alex, but it's wildly evident that it's not.

After Carly, Liam, Ali, and Vic go back to their house, Alex carries Claudia upstairs to her room. Paul follows. But instead of getting her pajamas on, Alex slumps down in the rocking chair. Claudia giggles when he starts rocking and grabs at the collar of his T-shirt. Alex smiles at her, but his eyes don't crinkle up.

"Do you want to tell me what that was all about?" Paul asks, leaning back against the dresser.

"My sister offered to be the mother of our child. I found that unnerving."

"You lost it about a completely theoretical suggestion none of us are interested in saying yes to."

"I don't like Delilah."

"You've said that before. You just haven't told me why."

Alex lets his head fall against the woven back of the rocking chair, and gives Paul a weary look. "Meth. Guns. *Prison.*"

"Insufficient answer."

Alex huffs. "Seriously, what would it take for you to think my feelings about her are valid, her being a serial killer?"

"Is she a serial killer?"

"What do you want, Paul?" Alex snaps.

"I want to talk about the fact that you are coping incredibly badly with a tweet from your sister, after coping badly with our current family situation. I'm not saying you're overreacting. I just have no idea what you're reacting to, and I need some help here."

"Okay. Small words time," Alex says pissily. "My mother didn't tell me Delilah was out of prison. Delilah keeps calling me. Delilah is now tweeting, to the world, about the kids. And Liam and Carly get pissed at me when I talk about the kids. Everyone is super into what boundaries the kids need. Or Liam needs. But when I need boundaries, I'm Crazy Absentee Parent Alex. Ow, Claudia, no, no hair pulls." Alex finishes, disentangling Claudia's hands from where she's wound them into his ponytail.

Paul nods, even if Alex isn't particularly looking at him. He waits to answer until Alex's breathing settles and he relaxes, just a little, into the chair.

"I hear you," Paul says quietly. "And I know things have been busy and hard for you since Iceland. Even more than usual, though I'm still trying to put together exactly how and why. So, what if we took some time away –" Paul suggests.

"Oh my God, yes."

"– and went to Indiana," Paul adds cautiously

Alex stares at Paul. "What the fuck makes you think that's a good idea?"

"A break would do you good."

"Yes, but to Indiana? Have you been planning and thought now would be an awesome time to mention it, or did you just get a random genius brainwave?" Franticness creeps back into Alex's voice.

"I'd been considering it vaguely, and then tonight happened. No, listen to me," Paul says when Alex starts to interrupt. "Let's go to Indiana. Just you and me and Claudia. Your mom will love seeing the baby, and you and Delilah can patch things up in person or scream at each other across the kitchen or whatever it is you need to do."

"I don't need to patch things up with Delilah. And I really don't need you manipulating me into trying. Or deciding you need to be my parent, too. In fact, how about you don't make decisions about any of my relationships for me?"

"I am really not trying to be your parent. This is me trying to be your partner."

"You offered me a vacation with just you and our baby to the place in the world I hate most."

"That's not manipulation, that's negotiation," Paul says. "Although while we're talking about bad habits, I know you're full of shit every time you tell me you've talked to her. Because if you were talking to her, you would not be freaking out like this and Gemma wouldn't have had to tell you to check Twitter. Lying is a thing you do."

"I don't."

"Victor's house."

"Fine."

"Delilah isn't going anywhere. No matter how much you wish she would," Paul says evenly. "You can't have this fight with her over Twitter or in the tabloids or on *TMZ*. And you clearly aren't going to deal with it over the phone. But what you can do is go to Indiana, get away from L.A. and our friends, and put this to rest once and for all. This isn't just impacting you anymore, or just you and me and Claudia. This is impacting Carly and Liam and our other girls, too."

"Ali and Vic aren't ours."

Paul stares at Alex. "Jesus Christ." He has no idea what that's about and doesn't even know if he wants to ask.

"What? They're not. We're not some weird baby-raising commune, they're our friends' kids."

"Who we're talking about adopting."

"We haven't yet."

"Also, you're being mean about a seven-year-old and an eighteen-month-old. For no reason that I can fathom or that you're giving me, so you should tell me or you should check yourself, because you can't keep doing this in front of the kids. Ali can snark right back at you when you're an asshole about how many kids you have, but she shouldn't have to deal with this from you."

Paul pauses to give Alex a chance to say something. When he doesn't, just jiggles his knee to bounce Claudia, Paul sighs.

"Someday, the place you grew up in is going to be gone. Your mom's not always going to be around, your terrible school's going to burn down, they're gonna build condos in the cornfields. And then you're never going to be able to make peace with that place."

Alex blinks. "You say that like it's a bad thing."

9

Alex schedules a meeting with Margaret to talk about the general clusterfuck that is his sister, Paul's idea about going to Indiana, and the social media nightmare of having yelled at a yoga kid on video. Margaret is matter-of-fact about Delilah, judgmental about his yoga confrontation choices and, to Alex's horror, completely on board with him going to visit his family.

"The sooner you deal with this, the easier your life is going to be," she tells him. "And the sooner you get to go back to complaining at me about how you're going to be on a cereal box."

Alex slumps down a little in the chair across from her desk. The afternoon sun pours down on L.A. outside the window but leaves the office in shade, which makes it feel cool and dark. Safe, for the moment, from the bullshit of the rest of his life. "You make me sound like a brat."

"I've known you since you were twenty. You are a brat. Now, do you want my advice?"

Alex shrugs. Which probably doesn't make him look any less petulant.

Margaret narrows her eyes at him. "If you're going to go to Indiana – which is a move that, personally, I think is a good one to make – I assume you'd prefer an angle other than your felonious sister got you to do exactly what she probably wanted?"

"Okay, now you're just being cruel."

Margaret gives an elegant shrug. "I'm doing

what you pay me to do. We can either release a statement about you being with your family in a difficult time while reminding people that your sister has paid her debt to society –"

"I really hate that phrase."

"Or…you can go visit your high school with a really big check for the arts and make the story a little cheerier."

"Not the arts," Alex says firmly, struck by a sudden idea. He still hates the entire concept of going to Indiana, but this might make it worthwhile.

Margaret looks at him curiously. "What do you mean?"

"New computer lab."

"Why?" Margaret asks, sincerely confused.

Alex smirks. He never wanted to be an actor. He never touched the arts in high school. He would feel ridiculous and dishonest to go back there and support them now.

"Come on," he says. "You know how I met Gemma. Fandom, and the internet. That's how I learned there was a chance for a life outside of Paragon. That's how I got out. And that's what those kids need."

◆

Gemma is in the middle of a meeting with Minette, Liam, and Jackson when her phone lights up with an incoming call. More accurately, Gemma and Jackson are sitting on the sidelines of a discussion between Minette and Liam that is rapidly turning into an argument. Jackson's given up on watching the tennis match and has started typing on his laptop. He's probably decided that dealing with his email or getting a new script idea on paper is a better use of his time than paying attention to yet another argument over Victor's legacy. Gemma's only listening in the unlikely event either Liam or Minette manage to solve something and someone needs to write their ideas down before the two of them forget.

She glances at her phone, praying for some sort of emergency to get her out of here. The caller ID says *Alex*, which may actually qualify. They haven't spoken since his sister popped up on Twitter.

Gemma stands from the table and mutters an excuse. Jackson nods distractedly at her, but Liam and Minette don't seem to notice.

In the hallway outside the conference room, Gemma answers. "What is it now?" she asks.

"Liam's freaking out at me about Indiana."

That's so far from anything Gemma cares about right now as to be laughable. "At this moment, Liam is actually freaking out at Minette about his dead boyfriend's work, so do you want to tell me why I should care about this now?" If Alex is burying the lede on a real emergency she wants him to hurry up and get to the point.

"I don't want to have to cope with Liam's spooky about a place I don't want to back to anyway. Bad enough Paul's making me go."

"You're an adult, Paul's not making you do anything, and if you have an issue with Liam, call him. He's my colleague. And your ex. I'm not stepping into the middle of this."

"He's only my ex in a weird and particular way, and he's not picking up."

"Yes, because like I said, he's freaking out at Minette right now. We're in a meeting."

"Oh. Is this a bad time?" When pennies drop for Alex, they do so slowly.

"You called me in the middle of the afternoon, when I am in a meeting and have deadlines for *multiple projects,* none of which concern you or your star power, to tell me Liam's being annoying and you have issues with Indiana. This is not the crisis I answered the phone expecting."

"Why'd you expect a crisis?"

Gemma sighs. "Because that's the only time you call me anymore."

Before Alex responds, there's a clatter from his end of the line along with what Gemma assumes is Ali's voice yelling "Allllllleeeeeex!"

"Fuck," Alex breathes.

"Baby emergency?"

"That sounded more like 'I have terrible seven-year-old judgment' than 'I have unleashed death and destruction.' But I should go check on them. Talk to you later."

With that, Alex hangs up.

Gemma stares at her phone. Her best, most absent friend in the world is still most definitely the worst.

◆

Alex hurries into the kitchen in pursuit of whatever trouble Ali's managed to get herself into this time. He finds her glaring at Todd, who is crouched on top of the refrigerator, flicking his tail and glaring back at her. Scattered on the floor are the mixing bowls and bananas that usually live up there.

Alex folds his arms and gives Ali a *Well?* look.

"Alex, the cat is throwing things at me."

"What did you do to the cat?"

"Nothing!"

"Ali."

"I just wanted to play." Ali sulks.

"Well, Todd is old and cranky and doesn't always want to play," Alex says. He starts picking up the mixing bowls, glad they're all plastic and that they don't keep anything breakable on the fridge.

"Like you."

Alex snorts a laugh and shoves the bowls onto the counter. "Okay, I know adults seem ancient to you, but thirty is not actually that old."

"Can I come to Indiana with you?"

Alex stares at her. Up on the fridge Todd gives him a look and a tail-twitch that clearly communicates that he is waiting for the small intense human to depart before he even considers coming down.

"What does that have to do with me being old and no fun?" He wonders if the complete non-sequitur of a question is more because she's seven or more because all of this is starting to take a toll on her.

"Indiana," Ali says, sliding herself very seriously onto a stool at the kitchen island, "is an adventure."

Alex has to laugh, even if he's kind of appalled. "It's really not."

"Then how come you're going?"

"Because I have to go deal with family stuff."

"*We're* family."

"Yeah, well, your mom and dad have work to deal with here. They'd probably go if I asked them, and if they could make the time, but they're busy and Indiana is boring."

"But you didn't ask and don't want them to go. Claudia's going! You could take me too! And Vic, I guess. If you had to," she adds.

"I really couldn't."

"But whyyyyy," Ali demands. "Things were supposed to go back to normal when you got home. Now it's like you don't like me anymore."

"Of course I like you."

"Then how come you keep saying how Claudia's your only kid?"

Alex feels a stab of guilt. He slides onto the stool next to hers at the island. "Because family is complicated and hard. And when Carly and Liam had you and Vic, none of us meant to be a family yet. We're still figuring it out. Sometimes it scares me."

"That's a bad answer."

"It's true, sweetheart."

"Still." Ali folds her arms over her chest. "You're a jerk about it."

Alex sighs. "I know. I'm sorry. My sister stresses me out, and I hate the place I grew up, and I really do not want to go on this trip." He's aware that the extent to which he talks to Ali like they are peers is somewhat fucked up, but Alex has never known how normal people do parenting. And his relationship with his own mother is surely anything but typical. "Like, when you're older, if you really want to go and you can talk me into it, we can go, but trust me, you're not missing out. On anything."

◆

Liam's chair at the conference table squeaks obnoxiously every time he moves, so he's trying to sit as still as possible. Not moving is hard for Liam in the best of circumstances. Right now he feels as antsy in a work meeting as he ever has.

They're in a room at the production company that's taking on *Scism*. Sitting around the table, in addition to Liam, is Minette, a junior marketing executive, and someone from finance. Jackson is walking back and forth near head of the table, pitching his latest concept for the show.

Liam twists the ring on his right hand, the ring he found in a metronome in Victor's house the year Victor died. It's a story that doesn't make sense to hardly anyone when he tells it, so he mostly doesn't. That he has the ring, a physical object to remind him that Victor was real and that their relationship – no matter how unusual by most people's standards – meant something to both of them, is enough.

For *Scism,* on the other hand, it's not enough for Liam to know that the story exists. It needs to be out in the world, not buried in a box and alive only in his memory and Jackson's increasing frustration. Other people need to experience it and enjoy it – or at least have reactions to it. Victor wouldn't have come up with the idea if it he wasn't craving a discussion of faith and power and politics. His shows were popular because they were good, but they were runaway hits because Victor always found a way to toss them into the world like a bomb. *Scism,* if done right, could be the biggest conflagration of all. The idea makes Liam nervous, but also excited. Fire is what Victor would have wanted.

The presentation Jackson is giving now is perfect. This *Scism* is dark and fucked up and everything Victor would have insisted on. Liam has goosebumps and damn well hopes everyone else at the table does too.

When Jackson finishes his presentation, it's obvious that the rest of the room is hooked too. Or that they at least see the logic of the pitch. This is what the show has always needed to be. Even Minette looks pleased, and Minette has spent most of this process looking dubious at *Scism* in general and skeptical of Liam in particular. She's always pretty, but she's prettier when she looks victorious.

"It's wonderful," Minette says.

Jackson looks relieved beyond words and collapses into a chair with a dramatic exhalation. But Liam can't relax yet. Because….

"It's wonderful," Minette says again, "But I'm not sure how advertisers are going to feel about it. Which means that selling it to the powers that be as it is now, is going to be hard." She looks at their visitors.

"You're not wrong," the guy from financing says. "But I'd watch it."

"It's dark," Liam agrees, because *of course* it is, "But audiences are loving dark. How many psychological thrillers and dystopian dramas are on right now?"

"I'll be sure to mention that to them," Minette says drily before turning back to Jackson. "Jackson, thank you, you're an angel. Everyone else, I want any and all feedback you have. Official and otherwise. I want to make sure our pitch – and our ask – is exactly what it should be before we go for broke. But I think we're done here for the day."

People start gathering up their things and making plans with each other for lunch, but Liam can't let such a perfect opportunity go to waste. He grabs his own phone and laptop and follows Minette out of the room.

"You really believe in what Jackson's been able to do, right?" he asks as Minette strides ahead of him down the hall to her office. "Because what he's done is amazing. It's perfect for what Victor's vision always was –"

He pauses briefly to duck out of the way of people coming the other way down the corridor. "And I know we always worry about selling to advertisers, but really after all the shows Victor has done – and all the shows people have done trying to be like Victor – I don't think we need to be fretting."

"Mhmm," Minette says, not turning around to look at him.

Liam is undaunted. "You felt the reaction in there," he says.

Minette's in heels, but he has to work to keep up with her. Somehow, it's his words that propel him forward. At least that's why he thinks he can't shut up. "That's not going to change when we go up the food chain. Sure, there'll be some angry newspaper articles and a bit of fuss on the internet. But then the ratings will go through the roof. I don't want you to undersell this thing because you think it's going to be hard or people are going to be pissed off by a critique of a very powerful and very flawed institution. I'm Catholic. Victor was Catholic. Surely we get to talk about these things especially like this. Because that plan, that pitch you just heard? Is *exactly* what it should be, and if we just commit…it will work. I know that."

They finally reach Minette's office. Minette steps inside. Liam hovers in the doorway, his best beseeching face on. "I know you think I'm an unreliable mess, but my gut is all I have and I am never wrong. I wouldn't be here with the career I have if I was."

Minette sets her computer down on her desk with a thud and turns around to face him. Her skirt flares momentarily around her knees as she spins. "Liam."

"Yes?" He has to restrain himself from adding 'ma'am.' Minette elicits that kind of respect from him, but he's also aware that, from a guy like him, 'ma'am' sounds either flippant, condescending, or both.

"What on earth makes you think I don't know all this already?"

"Nothing. I mean. I know you do. I'm sorry. I didn't mean to imply otherwise. I just…."

Minette sighs. "You just what?"

He smiles, because for as scared as he is, he is also happy. "I just really, really, want this to work."

"I know you do. Believe me, I do. And I am trying to make it so, but this job is emotional enough without a controversial show and your personal backstory. Meanwhile, you are exhausting, and I can barely do anything or even think about doing anything to get you this damn show when I can't stand being in the same room as you."

"Why?" he asks, taking a few cautious steps into her office. "Because we have to fix that."

Minette sighs. "Your brilliant, exhausting brain and your stupid, smug, attractive face and the fact that you know exactly how people react to both!"

"Wait, what?" Liam blinks. He's used to saying things that dumbfound other people – though he's not always sure why they dumbfound them. He's less used to being caught totally off-guard himself. Especially in a way that is kind of flattering, possibly awful, and fairly confusing.

Minette huffs and turns away from him again. "I did not just say that. I apologize. And don't read anything into it! It wasn't personal, just a general, 'ugh, actors' thing."

Liam shakes his head. "No, it wasn't." He knows he's not always the best at reading people, but several pieces have just fallen into place for him with rather resounding thuds. Maybe he hasn't been a mess over *Scism* this whole time because of Victor and his legacy. Maybe he's been a mess because Minette is lovely and smart and challenges him, and he's been an absolute fool not to realize any of that before this moment.

He comes to an abrupt decision and hopes it's not about to be the most ill-advised thing he's ever done. "I realize this is about to solve none of our problems, but can I ask you out?"

"*Ugggggh.*" Minette spins around again and stalks out of her own office, her heels clicking smartly down the hallway. Liam watches her go, then waits patiently. That wasn't a no. And if she wants him out of her office, she'll have to come back to tell him to leave. Or send someone else, if she's really mad. Liam's heart sinks. Maybe he did screw up. Badly. At work. Which is unkind when it involves a woman. Which is exactly why Victor shouldn't be dead. He needs advice for these sorts of things.

A moment later, he hears her footsteps return. He takes a breath – not because he's relieved, but because he doesn't want to faint. Air is important for conversations, especially ones that might be about to go super poorly.

Minette reappears in the doorway. "Yes," she says, looking supremely annoyed with herself, Liam, and the entire universe. But not displeased. "Yes, you can."

"Ask you out?" Liam says. "I'm just double-checking."

Minette rolls her eyes. "Yes!" she laughs.

Liam smiles broadly. "*Amazing.*"

10

Despite Alex's continued dubiousness, he eventually agrees to travel back to Indiana to visit both his family and his alma mater. Paul internally thanks Margaret for that idea. He's positive Alex never would have done this if he hadn't seen a purpose to it outside himself. After three weeks of phone calls, wrangling, and planning – and one very bumpy flight out of LAX – Paul, Alex, and Claudia land at the Indianapolis Airport.

Alex adjusts Claudia on his hip when they walk off the jetway and into the terminal.

"Huh," he says, looking around. "So this is what it looks like."

It's not until they're in the rental that it finally clicks for Paul that Alex left Indiana by car. He'd never been on a plane until *The Fourth Estate* sent him to New York to do press. He's likely not, until now, seen the airport that's an hour from his hometown from the outside, much less the inside.

Even though Alex has had this life of celebrity for over a decade, Paul suddenly understands how unprepared he feels about his new about-to-be-upgraded level of fame. The space between what was possible for him when he was eighteen and what he is now is massive. Having to go through another iteration of that cycle must be terrifying.

The drive from Indianapolis to Paragon isn't long, but Paul is shocked at how quickly the landscape changes from airport wasteland to a middle-American despair. It's intensely similar to parts of where he's from in South Carolina, just without the rich greens of its humidity. Even in July everything looks too used – the road, the grass, even the cows.

"Hey, can you pull over?" Alex says abruptly when they're about ten minutes from their destination.

"You okay?" Paul asks as he complies. It's the first time Alex has spoken since the airport other than to baby talk at Claudia.

"I really don't want to do this."

"I know."

For a few minutes, all Alex does is stare forward out the windshield. His breath is too loud and too shallow.

"Is this you having a very quiet panic attack?" Paul speaks softly.

Alex shakes his head but doesn't say anything. Claudia gurgles from her car seat in the back.

"Alex?" Paul's worried. Maybe Alex was right, and this whole trip is actually a colossal mistake.

Alex gulps a deep breath. "I just really, really need you to promise me that you're not going look at me differently once you see it."

"Why on earth would I do that?" Paul has known Alex for over a decade. He knows who he is now. He can't imagine that seeing Alex's town or school or anything else about his old life would change how he views him.

"Just promise," Alex persists.

"I promise," Paul says, a little bewildered.

"Okay. I guess you can drive now." Alex sits back in his seat.

Paul knows Alex doesn't believe him at all.

♦

Alex's mother lives on a stretch of broken asphalt named South Graveyard Road, which, surreally, isn't adjacent to a graveyard at all. The house is small and nearly as tired-looking as everything else they passed on the way here, even with its fresh coat of paint. It's still one of the nicest houses around, and Paul has to remind himself that this isn't actually the house Alex grew up in, but the one he'd bought for his mom years ago. He remembers well the endless phone conversations between Alex and Laura when she was house hunting. Despite Alex's repeated pleadings, Laura had refused to leave Paragon.

Paul slows the car to take it all in before they arrive on Alex's mother's doorstep. By the roadside are two white crosses, decked with faded plastic flowers and a sun-bleached teddy bear, the type of monument that probably means two teenagers died at that spot in a car crash who knows how many years ago. Paul wouldn't find it remarkable, except for the name of the road and the high odds that Alex knew them or their families.

"This is fucked up," Paul says in lieu of asking.

Alex nods.

Rather than carry in the car seat, Alex unbuckles Claudia and picks her up the way he'd carried her through the whole airport. When he stands unmoving in the driveway staring at the house, Paul realizes he may not be capable of walking up the front steps.

"What do you need me to do?" he asks carefully, aware that grabbing Alex's hand and leading him into whatever this is will not be helpful to anyone.

Alex huffs at him but at least starts to walk. "I'm fine."

Paul trails Alex as he gets up on the porch and looks for the bell before he realizes there isn't one. He raps on the frame of the screen door instead.

"Oh my God, you made it!"

The door is practically yanked off its hinges by a woman who looks so much like Alex that Paul takes half a step back. Alex gives him a sharp look that he suspects is less about his manners and more about the I-told-you-so of the moment.

"What was I going to do, decide to take a holiday in Indianapolis instead?" Alex says sharply.

"Not what I meant but, you know, bad things happen to planes," she says with a shrug. "You brought your baby!"

When she reaches for Claudia, who looks dubious about the entire situation, Alex takes a step back. "Where's Mom?"

"Out back. I told her I'd get her when you guys got here."

"Well, can you get her?"

"I want to say hi first. You must be Paul," she says, turning to him.

Delilah is younger than her brother, but she looks older, with fine lines around her eyes and mouth that Alex – because of sunscreen and moisturizer, because of a gentler life, and because he's a TV star – doesn't have yet. She has the same red hair, though, and the same striking freckles. Her eyes, really, are the only thing that are different: gray instead of Alex's nearly black brown.

"I've read *so* much about you," she says.

"I did not know my creepy stalker fans

included my sister," Alex bites.

"Most people don't have to search the internet to find out anything about their brother-in-law," she shoots back. She pulls the door open again before Alex can get to it himself. He rolls his eyes and stalks inside.

While Paul debates what will count as being supportive right now, Delilah regards him for a moment, head tipped to the side and eyes narrowed consideringly.

"Welcome," she finally says, "to Indiana."

The house is bigger than it looks from the outside, but it's still small compared to any place Paul has ever lived. There's two bedrooms, a living room that faces the street and a kitchen-slash-dining room with windows that look back over the fields.

Paul wonders what the house Alex grew up in looks like. Alex won't tell him anything about it, except that it's on this same street. Paul decides to take a walk later regardless of whether Alex is interested in joining him.

Here in Indiana, Paul feels perilously close to all the stories Alex has never wanted to tell him. Alex still may never tell him everything, but he won't have to. Paul also works in television. Landscape and architecture are as much a character – and as expressive – as any human being can be.

As Laura puts on a pot of coffee and asks Alex how their trip was, Paul stops and looks at the pictures hanging in the small living room. He's never seen childhood pictures of Alex before. He smiles at how much of Claudia there is in toddler-Alex's face.

Alex at eight was a scrawny, gap-toothed kid, covered with freckles. The photos are adorable, but what Paul is startled by is the gaze tiny Alex has locked on the camera. It's as much an indictment as any he gives now.

♦

Alex doesn't put Claudia down once. The baby doesn't mind; she loves clinging to Alex any day and is shy and in need of assurance when there are new people around. But watching Alex bounce her on his hip, Paul can't help but think he's using his child as a security blanket. Or, maybe, just a living reminder that he got out and has a life beyond this town.

Paul is taken aback to find that, after the initial round of sibling bickering, Alex and Delilah fall into a repartee that he completely did not expect. Alex may harbor every resentment against his sister in the world, but they also get along amazingly.

"Wanna watch the game later?" she suggests.

"At the school? Yeah no, I am not doing the *Friday Night Lights* thing."

"No. *Asshole*," Delilah says and winks at Alex when Laura scolds her for language. "On TV."

"Sports are horrible."

"Says the high school wrestling champion. Also you're built like a truck now. A very small truck," she adds, tipping her head. "You were not that built before, were you?"

"No, but I could run faster."

"Yeah, no. I was faster than you."

Alex grins. "Remember that time the neighbors caught us out in their shed?"

"Yeah, and you ditched me." Delilah sounds angry but she's also laughing.

"Because you were cuter and better at talking

your way out of shit."

"Yeah, real good that did me."

Paul watches the whole thing, amazed, while Laura goes about reminding them to set the table and telling Alex where the glasses are when he gets confused by the cabinets. He can easily see how Alex and Delilah were scared, fucked-up kids together. They must have been some source of constancy for each other in a life that was very uncertain.

But what Paul is most struck by is that, for all Alex's fears, Delilah is not a monster. She's just a girl.

Alex puts Claudia down only when it's time to eat. He sets her down carefully in a high chair that's so old Paul suspects it's the one Laura had when Alex and Delilah were babies. He wonders what made her keep it for so long and go to the trouble of moving it from her old house to this one; certainly there were no grandbabies on the horizon then.

♦

When they're getting ready to leave to go check in at their hotel, Delilah hugs Alex – getting her arms as best she can around him and Claudia both – and calls him Jay.

"I'm Alex," he says petulantly. He sounds so very young.

Alex doesn't talk at all during the fifteen-minute drive to the Best Western in Martinsville, the next town over. Paragon, population six hundred, doesn't even have a motel. Paul gives him quiet. Sure, he wants Alex to feel as easy as he can, but he also knows he's not going to get anything out of his husband until the man decides to talk.

Which takes far less time than he expects. Alex changes Claudia's diaper, makes sure all cords and outlets are out of her reach, and puts her on the floor to play with a set of stacking cups. Then he digs out the beer they bought from a gas station – which had reminded Paul unnervingly of the set for *Winsome* – and plunks one for each of them on the tiny table.

Paul looks up from his laptop, where he's trying to get a little work done from the road. He may be on some sort of vacation, but at this point in the process things are too busy to leave Olivia entirely on her own.

"My mom and I used to do this," Alex says, sitting down on the edge of the bed and opening his own beer.

"Sit in a sketchy hotel room?" Paul jokes.

"No, although if you want the premise for your next network hit, go for it."

Paul doesn't know what to make of his shift in mood.

"I mean, we'd sit on the porch and share a beer. After we both got home from work. It was nice, in a profoundly fucked-up way. I was like sixteen."

"Where was Delilah in all this?" Paul asks.

"Juvie. Or out with her boyfriend. It depended on the month."

There's something almost wistful in his voice. Paul is confused. "Are you telling me now, after all your whining, that you *miss* being a fucked-up teenager here?"

Alex gives a disconcerting laugh. "No. But…something. You were right. Maybe. It's just a place. I'm here with the baby I have with you. That's not something that seemed possible. Ever. At all. This place feels less awful when I know I can leave."

◆

In the morning, Paul braves the continental breakfast buffet alone to bring bagels and juice back up to the room. They'd booked it in Paul's name and no one's spotted Alex yet, as far as he can tell. But it's only a matter of time before somebody tweets something about seeing J. Alex Cook at the Indianapolis airport or a shitty Paragon gas station.

There is very little to do. They spend most of the day at Laura's house sitting around the living room, sometimes talking and sometimes not. Alex is ill at ease, like a cat in a new space. He spends long stretches of time silent and looking around the room – at the walls, with their faded pictures and memorabilia of Alex and Delilah's childhoods; at the furniture, that is far lumpier and shabbier than anything they've ever had in their own house; and at the corners of the room, where dust has gathered out of the reach of a vacuum cleaner.

"What are you thinking?" Paul asks him quietly at one point, when Delilah's gone outside to get the mail and Laura is in the kitchen.

"That I haven't done a load of laundry in three months, we pay our housekeeper more than my mom makes in a year, and nothing about this place feels comfortable or familiar."

"Did you expect it to? You were so pissed off at the idea of coming here."

"It's still home. Or it was. L.A. isn't. And apparently Indiana isn't anymore either."

Paul starts to say something in reply, when Delilah comes back in the room with a few thin envelopes. Claudia, for no reason that Paul can discern, starts to cry.

"Do you want me to take her?" Delilah offers, tossing the mail on the arm of the couch.

Alex laughs. In contrast to the still-confused and searching look in his eyes, it's unsettling. "Oh fuck no."

♦

Alex disappears before lunch with a murmur that he's going to get some air and an exhortation for Paul to keep an eye on the baby. Paul gives him ten minutes, then leaves Claudia under Laura's watchful eye and goes after him.

He finds Alex on the back porch that looks out over the scrubby lawn and the fields behind the house. He's hunched over in some position Paul assumes is meant to be healthy or strengthening or something, because it doesn't seem like it makes much physical sense.

"Nice view," Paul observes. He takes a seat next to Alex on the old plank steps of the porch.

"If you want dead grass and dying trees, we can get that in California."

"Wasn't talking about the trees," Paul says. He slides a hand down Alex's back.

Alex straightens up and untangles his limbs to sit more normally. "You can get that in California too." He looks around. "My life is fucked up in eight hundred ways, but the most fucked-up thing is doing yoga on my mom's back porch in Indi-fucking-ana."

"Is it making you feel peaceful and at one with the earth?"

"It's making me feel murderous and like I want to eat half a cow."

"If it helps, I don't think your mom's making

salad for lunch."

Alex bows his head over his knees and sighs. "I really don't want to be here."

"I know."

"I spent high school on the wrestling team so people couldn't fuck me or kill me."

Like many of Alex's confessions, the one is out of nowhere and more weary than sharp. The information isn't really new, but something twists inside Paul to hear Alex say it out loud, his voice swinging a little more sweet and rural than it does anywhere except in South Carolina. Or when Alex is very drunk.

"I figured. I didn't know you were a wrestling champion, though," Paul says to give Alex the out if he doesn't want to talk about this.

"I was." Alex grins sharply. "Did you see my medals?"

Paul nods. They're on the wall opposite Alex's baby pictures, hanging next to his high school diploma.

"And now I'm super buff, and nobody here could even touch me if they tried, except I'm doing fucking yoga on my mother's fucking back porch so I can make myself *less* buff. But, I'm still not back to looking like a twink which means I still look like the thing that used to be able to kill me. By the way, my relationship with my body is incredibly fucked up right now and why can't I go back to Iceland?"

"Is this why you've been really into the service-sub stuff?" Paul says with a mellow chuckle, in an attempt to defuse some of this tension.

"You've been spending way too much time with Liam, and can you not say that out loud this close to my mother?"

Paul smiles at the slight flush in Alex's cheeks. It's better than worrying about Alex saying he wants to go back to Iceland. Alex ran away from everything that was limiting and hard in his life back when he was eighteen and terrified. His tendency to withdraw, disappear, and lie hasn't entirely gone away between then and now. Paul will never forget the first time they argued and Alex had run. There's no reason Alex might not decide to do that again.

"The question stands," Paul says, quietly this time. He rubs Alex's back and can't resist the temptation to slip his hand under Alex's T-shirt.

"Paul," Alex protests. He squirms forward, away from Paul's hand.

Paul pulls back. "Sorry."

"It's fine," Alex says distantly. He doesn't settle back, though.

Paul puts his hands in his lap, both concerned and fascinated at whatever is going on in Alex's head. "What can I do?"

"Not a fucking thing. No one's ever been able to do anything about this place. Least of all me."

◆

After lunch, neighborhood ladies that Paul suspects Alex can't remember the names of come over to visit. They coo over the baby, but when they reach for phones to take pictures of her, Alex practically leaps between them and Claudia. Paul can't blame him when Alex gathers her up, announces she needs a nap, and takes her into Laura's bedroom.

Paul wants to go after him, but he stays in the living room and makes pleasant small talk with the women until their disgruntlement over being practically chased away from the baby subsides. Any pictures anyone takes of Claudia Keane are almost guaranteed to end up on the internet, and neither he nor Alex feel good about that prospect.

Paul knows he should be less surprised than he is that nobody Alex's age stops by the house. He may be a celebrity now, but apparently Alex was not kidding when he said he had no friends in high school.

After dinner, they sit out on the front porch in the mellow evening light. Alex tentatively sets Claudia down so she can pull up fistfuls of scrubby grass on the lawn. After about half an hour, a rusty pickup truck pulls into the driveway.

"Him again?" Alex asks Delilah scornfully.

"What? He has a job."

"Tell me he doesn't still work at the car shop," Alex says under his breath as the guy – a former or possibly current boyfriend of Delilah's, Paul guesses – walks across the lawn.

"At least he's not the one who landed me in jail. Heyyy, Billy." Delilah stands up from the steps where she was crouched next to Alex. Their visitor hugs her. "Look who came home!"

Alex looks warily up at the guy, who seems to be about his age, while Paul exchanges glances with Laura.

"It's Alex!" the guy says, smiling broadly and offering Alex a hand.

He stands up carefully to take it.

"The big TV star comes to visit the little people." It's jocular rather than sharp, but Paul can still see Alex bristle.

"Hello, Bill."

"So you're gay now." The guy looks between Alex and Paul.

"I was always gay."

"Is that why you did wrestling? So you could touch guys?"

The sentence is such an archaic one, from a world Paul hasn't encountered since he was in middle school, it nearly takes his breath away. How do attitudes like that still exist? Except they do. Clearly.

"I did wrestling so I could protect myself from guys. Get off my porch."

"Hey, no offense. Nice to meet you," Bill says to Paul, who just nods at him. He's afraid to say anything that will make this situation more miserable or provoke Alex into doing something really ill-advised.

Alex doesn't sit down again until Bill and Delilah have driven away, and when he does, he slumps into Paul's side.

11

The last thing Alex wants to do the next morning is get in their rental car and drive from his mother's house to his high school. The house he was leaving then was different, but it's too familiar and feels too much like everything he ran away from when he pulled out of this street and onto I-67 to head west, leaving Indiana behind in the dust where it belonged, forever.

The school is smaller than he remembers and even older and sadder looking. He feels immensely self-conscious of the car as he pulls into the parking lot. It's a rental, a few years old and grubby from the roads here but still so much nicer than anything else here.

Margaret had been the one to make most of the arrangements with the school, and part of the agreement had been no cameras allowed. That had been one of Alex's few stipulations. He cannot deal with the world seeing this place.

There's a teacher waiting for him by the front door, by a trio of benches that were new at some point in the last decade. Alex is slightly shocked when he realizes that it's his old chemistry teacher. Of course a lot of the staff would still be here. He's not that old and high school wasn't that long ago.

He's glad he managed to talk Paul into staying behind at his mom's house. Alex definitely doesn't want to deal with the added attention his husband and daughter attending the event would bring.

The inside of the school is as disquietingly familiar as the outside, and Alex doesn't know how to make small talk as Mr. Miller leads him to the gym. The practiced patter of the red carpet won't work here. Alex feels his shoulders tense in a very un-yoga-like way. In this moment, he hates everything about who he is now, because it feels like such a betrayal of everything he came from. Indiana may be terrible, but being poor is just being poor.

The students seem younger than he expects. He deals with teenage fans all the time and usually hates it, but he's forgotten how very small fifteen can be. The gym bleachers are pulled out for everyone to sit on. When the principal, who is new, introduces him, he thinks, absurdly, of all the wrestling matches he ever competed in.

He spends so much time standing in front of mics and chattering these days, that it seems a little ridiculous to be stuck behind Martinsville's ugly chipboard podium. Still, he's glad to have something to hold onto.

His speech isn't much. He considers confessing his fear at being here, or the abject misery of the place when he was a teen, but the people he's afraid of and angry at don't deserve the satisfaction. Instead he talks about how much he'd wanted to get out and how hard it was, and how much he was only able to because of hard work, dumb luck, and the internet. To the extent that he can let his eyes focus on the students – which is very little – they look bored.

When he tries to open the floor to questions, the principal says there's a list of vetted questions he'll read.

"Seriously?" Alex says into the mic.

"We wanted to weed out the inappropriate

ones."

In other circumstances, Alex would be grateful. In this one, he suspects he'd prefer the inappropriate ones. "Do you have any idea how many inappropriate questions I get whenever I do anything?" he asks, half to the principal and half into the mic.

The students laugh.

Alex realizes that, now they have a common enemy, they are totally interested in the proceedings and completely on his side. Seeing what they can get away with together is, suddenly, like a sheer cliff face – a challenge Alex can't resist, even though he probably should.

"Hey," he says turning back to them. "Anyone got any real questions?"

There's silence for a moment and some rustling from the bleachers while the kids look at each other and consider their options. Finally a kid toward the back raises his hand tentatively. Alex points at him.

The questions are intrusive, as everyone had expected. They ask about how he and Paul met, what life is like with a baby, how he learned to shoot. But getting those questions from people like him feels a lot better than getting them from journalists and fans who have far less of a right to his story than they think.

Eventually a girl with blue hair and a lot of eyeshadow in the front row asks if he went to prom.

"Yeah, no. That was going to happen never," Alex says. People laugh, even though Alex doesn't think it's funny. He hadn't had the money to go even if he'd had the faintest desire to, which he didn't.

"'Cause I want to go to prom. With my

girlfriend. And the school says we can't."

"Really?" Alex says slowly. He feels a frisson of something strange, like Liam's charm mixed with Victor's viciousness; it feels like Christmas. Alex turns to the principal. "Did you really tell her she can't bring her girlfriend to prom? Because I think she can call the ACLU about that."

The principal looks vaguely uncomfortable. "School policy is..."

"You did catch the part where I'm super gay and they were all asking me about my husband, right?" Alex says, not remotely interested in making him more comfortable. "Also, I'm totally serious about the ACLU."

The principal clears his throat. "The policy has nothing to do with orientation, Mr. Cook. The school district felt –"

"They told me," the girl pipes up, "that if two girls paired up then maybe there wouldn't be enough girls for all the boys to have a date."

"You have got to be kidding me." Alex is shocked only by how creative his alma mater has gotten with its conservative bullshit. "That is – I am not going to swear, because this is a school," he says and grins when he gets a laugh out of the kids. "That is profoundly effed up. One, I guarantee you there are actually gay – and bi! – boys here who would happily go to prom together if the rest of this town didn't live in the dark ages. Two, guys are not owed girls. What even is that logic? I did not expect to have to have the 'gays and women are people!' conversation today, but hey, since I'm here. Public service."

"Mr. Cook, we're very grateful you've given us so much of your time –"

"Oh no, no, no," Alex interrupts. "I came a long way, and the more you talk, the more time I've got to give. I haven't even written the check yet!"

The principal looks baffled as to how this got out of hand so very quickly. Some of the teachers, on their folding plastic chairs, are making sour faces. One or two, though, are hiding smiles, and Mr. Miller – his old chemistry teacher – is grinning broadly, clearly on Alex's side. That's something.

"I could not write the check," Alex offers with a wink first to the kids. He would never withhold resources from them because their administration was intolerable. He suspects the kids know that. The administration probably doesn't.

The principal splutters. Alex suddenly wishes he'd had the chance to be in a teen movie when he was younger.

"How about this," he says. "Double or nothing. You bring your prom policy into the twenty-first century. I don't walk out of here right now, and I stay and answer some more non-vetted questions. Then I write a really nice check for the computer lab...."

He hardly has to let it hang for a second before the whole administration collapses in on itself and nods helplessly at him.

Alex smiles and turns back to the kids. "Okay. Anything else you guys want me to help blackmail the school for? Because this is spectacular."

◆

With Alex at the school, Paul is a bit at a loss of what to do. The quiet here feels less like the calm and peace of his hometown of Marion and more like a thing he's trapped in. Paul is, however, willing to chalk that up to his own discomfort rather than Alex's repeated assertions that this place is bad news.

He asks Laura if there's anything he can do to help around the house, but she turns him down. If there's actually anything that needs doing, Paul gets the distinct impression that Laura is used to, and prefers, dealing with it herself.

He ends up at the battered kitchen table by the window that looks out over the yard. He pokes at notes from Olivia on his laptop while keeping an eye on Claudia as she plays with a set of old wooden blocks Laura pulled out from somewhere. After a little while, Delilah comes down from whatever she'd been doing upstairs and slides in across from him at the table.

"Whatchya working on?"

"Production stuff for *Plague*."

"Is that your new show?"

Paul nods.

"We watched *Winsome* in the place. Is that blonde chick that crazy for real?"

"Darcy? She's something special." Paul can't think of how to respond to Delilah referring to prison as *the place*.

"It was weird seeing Jay on that."

"Yeah, I bet."

Paul's uncertain how engage with Delilah. Whatever fierce repartee she has with Alex, he clearly can't match it. Their striking resemblance to each other keeps throwing him, too, even if the way she holds herself is so very different. Paul wonders if Alex looked like her more in that regard, too, before he came out of the closet and moved to L.A.

"You know, he taught Darcy how to shoot for

that part," he says, searching for something they can chat about.

"Yeah?"

"He says nobody in Hollywood knows how to hold a gun."

"They don't," Delilah says scornfully, but then doesn't have anything to add.

Not a conversation starter then. Paul punches a few more keys in awkward uncertainty.

"Hey," Delilah says, suddenly brightening. "Do you want to see the place we grew up?"

◆

Paul leaves Claudia with Laura, who's more than thrilled to have her. Other than the couple of weeks after she was born, when Laura came out to L.A. to visit and help with the baby, she's not seen her more than a couple of times. Paul feels guilty about that, even though it's not his issue and is, Alex's crazy aside, just a reality of living on the other side of the country from their families. His mother and Sarah haven't seen Claudia much more than Laura has. He's aware that Alex may freak out at him for leaving their daughter alone with his mother, but leaving Claudia with her is certainly preferable to bringing the baby to the scene of Alex's anxiety.

Delilah leads Paul down the gravel driveway and onto the shoulder of South Graveyard Road – there are no sidewalks here – away from the main road and further back along the fields. They pass the two white crosses with their faded flowers and teddy bear. Paul tries to read the names on them, but the little plastic letters, the kind used for labelling mailboxes and the like, have mostly fallen off.

"Jay never told you anything about the old house, I bet."

"Not much. I just remember when he was helping your mom move."

"Sending a check does not count as helping," Delilah says. "Just so we're clear. Also it would have been nice if anyone had bothered to tell me Mom moved before I got out."

Paul is less surprised by that than he thinks he should be. "So everyone in your family is shit at communicating? Not just Alex?"

Delilah smiles sharply at him. "That's what happens when nobody's got anything to say that anyone wants to hear."

They walk in silence for a few minutes, along the gravel and occasional bits of broken glass at the side of the road. No cars drive past, and there's not even any hum of farm equipment. Aside from the few houses that dot the landscape, it feels as isolated as Iceland. Although, so much of Iceland feels like humans have barely touched it. Here, it's as if they've done too much and then fled.

"Here we go." Delilah points when they come around a long curve.

It's hardly, strictly speaking, a house at all, just a trailer up on blocks. There are places like this in Marion, and Paul knew people who lived in neighborhoods almost like this one when he was in high school. Except that those places were clearly homes, small but loved, and kinder sometimes than the house he grew up in. This one looks abandoned and ready to collapse in on itself.

The roof sags and some of the siding is missing, exposing the studs. More than that, though, it *feels* worse than any of the places Paul knew in South Carolina, and not for any reason he can put his finger on. The land feels wrong. Like it wants to take hold of him and never let him go. Not unlike the haunted pond at his family's farm that tried to drown him as a child. Paul wonders if Alex feels that here too, wonders what it was like growing up in a place that felt like it wanted to consume him and leave nothing but a blurred memory, like white crosses with their plastic letters falling off one by one.

"Dunno who lives there now," Delilah says. "Looks empty. Wanna snoop?"

"Ah, no. That's okay." Quite aside from having no desire to get caught trespassing with Alex's sister the felon, Paul feels uncertain whether, if he walked through that door, he'd ever walk out again.

Delilah shrugs. "Have it your way." She leaves Paul standing there on the side of the road and walks up to the house herself. To Paul's relief she doesn't try to open the door, but she does cup her hands around her eyes and peer in the windows.

Paul squints into the late-morning sun at the battered trailer with its rusting window frames and siding that's so faded he can't tell what color it used to be. "What was he like as a kid?"

Delilah turns around from her inspection of the house. "Who? Jay?"

"Yeah." Paul realizes for the first time that maybe Delilah calls him JJ not to annoy him but because he never was Alex to her.

"I dunno. He was a brat. He and I used to break into the neighbors' houses."

Paul stares at her. It's not that he thinks she's lying – she and Alex have both told stories about such adventures in the last two days. He just has no idea what he's meant to say, only that he's meant to say something. There is, somehow, more to this story.

"It's not like we took anything anybody would miss. Just little stuff. Sometimes food."

That takes Paul aback. That Alex had been poor growing up is demonstrably obvious. Paul didn't know he'd been hungry. Until this moment, he'd never realized just how bad Alex's childhood really was. He looks at the house again and wonders if it was in any better shape when Alex was living in it.

"He told me about the time you tried to stab him in the kitchen," Paul says.

"I bet he did." Delilah laughs. "Did he tell you it happened twice?"

"Yeah. Never told me why, though."

"'Cause he was my brother. Duh."

There is no appropriate reaction to that, so Paul says nothing. For a long moment they stand together in silence.

Finally, Paul speaks. "I grew up on a farm in South Carolina. We had a pond that tried to drown me when I was little, and in the end my parents got divorced because I was gay. Whatever scary shit you tell me, and whatever the hell it is that upsets Alex about this place so much, I'm not going to run away screaming. I've spent a lot of time trying to convince him you're not evil, just messed up, and I've seen too much weird shit – most of it in my own head – to waste time on you trying to freak me out."

"Are you saying that you're on my side?" Delilah says. It's almost a flirt.

Paul shrugs and doesn't look at her. "Could be. Maybe I'm just on the side of the angels. What happened to Alex?"

"Nothing."

Paul sighs and turns away. "Fuck you," he says.

There's no real anger in it. He's just tired of everyone's fear and misery and silence, including his own. He can walk up the road back to the house with or without Delilah by his side.

♦

Paul is surprised and then worried when Alex is late getting back from the school. He gets even more concerned when Alex doesn't respond to texts asking how the talk went. He'd assumed that he would get out of there as fast as he could. He can't imagine anything good he would have stayed for. Paul keeps glancing out the window at the road. The third or fourth time he catches Laura's eye as she does the same thing.

She gives him a tight smile of solidarity and looks away. Delilah, who'd returned to the house not long after Paul, seems unconcerned.

Alex finally pulls into the driveway as Laura starts getting dinner together. Paul meets him on the front porch.

"How did it go?" he asks carefully, despite the fact that Alex is glowing.

"Very, very well," he says. He grins and grabs Paul for a kiss. "I gave an awkward speech, and the kids helped me blackmail the administration!"

♦

Alex tells the whole story over dinner, clearly delighted by his performance and the belated fuck-you to the school administration. Laura takes it all in stride, reminding Paul of nothing so much as his own mother's reaction to anything odd that happened around him growing up. She's clearly seen it all – especially with Delilah's track record – and nothing Alex does can surprise her anymore. Delilah thinks Alex's exploits are hilarious. Paul, however, feels mildly concerned.

Yes, Alex clearly enjoyed himself, and maybe the trip to the school will, in time, prove as therapeutic as Paul had hoped. But these choices are out of character and not the work of a well-adjusted adult. Paul has no idea what the fallout from this performance will be like – either for Alex or for the kids at the school.

After dinner they gather in the living room. Alex pulls out his phone and discovers – to his elation – that one of the kids at the school filmed the whole talk and posted it online. Paul sits on the couch and watches the video on his laptop while he scrolls through his inbox. There are a few emails from the *Plague* medical consultant, a brief note from Carly filling him in on what's going on with Ali and Vic while they're gone, and a number of messages from Olivia about subjects ranging from a meeting with some executive bigwig to a pissed but hilarious screed about the AC unit in her office leaking and destroying the carpet.

Alex sits on the floor playing with Claudia. He also keeps tapping at his phone, presumably poking his audience of Twitter followers. Paul is reminded of Victor, and while he should probably be concerned about that, all it does is leave him fond.

His performance at the school is masterful if unnerving. Paul's never seen him be quite so vicious or delighted in public. He wonders what

Alex would have become if Victor hadn't died.

"What did you do all day?" Alex asks him eventually. He pulls Claudia onto his lap and leans back against Paul's legs.

"Worked," Paul says. He glances over at Delilah as he does.

"All day?"

"Would you prefer I went out and shot bottles in the back?" Paul asks.

"You deserve a break."

Paul wonders how sarcastic Alex is being. Certainly Alex finds nothing relaxing around here.

"Actually, Delilah and I walked down to see your old house," Paul says. Better to admit it now than leave Delilah to tell Alex in private, probably with her own dark spin on it.

"Why?" Alex directs the question at Delilah, not Paul.

Delilah shrugs. "He wanted to see."

"You asked to see the old house?"

Paul nods. It's not the technical truth, but it seems the better option than bickering with Delilah.

"Why?" Alex demands, more urgently this time.

"It's just a house."

"Nothing here is *just* anything," Alex snaps. "Did you bring Claudia down with you too?"

Paul shakes his head.

"You left the baby alone with my mom?"

"Alex, I'm right here," Laura puts in.

"Whatever your problem with this place," Paul says quietly, his voice warning, "it is not your mother."

Alex tosses a somewhat apologetic look at Laura. "Package deal."

"Sometimes, I don't get you at all." Paul is baffled both by Alex's changeability and the ongoing dramatic specter of, as Delilah had so cryptically informed him, nothing.

"Good thing there's nothing to get," Alex says sharply. "I'm not a puzzle."

"Really?" Delilah drawls.

Paul is disconcertingly reminded of Alex at twenty, coy and terrified.

"God, fuck off, will you?" Alex says.

"Language," Laura says. Which is totally fair but also a losing battle. After all, Carly's helping to raise their child.

This time Alex snaps at Paul. "Yeah, that's what's wrong with this place. Why the fuck did I let you talk me into coming back here?" He stands, hoisting Claudia up with him. He stalks out of the living room and bangs through the screen door onto the back porch.

"Goddamn delayed reactions," Paul mutters. He sets his laptop aside and gets up to follow Alex and the now-whimpering Claudia. At least Laura and Delilah don't come as well, although he's aware of them watching from their seats through the door.

"Okay," Paul says, once he gets outside. He tries his best not to let the door slam. His best isn't good enough, though, and Alex flinches at the sound. "You have been a rollercoaster since we got here. Which is fine. I get that this is hard. But I know you, and I know we're getting to the place that turns into screaming matches for us. I don't want that."

"What, no trailer trash arguments for the Hollywood couple?" Alex's smile is vicious.

Paul is not going respond to that. Especially with Laura and Delilah in earshot.

"You told me to come here so I could sort out my shit and realize all the monsters under the bed were just my imagination," Alex says. "They don't feel like my imagination. It's like you and that fucking pond at your mother's house." He gives a despairing sort of chuckle. Then his face goes still as he swings Claudia back and forth on his hip and looks out at the fields behind the house.

Paul comes up beside him and bumps their shoulders together but doesn't say anything.

The silence between them stretches. If it takes all night for Alex to speak again, Paul is perfectly willing to wait for him.

"I'm sixteen," Alex says, after a long time. Paul looks at him sharply. Alex's voice is low and flat, and it makes the hair on the back of Paul's neck prickle. "Delilah's dating a guy five years older than me. It's a Sunday afternoon in summer. We're out in front of the old house. Everything is hot and bright and dry. And her boyfriend points a gun at me and suggests I either let him fuck me or I let him shoot me."

Somewhere, in the distance, Paul can hear the whine of insects in the fields and the scrunch of tires as a car drives down the main road. "What...?" he starts. His is voice breathless, captivated by the looming horror of Alex's words.

"Nothing happened," he says with a shrug.

"Jesus Christ, would everyone stop saying that?"

"He's not lying." Delilah edges the screen door open and slips out.

Alex bounces Claudia on his hip, head bent down into hers to baby talk like none of this is real.

"Alex, what happened?" Paul says firmly in the

voice he hates to use because Alex always too readily obeys it.

"I just told you. Her boyfriend pointed a gun in my face and threatened to rape me."

"Yes, I got that. And then what?"

Alex shrugs. "I told him to fuck off and went back in the house."

Paul lets out a long sigh, but it's not relief. The story is horrifying. Alex had every right to be traumatized then and has every right to still be living with that trauma now. Paul wonders if the worst part for Alex is how long he has kept this particular secret.

12

Between Liam's obligations to his family and Minette's obligations to work, three weeks and two cancelled attempts go by before they both have a night free at the same time. Dating with kids is hard. Dating in Hollywood is hard. Combined with the complications of his family structure, sometimes Liam wonders if he should be dating at all. But Minette is the first new person who has made him inclined to try since Victor died.

Liam is late, as he really should have known he would be. He texts Minette frantically from a stoplight. *So sorry. Be there in fifteen. Baby drama followed by traffic drama.* He finds a parking spot mercifully close to the restaurant they'd picked and hurries inside. He hopes Minette hasn't decided to give up on him entirely.

But there she is, sitting at the bar in a brightly colored dress, a glass of wine in front of her.

"Should I get used to this?" she asks, standing so she can accept Liam's kiss to her cheek.

"Dates at restaurants, or me being late because everything's hard, even when it shouldn't be?"

"The second one."

"Basically, yeah. It's not personal though. I never was good at schedules and having kids did not improve that."

"So I see."

Minette's judginess of him hasn't slackened any, but she's regarding him now with less exasperation than she ever has in a meeting room. Liam decides not to test her patience further. At

some point, he'll need to explain his everything –
from autism to relationship structures – but they're
not there yet, and he worries it would just sound
like more excuses. He didn't tell Alex for years;
actually, he never told Alex at all…which is a
problem he'd like not to repeat.

"Let's get a table?" he asks.

They're seated in a cozy corner. The space is
sort of industrial hipster chic with exposed
ductwork painted black and garden lights strung
from the ceiling.

"Victor would have hated this place," Liam says
when their waiter lights the candle on the table
between them and departs.

"Okay?" Minette laughs uncertainly.

"I mean, that's not why I wanted to bring you
here," Liam hastens to clarify. "But it's true, and –"

"And you have no filter, especially when it
comes to him?" Minette finishes for him.

"Yes. Exactly. Although filters aren't my strong
suit in general. And I should probably explain more
about my relationship with him at some point."

"Is there more to tell? I do know Victor was
your boyfriend."

"*Everyone* knows Victor was my boyfriend. But
he wasn't 'just' my boyfriend." He uses finger-
quotes because boyfriends are important, too. "I
mean, if you really don't want to know, tell me and
I'll stop. But I've been a total thorn in your side
for…kind of a long time now, mostly because of my
feelings about him and his work. But he was also
my partner, as much as Carly is and for longer,
even. Our relationship wasn't about the work, but
the work was a big part of how Victor showed that
he cared for people. Nobody's replaceable, but no

one can ever come close to playing the role in my life that he did. When he died, I kind of had a massive breakdown. There were a lot of things I couldn't do that I'm normally able to. Moving past that is my day job. Which totally isn't an excuse for anything I've done, because I know I've been a massive, massive hassle for you and a lot of people around *Scism*, and I don't expect you to forgive me on those grounds, but as far as context goes...." Liam trails off and shrugs. "I thought it might be useful."

Minette stares at him.

Liam wonders, with a brief sense of panic, if he has far overrun what Alex calls Normal Human Monologue Length.

"So," Minette says slowly, and with what might be a smile dancing at the corners of her mouth. "What you're telling me is that you're a flaky asshole with a heart of gold, but not actually as big of an asshole as that makes you sound."

Liam considers that. "Basically, yeah. Why did you agree to go on a date with me again?"

"Self-effacement doesn't work on you."

"I'm still curious."

Minette fiddles with the little cut-glass holder the candle is bobbing in. "I have a few answers, but all of them would stoke your ego and I think that wouldn't be good for either of us right now."

"Tell me more." Liam leans his elbow on the table, his chin on his hand, and gives Minette his most charming smile.

"Oh no. Here's how this is going to work. You and I are going to gossip about other people tonight, and other people and I are going to gossip about you tomorrow. We're going to see if we have anything to talk about that isn't work, because you can't be dating me because you're used to dating whoever is in charge of this project."

"That's not –"

"Then prove it."

"All right." This might not be going quite how he wants, but at least Minette's instructions are clear. "Where are you from originally?"

"Because no one is really from L.A.?"

"No one is really from L.A." Liam confirms, although Victor was.

"Atlanta."

"How'd you wind up out here?"

Minette shrugs. "The gravitational pull. You?"

"New York. I needed to know I could. And then I was lucky enough to be able to stay."

Minette gives him a crooked smile. "I don't know what that's like at all. Except I suspect I know exactly what that's like. So, first job…this is a classic nightmare L.A. story, but I think you'll get a kick out of it. I was a personal assistant which is a job title that never ends well."

This date is going nothing like he'd expected. By declaring work off-limits their friction and the hint of the elicit are gone. But this is still totally working; Liam wants to laugh with the wonder of it all.

◆

Paul and Alex have two more days in Paragon after the event at the school, about which word spreads thanks to the magic of both small towns and the internet. Every time they stop at a gas station for snacks and beer or walk into their hotel, people recognize Alex. Multiple times, people try to take pictures of him through their car windows. Traffic down South Graveyard Road increases.

Whatever relief Paul expects when their plane finally takes off from Indianapolis never comes. The Alex he brings home to LA is, very clearly, not an Alex who has his shit together. In the days that follow Paul wonders just how big a mistake he made insisting on going to Indiana. Alex probably has – and has always had – PTSD of one form or another. He definitely needs more structured help than Paul alone can provide.

Thankfully, Alex remains good with the kids. In fact he seems brightest and most like himself when he's taking care of the babies or hanging out with Ali – horsing around, reading with her, or even just going to the yoga classes he still hates.

Aside from the kids, though, Alex wants nothing to do with anyone who is not Paul. He refuses to go to family dinners or spend evenings together with everyone. Even afternoons with Liam are intolerable to him. When Paul insists – or Alex can't otherwise avoid them – he's chipper and animated in a way that's definitely a performance. Alex probably means it to be reassuring, an attempt to brazen his way through coping with people, but it comes across as grotesque. Liam is clearly worried, Carly is concerned and pissed off, and Paul doesn't know what to do about any of it.

At this point Paul isn't surprised Alex refuses to talk, but it is exhausting and it is not making their collective lives easier. *Plague* premieres soon, which means Paul's days – already long – are getting longer. Aside from the general stress of that, the work means being apart from Alex far more than he wants while Alex is not okay.

When Alex tells him two weeks after they get back from Indiana that Gemma is coming over for lunch, Paul's surprised. It's been so long since Alex has been able to stand anyone's presence except his and the kids', he can't help but wonder what his reasons are.

He hopes it will be a good thing for Alex. Certainly, Gemma is the only one of them who actually knew Alex when he was still living in Indiana, and the one he hatched his escape plan with. Even if it won't solve everything, maybe having her around will put Alex back on something of an even keel.

◆

For the first half an hour or so after Gemma arrives at their house, she and Alex don't make much more conversation than small talk. Alex doesn't mind. He's had enough of telling stories. He just wants to enjoy Gemma's company. She was the first person he ever felt really safe with, and he lets himself soak in that feeling as they make lunch together.

"So, business proposition," Gemma says, digging in the refrigerator for vegetables.

"Yeah?" Alex asks from the stove where he's sautéing chicken.

"Come be in *Scism*."

Alex starts laughing. The sound is rich but distinctly dark even to his own ears.

"Excuse me," Gemma says, straightening up from the refrigerator with a bag of broccoli slaw. She looks affronted, but Alex doesn't have any bandwidth to be kind.

"Seriously?" he retorts. "Victor is dead. I am

done with his shows. No, no, and no. Why are you even asking me?" His plan for today had been to escape with Gemma into reminisces of their (relatively) carefree existence in a crappy L.A. apartment a dozen years ago. Gemma bringing up the man who still lingers in his memory as an evil fairy godmother does not make him feel safe. Especially when she's using him to guilt Alex into something.

"Because you are my friend, you're not currently attached to anything, and you have three kids, you could use a job close to home that doesn't require travel." Gemma's voice is as sharp as Alex's. "Also, tell me you don't want to be an awesome evil bishop."

"Yeah, no. Look, I am so relieved Paul isn't a part of the clusterfuck this show is surely going to be. I'm certainly not going to step in it."

"Wow, way to be supportive," Gemma says.

"How do you want me to be supportive?"

"For one, I'd like you to not be a dick about a major project that has been a major pain in my ass for months now."

"You work in development. What did you expect? You talk about how you never see me and how TV is hard, like you're the only one with those issues. I'm married to a showrunner in case you forgot." Fighting with Gemma is not good choices right now, but that's kind of the point.

"I never see you, and development *is* hard," she insists. "People say yes when they mean no, they promise you money that never shows up, and I deal with the worst of everything we hate in this town all day, every day, and usually at The Ivy, which still has the worst salads. And if you call me to bitch about your fabulous life, I will damn well bitch to you about mine. I know you have fucking trauma over Indiana, but you're being awful. What is happening in your head?"

Alex shrugs. "You say that like trauma over Indiana's not enough."

"I'm not saying it's not. I'm saying something's worse now." Gemma frowns. "Are you sure you're okay?"

"I'm sure I'm not, and I'm sure you asking me to be a part of dead, fucked-up Victor's fucked-up project is not going to make me better." Alex doesn't want to talk about any of this, and he'll fight his way out of this nightmare discussion if he has to.

Gemma sighs. "You know, I am trying here, but I am rapidly running out of ways to try. You never talked to me about going to Indiana or whether I thought it was a good idea. If you had, I'm not sure what I would have said. But I did think that maybe taking some time to face your shit would make you less of the asshole you've become in the last however many years. I was, as usual, wrong."

"What's that supposed to mean?" Alex says sullenly.

"Do you want the part about fame making you awful or the part about how you've exploited your whole Indiana poverty schtick for years so you can be America's Cinderella story forever? It's creepy, it's weird, and it's rude. The most annoying part is that I know you know it, and yet I'm still standing in your kitchen explaining it to you. What I can't figure out is if you get off on me going through these motions or if you just don't care."

He bangs up from the island to refill his glass at the sink so he doesn't have to look at Gemma. "I was always this awful. You and the rest of America just didn't want your precious little J. Alex Cook to be anything but perfect or to think too hard about why I might not be. So don't put that on me."

"Bullshit. I lived with you for a year before...." She trails off and flaps her hand around to mean *fame.* Alex doesn't understand how everyone still does that to him. Even people as enmeshed in the business as she is. Especially in the middle of this fight.

"Oh, you mean the year you were too wrapped up in your own failed career plans to notice you weren't the only awful person living in our apartment?"

Gemma pulls back and goes cold. "Are we seriously going to do this?"

"Do?" Alex says casually. "Seems already done."

◆

The next day Ali has a dance recital. Liam takes her there early so she can get ready. Paul and Carly are going to the venue once they get out of work; Alex is supposed to join them just as the recital starts. Meanwhile, Risa, Carly's long-term girlfriend, is watching Vic and Claudia for the evening.

The arrangements are the kind of logistical headache that would be difficult to keep track of under any conditions. Trying to re-enter life in L.A. after a week in Indiana, Alex finds the constant back-and-forth emails working out the schedule unbearable. The constant reminders on the damn polyamory app Liam made him get are even worse, at least until he figures out how to silence them. He just wants someone to tell him where to be and when, and for that to be the end of it.

What makes it all worse is that Alex can't even get there early and hang out in the auditorium with Carly, Liam, and Paul before the recital starts. He gets too much attention in public, which has always been true but these days is getting worse. The last place he wants to pull focus is at an event for one of their kids.

He decides to go climbing, because he doesn't know what else to do with himself. Maybe some time alone on the rocks will help him clear his head after the mess of the last few weeks. For the first few minutes as he gets his gear together, Alex thinks it might actually work. Ever since his disastrous fall years ago, he's always been meticulous about setting up for a climb.

But once he starts up the face of the rock wall, he has time to think again, and as always of late, that's not good. He keeps churning over memories of being in Indiana with Paul and Claudia, which in turn leads to memories of living there years ago. It's like an extended daydream, but a terrible one filled with inexorable grinding underlying misery. He'd thought a decade of building a life and a family far, far away would eventually remove the power of the place he'd come from. But he'd been wrong. Going back to visit had merely fed a monster he'd locked in a box but not destroyed.

He tries to focus on the work ahead of him: looking for the next handhold, getting the right grip on it, keeping the right proportion of his still-uncomfortable weight supported by his legs and not his arms. But Indiana keeps intruding.

At the top of the cliff – sweaty, chalky, and

unpleasantly sore – Alex checks the time on his phone. Then he swears. The climb took longer than he'd planned. Probably because he was distracted. Possibly because he's still not totally in sync with the current and changing state of his body. Unless he starts back down right now, and takes some risks on the descent, he is so not going to make it to Ali's recital on time. And he learned years ago not to take unnecessary risks on the rocks.

He groans and pushes back some of the hair escaped from his ponytail. He has no good way out of this, and being late to the recital would be a disruption that wouldn't be fair to Ali or anyone else's kid.

There's going to be hell to pay, but there is only one obvious choice here; he feels uncomfortably guilty already at the prospect. But what else can he do? He pulls out his phone to text Paul not to expect him, so Paul doesn't freak out and call 911 when Alex doesn't show. Then he sighs and pulls water and a granola bar out of his pack. Even if he's letting everyone else down, he still needs to take care of himself.

♦

Alex's return home is exactly as miserable as he expects. Carly opens the door of her house to his knock with a positively murderous expression on her face. Any protest Alex was going to make dies on his tongue when he hears Ali crying from the living room.

"Shit," he says.

"You think?" Cary bites back at him. She turns and heads back, presumably to Ali, leaving him standing there in the doorway.

♦

Alex's attempts to apologize to Ali are, reasonably, rebuffed. When he slinks back to his own house, Paul is sitting at the dining room table with his laptop, waiting for him. He looks at Alex over the top of his glasses when he walks into the room.

"Before you say anything," Alex says as he drops into a chair across from Paul. "I know."

"What happened?" Paul asks quietly.

"I lost track of time. Because my body still doesn't work the way I want it to anymore, even with the yoga and the ballet and the never-ending diet. And now Ali is sad, and Carly and Liam are pissed, and I know you're pissed even if you're sitting next to me all calm and good cop right now."

Paul doesn't even try to deny it. He calmly shuts his laptop. "Getting verbally upset doesn't seem like it will do much good. I don't know if you want to feel bad or just don't care or know how to fix it."

"Can we just go with yes?" Alex says.

"Yeah. We can. Look, because someone needs to say it, thank you for being safe today and thank you for communicating. I don't know why you thought there was time for you to climb but...I know it could have been worse. I'm glad it wasn't."

Alex grimaces. "Too bad that doesn't fix anything."

"You haven't been in a good place since you got back from Iceland. You're in a worse place now. I want to help –"

"That worked out so well with Indiana."

"I know. I'm sorry. I also know our extended

network of friends and kind-of family is making that harder. Both for you and my ability to help you."

He pauses, like he's giving Alex a chance to say something. Alex doesn't know what to say, so he just shrugs.

Paul folds his hands on top of his laptop, looks at them, then looks at Alex. They've been together for ten years now, through breakups and makeups and more fights than Alex cares to recall. But for however much the shape and status of their relationship has changed through the years, the sheer fact of Paul in Alex's life hasn't. Paul's hair, once sandy blonde, is liberally sprinkled with salt and pepper, and he's had a beard for so long Alex sometimes forgets he was clean-shaven when they first met until he sees old pictures. He's grown into his role as showrunner, he's a model father, and he's mentally healthy in a way Alex couldn't have imagined for him when they first got together.

The narrative of Paul's life has been about growth and improvement; next to him Alex feels like an abject failure. He's had work he relishes, friends he adores, a daughter and sort-of-daughters he loves more than he ever thought possible. And yet, this long after he left Indiana, he's still a mess who can't cope with the rewards of luck and sheer hard work life has given him.

Looking at Paul as they sit at their dining room table, the baby monitor next to him humming softly from the sounds of the white noise machine in Claudia's room, Alex feels like nothing and no one.

"I'm not a mind reader, Alex," Paul says gently. "If you want me to know what's wrong, you have to tell me."

"You mean aside from the fact that I'm fucking up at every turn here?"

"I can't and won't argue that, but nobody does shit without reason. What's yours?"

Alex can't make himself meet Paul's eyes and instead stares somewhere past his shoulder. "You've been to Indiana now. You saw where I grew up. Literally, because Delilah took you to our old house even though I didn't want you to see it."

"You don't have anything to be ashamed of."

"I wasn't *ashamed*. I didn't want Indiana to get you, too."

"Alex?"

"When I was a kid, my life was a disaster of unreliable, crazy, distracted people. A lot of whom were dangerous. My mom tried, but she couldn't be there all the time. So, the smaller my world was, the better it worked. I was safest when it just me and everyone else was a potential threat."

"Okay. That makes sense. Can you keep talking?"

"And now, here, today, in this timeline, there's too many moving parts. There's too many people policing me. There's too much external judgment. And now the past – Indiana, Delilah – has literally come back to haunt me. I know it sounds crazy to you, because it sounds crazy to me, but I've gone from feeling left out of the family you all made when I was in Iceland to feeling like there are way too many people available to try to stab me in the kitchen."

◆

Paul completely sympathizes with Alex, but they still need to find a way to move forward as a family. The night after Ali's dance recital, everyone gathers on Carly and Liam's back deck after dinner. Ali is over at a friend's house for the evening. Vic and Claudia are chattering with each other in some mutually intelligible baby language as Vic tries to show Claudia how to put together a little wooden puzzle. Claudia's much more interested in chewing the pieces than connecting them. The adults gather around the table, Alex more reluctantly than the rest.

"Getting called into Victor's office to get yelled at was not as intimidating as this," Alex says sullenly as he slides into the chair next to Paul's.

"You got called into Victor's office to get yelled at?" Liam asks curiously.

Alex sighs. "No, it was a figure of speech. Victor just screamed at me in front of people."

"Only that one time. Because you and Paul fucked in your trailer," Liam points out. "Loudly."

Carly puts a hand on Liam's arm. Paul agrees with her sentiment. Liam's commentary is generally fine, but right now it is a universe away from being helpful.

"Okay, whatever is going on right now, that is not relevant," Alex says. "Also, that was vastly unpleasant. Much like this."

"So let's get it over with as quickly as possible then." Carly says.

"Sure, if you can keep Liam from interrupting every two seconds," Alex says.

"Hey," Liam says as sharply as Paul's ever heard him. He's relieved when Alex looks at least faintly guilty, though he doesn't say anything.

"And this will go a lot faster if you are not mean or unnecessarily an asshole." Carly's voice goes steely.

Alex nods.

"Okay," Carly says, her voice gentling now. "We know you've had a fuck of a time recently. Definitely since Iceland, maybe before that, but you've been a mess since you got back and Indiana hasn't made things better."

Alex gives an awkward half-shrug.

"And now," Carly continues, "It's negatively affecting us and, more urgently, having an effect on Ali. Clearly, you are having reservations about our family. And whether you've always had those, or they're new, or you are just being an asshole, we need to talk."

"These family meetings are one of the things I have reservations about," Alex snarks.

"Alex," Paul says softly.

"Way to be supportive," Alex bites at him.

"I'm right here next to you," Paul says carefully. "But we do need to put everything on the table. Us adopting Vic and Ali as their third and fourth parents, your job, the house next door – because I think we're approaching the point where you need to fish or cut bait."

"That's the expression you go with, Mr. Crickets?" Alex asks.

"It's as apt as any," Paul says steadily. He has to quash the urge to snap at Alex's continual attempts to deflect. He wants to push back as forcefully as Alex is goading him. In these circumstances, Victor might have. But that's not who Paul is or can be, as useful as that ability would probably be right now.

Alex gives him a faint grin, and for a moment

Paul thinks this is all going to be okay.

But then, Alex sits back in his chair, and says, "What if I want to cut bait?"

♦

After they get home and put Claudia to bed, Paul takes the baby monitor and Alex's hand and leads him out to their backyard. They climb into the weird wicker daybed they got last summer. Paul loves it because when Alex is tucked against him they're completely cocooned away from the world. All he can hear is the wind whistling through the canyon, the faint gurgle of water in the pool, and the sound of Alex's breathing.

"I don't understand why you're not mad at me," Alex says eventually.

"Were you trying to make me mad?"

"Not this time," Alex says with the faintest breath of a laugh.

"Were you trying to make Liam mad?" Paul asks.

"Definitely."

"Will you bite my head off if I ask why?" That's the question Paul keeps coming back to in this clusterfuck.

"No," Alex says and tucks himself closer against Paul.

No more words are immediately forthcoming, but Paul's willing to wait him out.

"Everyone else is mad at me," Alex eventually mumbles.

"You've kind of been on a tear," Paul says gently.

"I mean they should be pissed. I've been an asshole."

"No disagreement here. Although at least you haven't tried to punch anyone."

Alex gives a soft chuckle that's a little wet. "It pisses me the fuck off every time I miss him."

"Victor?"

"Yeah."

Paul feels the tug of his own grief at Victor's loss. The man is irreplaceable on so many levels. "Is he what this is about?"

Alex shrugs.

"I would understand if it was," Paul says. "You need a villain in your life. Which I think was Indiana, and then it was Victor, except now you live here and Victor's dead, and you're trying to figure out who to hate next. I appreciate the work you've done not making it me, but it's not your sister, no matter what happened when you were a kid. It's not Gemma, and it's not Liam just because he makes your life complicated."

"Okay, but you understand that Victor was actually a villain and actually tortured me?"

It seems best not to ask too much about that right now. In order to get Alex through this conversation he needs to stay on topic. Letting Alex linger on subjects that seem likely to only upset him further would be counterproductive. Alex isn't flying off the handle at him or anyone else right now, and Paul would like to keep it that way.

"Still," he says. "Victor's dead, and you need to not make anyone in our family your next nemesis. Besides, you know Victor only put you through the dead Zach wringer because of how much respect he had for you."

"Paul? You literally just told me somebody victimized me because I'm special or some bullshit.

Like, fuck you," Alex says so easily it throws Paul off.

"You're right. I'm sorry," Paul says, because an apology is surely necessary. "Did Victor know about what happened in Indiana?"

"No. At least I never told him. God knows what he would have done if I had."

"So, just you and Delilah since you were a kid?" Paul presses. He knows he'll have to think about what Alex has just, very legitimately, pointed out about Victor's relationship with consent, but he can't quite bring himself to do it now with Alex in his arms.

"Who was I gonna tell? *Nothing happened.* Also, gay kid, Indiana. Even if anything had happened…." Alex gives a dark chuckle. "God," he says. "Nothing fucking happened to me and now I'm a big rich famous movie star who can't even cope with a trip home. How does everyone not hate me more?"

"It wasn't nothing. And you can't feel guilty about that," Paul protests. "Your trauma is real. Your sister's trauma is real. They don't cancel each other out."

"Why not? Delilah was the one dating the guy. I was just…there. She was fourteen. And she went to juvie and then prison for him. Not then, but later. And I graduated high school and got the fuck out of there and still have nightmares about a *thing that did not happen.*"

Paul finds Alex's hand and tangles their fingers together. Alex squeezes tightly.

"Threats and danger are both legitimately traumatizing. The things that happened to your sister and how she tried to cope with them were also legitimately traumatizing for you. You get to be affected by that," Paul says. "You get to ask for support. You get to feel not okay."

Alex rubs his face against Paul's chest. His long hair catches in Paul's beard, but Paul would have to let go of him to fix that and that is so not happening.

"Delilah and my mom are still in that place," Alex says. "And despite having all the resources in the world there's nothing I can do about it. My mom won't leave, and I don't get why. I don't know what's going to happen to her there. And I'm scared of what happens if I'm generous with 'Lilah."

Paul presses a kiss to the top of Alex's head. "Right now, it seems like you're scared of what happens if you're generous with anyone," he says. "Because I've done the thing you're doing, where I'm an asshole because I think people should hate me, and it's not a good thing. It's also not your style."

Alex squirms out of Paul's grip and flops onto his back. "Remember how I never wanted any of this?"

Paul nods.

"That hasn't changed."

Paul props his chin up on his hand. "You love the travel, though. And the work. And being a Viking for four months, and the stunts, and whatever crazy shit you do that's going to make my hair even grayer."

"The gray is hot."

"I'm glad you and the internet think so. My point is, however, that you love this life, and I'm not saying that just because I'm a big part of it." Paul reaches out his free hand and strokes up and down Alex's side.

Alex takes in a deep breath. "Yeah, but I'm back from Iceland now and I have to deal with the media junket soon. I will be on a plane every twenty hours – or less – for two weeks. I mean, that's fine, I guess, except for being away from you and Claudia." Alex bites his lip and stares up at the wicker ceiling of the daybed. "I thought my life couldn't get any more disrupted than it did when I was twenty and Victor turned it upside down. Except there's *Saga*, and apparently I'm a movie star now. It's orders of magnitude, and I am just not prepared for this. Meanwhile, while I'm freaking out about fame, my family is still in fucking Paragon. I'm a fucking mess, and everything that should make things better – like my friends, like Liam, even you sometimes – feels really, really hard."

"What do you want to do?" Paul asks, after a long silence where they just listen to the wind and breathe.

Alex rolls over onto his side to face Paul. "I don't know. Not feel like I have to figure that out tonight. All the choices feel too big and too frightening."

Paul finds his hand again. "Did you mean what you said about cutting bait?"

"Yeah. In the moment, I did, at least." Alex looks down at their twined fingers. "I feel terrible for saying it. But it would definitely be easier."

"In some ways," Paul says. He's a little afraid of what might happen should Alex decide he really wants out of this life. For now, he can't do anything about any of it except wait. Alex is still trying to work out for himself how not to feel guilty about Indiana, much less what he wants in this life he never chose.

"In some ways," Alex echoes wistfully.

Paul is quiet for a long time. That the silence doesn't feel ominous is a relief, and it's what gives him courage to say what needs to be said next. He's been thinking about this possibility for a while. He'd hoped it wouldn't be necessary, but now it definitely seems to be.

"So, hey," he finally says. "I'm not telling you to leave – I am never telling you to leave – but if you need to get out of here and take a break before the junket and everything else, you should do that."

"Is this you trying to get rid of me so you can have a happy sane family with Liam and Carly?"

"Okay, seriously, Alex? I know everything is hard for you, but come on. I love them like the family they are and we have systems that work. But they work because you're a part of the story too."

"Yeah, okay," Alex says, a little sulky, but he gives Paul a faint smile.

"Figure out what you need and want from a distance where you feel safe to deal with everything. You taking the time to do that is way preferable to what's going on right now."

Alex takes a deep breath and lets it out slowly, but doesn't say anything.

"Just think about it, okay?"

"I will." Alex props his chin on his hand and runs a fingertip down Paul's chest. "But not right now."

"Too much all at once?" Paul asks fondly.

Alex shakes his head. "No, actually. It's just no matter what I do, I don't want to take a break from you."

13

In the weeks that follow Alex is thinking, that much is obvious to Paul. Whether that's what to do about his sister or what he has in mind for the future of their family arrangement or where he wants to take off backpacking for a week, Paul doesn't know. All he can do is wait for Alex to tell him.

It's not the worst thing he's ever waited for from Alex, even if Paul has to remind himself of that some days. He's fairly sure that whatever is going on, isn't about the two of them and their future. That said, they have commitments to three little girls, not just one. He worries about how to navigate a scenario where Alex wants there to be no one else in the world other than him and Paul and Claudia.

Alex does, however, manage to at least contain whatever he's going through. He attends family dinners, and even apologizes to Liam for threatening to leave the arrangement they all have. Liam accepts it, then quietly asks Alex not to mention it again, unless Alex has a specific plan he wants to discuss.

For himself, Paul is busy enough with the run up to the *Plague* launch. It's a good distraction, but he works hard not to lose himself in it. Whatever disaster is or isn't looming, Paul is determined not to let himself contribute to it by his absence, physically or mentally, from their family.

Still, he's a little nervous when Alex rolls onto his side one night after they fuck, grabs Paul's hands, and says, "So I've been thinking."

Paul looks down at their intertwined hands and squeezes them. It's better than prolonging the time it will take Alex to say whatever is coming next by making any sort of quip.

Alex gives him a small smile. "I do want to get out of here. Before the junket. Just for a little while. But maybe for longer than you were thinking and farther than you were thinking."

"Okay," Paul says. "Whatever you need. Where and how long?"

"The whole time I was in Iceland – people didn't notice me there. I keep wondering if all of Europe would be like that. And if I go, it's far away, which makes it harder for me to be lazy and come home before I'm really ready. I think I'd feel safe there. So, basically at random, but maybe because of the whole *Scism* situation and whatever business I still have with Victor, Italy?" He says it like a question, and searches Paul's face until Paul nods. It's farther than Paul might have expected, but he also wouldn't have been shocked if Alex went back to Iceland to climb glaciers. On the list of stuff he's worried about, location is pretty low.

"How long?" Paul asks again.

Alex looks down. "I'm not sure."

"Okay," Paul says gently, although he is concerned now.

"I think I need to not have a deadline for my escape. I want to be gone and not have to think about counting down the days to when I have to feel better."

Paul makes himself take three long, deep breaths before he even tries to respond. Because what Alex is saying makes perfect sense. It's also terrifying. "Won't you just be counting down to the junket?" he asks. The question is a cowardly one and he knows it, but he hates the idea of Alex not having a return plan no matter how good the argument for it.

"Hopefully I'm not going to be gone *that* long," Alex says. "If I am, we'll figure things out. Just like anything else." Alex hesitates before he speaks again. "I love you. That's not the question here. I just don't know if I can be with you the way we are now."

Paul's breath catches. It's not anything he didn't know already. Certainly Alex has been struggling with whether he can handle Carly and Liam's place in their lives. But hearing Alex say it out loud is terrifying.

"I know," Paul says softly. Alex presses their foreheads together and closes his eyes. Clearly, he's as overwhelmed as Paul is. Paul disentangles one of his hands from Alex's and cups it around the back of his head.

"I'm afraid you're going to ask me to make a choice," Paul says quietly, offering his own confession to match Alex's.

Alex blinks his eyes open and looks confused. "Between what?"

"Between you and the rest of our family. Because I have obligations to Carly and Liam, not to mention Ali and Vic. So while you're in Italy sorting yourself out, I also need you to work out where you are on our friends and how many daughters we have. Because god knows I can't ever say no to you, and this is hard."

◆

"You're going *where*?" Ali drawls in a remarkable impression of Carly's judginess. She and Alex are walking from their weekly yoga class back to Alex's car.

"Italy," Alex says again.

"Don't say it's boring like Indiana. I'll know you're lying."

"How's that?"

"Half the kids at school have been to Italy. Duh."

Alex chuckles. Ali certainly has reasonable grounds to be upset with him, which is why he'd decided to wait until she'd forgiven him for the dance recital to tell her. God knows what she'd tell the other tiny, terrifying yoga kids if she'd had this ammunition in class. "Oh don't worry, I won't."

"So *why* can't I go? I mean, if you and Paul are gonna adopt me and Vic at some point, don't you think you should take me?"

Alex admires her logic. "Because I have to sort some stuff out with myself, and Paul and I think the best way for me to do that is to take a break from everything. A temporary break!" he adds hastily when Ali crosses her arms over her chest.

"This is just 'cause your sister is mean and you don't like Indiana?"

"In part," Alex says. "In part it's because I never really got time to take stock of my entire life ever since I got this one. And I'm making things harder for everybody now by being around."

Ali turns to Alex and narrows her eyes as they get to his car. "Are you asking me to see if I'm okay with you going? Or like seeing if I have any wise magic kid-advice?"

He so wishes she did. "You are sort of my kid, so you get to be mad at me if you're not okay with this plan. Also, you've been watching too many movies."

Ali tuts. "Yeah, because my father won't let me be in one."

"It's less fun than it looks," Alex admits.

"What do Mom and Dad and other-Dad think?"

Alex is torn between guilty curiosity if he also ranks as some sort of dad on Ali's ordering of the universe, and being really, really glad to be getting out of here for a while. He also doesn't want to answer Ali honestly, but knows he'll get caught out in a lie.

"Carly and Liam aren't thrilled. Paul suggested it."

Ali spends a long moment in deep concentration. Finally, she says, "I'm not cool with your shit, and I don't know how to fix it. Just so we're clear. Can we go get smoothies?"

Alex laughs and pulls her in for a hug she grumbles against.

"Eww, you're sweaty!"

"Yes, you're gross too." He kisses the top of her head. "Make Paul go with you to yoga while I'm gone."

She wrinkles her nose at him. "He's not the yoga type."

"Would you rather go with Liam?"

Ali frowns theatrically. "Point."

♦

In the week after Alex decides to go to Italy, he seems steadier with something to plan. Paul does his best to take that as a good sign. Usually, Alex goes quiet and withdraws when he's getting ready to go away. This time, though, he seems more engaged and happier than he has in ages. It's charming to come home from work to find Alex at the kitchen table, Claudia on his lap, reading to her about the Forum while she tries to eat his pen.

But as he stands in the doorway to the kitchen, watching them, Paul can't help but think that soon Alex is going to be gone from his life again, with no plan or schedule to come back. He digs out his phone to take a picture of them before either of them realize he's there. And as he finally walks into the room to kiss Alex hello, he tries just to enjoy the time they have together now. Better to enjoy the moment than dread all the days or weeks or months when the only part of Alex he'll get to see, will be on a screen.

♦

"So I'm leaving in three days," Alex says one night as they lie together quietly in bed. "What do we need to talk about before I start packing?"

"You tell Ali yet?" Paul asks. He knows she's sort of part of the problem Alex is getting some space from, but it still has to be asked.

"Yes. A while ago. I tell Ali everything," Alex says smugly.

It's true. Alex does. While never being inappropriate, he definitely walks the line between cool dad and friend, and indulges their mutual brattiness in ways none of the other adults really approve of. That said, his honesty and openness with her probably goes a long way towards her not being screwed up by the constant tornado that is Alex's own struggle with adulthood.

"How's she taking it?"

"I think she's more pissed I'm not taking her to Italy than she was about me not taking her to Indiana."

"Sensible child," Paul says in lieu of having any wisdom to offer.

"I know this is running away," Alex says. "But I also know this is me trying to do right by everyone else. Or so you're letting me think."

"Put your own oxygen mask on first," Paul says almost by rote. It's been a joke from therapy for both of them for years now.

"Yeah. Am I going to get to stop feeling guilty about that?"

"Maybe not, but you can work on it. And, well, speaking of things you shouldn't feel guilty for..." Paul has been planning this conversation almost since the moment Alex decided to go to Italy. He hadn't been able to decide whether having it in bed was to the good or not. But they're here and it's apparently happening now, so he rolls with it.

When he hesitates, Alex tucks his arm under his head. "What?"

"I want going away to be a good thing for you. And God knows I want you to come back to us when you're ready. Which also means, I want you to do whatever you need to do while you're gone."

"That is vague and nonspecific."

"And you're not Liam. You know exactly what I mean."

"Maybe you should say it for real then, so I can yell at you for it."

Paul cups Alex's face in his hands and kisses him. "I'm not saying add random dick to your sightseeing list. I'm just saying, have whatever adventures you need to."

"Without you?" Alex says. He sounds a little scared and incredibly vulnerable. It makes Paul want to wrap himself around him and never let go.

Paul smiles. "We've always allowed each other to have relationships – as in friendships and emotional connections – that don't involve each other. That includes Liam and Carly. That can also include anyone you meet in Italy."

"Okay, is this you trying to use my crisis to transition our marriage to polyamory? Like with whatever random Italian boyfriend you think I'm going to pick up?"

"No, but I want us to stop being codependent and stifling each other and living in fear."

"Why are you saying this to me when everyone is pissed at me for leaving, and wants me to stay home and not be gone on movies, and being all 'Alex, you're being bad for the kids?'"

"Because it needs to be said. Because I'm not mad at you. I'm telling you to go to Italy," Paul reminds Alex gently. "And to do what you need there, whatever that looks like. If that includes sex, so be it. You can't keep demanding your freedom and then getting pissed off when I remind you you've had it all along."

"Is this a test?"

"Absolutely not. Go figure out how much human contact you need however you need to figure that out. Then tell me, so we can plan what our lives should look like for the next decade. You forget this all the time – which is not your fault, because the world lies to you about it all the time – but the only person you belong to is you."

"Then what's all this?" Alex smirks and gestures between them. He's clearly fishing for both compliments and reassurance.

"Love," Paul says. He means it too, even after Alex squawks at the sappy indignity of it.

"So what's the deal?" Alex asks, still grinning. "Give me some terms."

"When it comes to what you do – tell me, don't tell me, I don't care. When it comes to what you need – tell me. That's it."

14

Alex's flight is scheduled to leave on a morning in mid-August. The night before, he's pleased but not surprised when Paul comes home from work early. His worry over Alex has been quiet but insistent. Paul can't do much to help him at this point, but Alex appreciates the thought.

Alex is in the living room with Claudia when he gets in. Vic and Ali are with Carly and Liam, but Alex wants as much time with Claudia as possible tonight. Especially when he's not sure when he's going to be back. They eat dinner together, not talking much and not needing to do more than be in each other's presence. The mood is heavy, solemn, and Alex isn't comfortable. He feels like something momentous is about to happen, the way he's rarely felt in his life, and he doesn't know what to do about it. Certainly the night before he ran away from Indiana to L.A. didn't feel this heavy.

After dinner, as they get ready for bed, even Todd knows that something is up. He winds around Alex's legs, mewing mournfully while Alex changes Claudia and gets her into her pajamas. The cat's sadness reminds him unpleasantly of the night he and Paul broke up, years ago, back when Paul was a mess and Alex was a confused and terrified kid. Alex had been trying to pack his stuff to leave, and Todd had kept climbing into his suitcase like he was trying to make him stay. He didn't have a plan for coming back then, either. Although that time, Paul wasn't home, and they'd just been screaming at each other.

Alex smiles to himself as he puts Claudia down in her crib and fishes her favorite stuffed animal out from underneath it. Fraught as this evening is, he's definitely leaving on better terms this time.

Both he and Paul stay in Claudia's room until she's asleep. Then, Paul takes Alex by the hand and leads him down the hall and into their bedroom.

Alex isn't sure how he doesn't sob the entire time they fuck. He feels too much of everything: Anxiety and dread about leaving the house in the morning. Fear of everything terrible that happened, and didn't happen, to him when he was a kid. Worst is the nearly unbearable tenderness with which Paul touches him.

"It's okay," Paul whispers to him at one point, moving in him gently, the weight of him on Alex's body the only thing keeping him together. "I've got you. I'll always have you."

Alex has to close his eyes. Paul brushes the tears away from his cheeks with his fingertips and kisses him softly.

After they both come, Alex doesn't want to sleep. They only have hours left together and he doesn't want to waste any of them being unconscious. He curls against Paul's body. Paul wraps his arms, warm and protective, around him. Alex tries to let everything else go and just be.

Of course he falls asleep within minutes.

The next thing he's aware of is his alarm is going off. It's morning. He blinks his eyes open to see Paul already awake, gazing back at him from the pillows. Alex is sure he hasn't slept at all.

"Time to go?" Alex asks softly, his voice raspy.

Paul nods.

◆

By the time Alex lands at Fiumicino, Rome's airport, he's sore, exhausted, and entirely not prepared for the complete clusterfuck at the arrivals terminal.

Twelve hours in the air was pure torture. Now that he's here, he wants nothing more than to get back on the damn plane and fly home again. But that's the point of having come this far; the distance is meant to keep him from turning right back around.

Going home again without doing what he came here to do would make things so much worse. The only way out of this, is through. The only way to get distance and figure his shit out is to actually take the time and do the work. No matter how much it hurts right now.

Alex video calls Paul from the hotel as soon as he gets in. He desperately wants to see Paul's face and hear his voice. But he's also reluctant as he waits for Paul to pick up. Seeing Paul as a cluster of pixels on a screen and not a warm, living body he can touch will only make the distance so much harder. But Alex needs to see the kids – Ali, because she'd asked and he'd promised, and Vic and Claudia, because they are babies and don't understand why Alex is gone. They should be able to see him every day.

The conversation with each of the kids is short, and when it's just Paul on the screen Alex stares at him from six thousand miles away and doesn't know what to say.

"Alex," Paul says gently.

"Yeah?"

"Go get some sleep. I'll be here when you wake up."

♦

Alex spends most of his first two days in Rome sleeping, interspersed with the occasional call home to the kids. He's done enough travel, and enough pushing through jet lag over the years, that he feels justified indulging in rest. When he wakes up on the third day he feels more rested than he has in months, possibly since before Claudia was born. Or maybe even since Victor died.

It's not just the sleep. It's not having a schedule – filming, press, kids, or otherwise. For all the luxury in his life now, this one is entirely new. Even when he left Indiana for L.A., he'd had a destination and a plan.

When he finally does venture out of his room he snags a map from the front desk of the hotel. It's not to scale, and the downright weird illustrations on it mark him out as a tourist. He isn't planning on sightseeing, but he figures having a vague sense of where landmarks are in case something does strike his fancy is a marginally worthwhile plan.

Alex quickly becomes aware of how much he does and does not stand out in Rome. He's paler than most everyone, and the man in the tobacco shop who sells him tickets for the subway speaks to him in English before Alex can even open his mouth. When Alex does the man is surprised he's not British or Irish. Alex is thrilled to not be recognized. Not as an individual, and not even as an American. He wishes he could strike up a random conversation with the guy, but is at a loss as to what to say. Also, having lived in California with its draconian health consciousness for so many years makes the idea and ubiquity of the tobacco shops – tabacchi – deeply strange to him. He'll have to bring a box of the slender cigarettes wrapped in black paper with gold foil home to Carly, who still occasionally indulges.

The subway only has two lines, the A and the B, but Alex somehow still gets turned around trying to find the one he thinks he wants, even if he isn't entirely sure where he's going to get off. He just wants to go and see how things work so when he feels capable of making decisions, tomorrow or next week or next month, he'll at least be capable of acting on them.

People are in his way, the signage is poor, and he's not entirely sure the ticket machine has taken his ticket and that he didn't just hop a turnstile. The train cars are covered in graffiti and smell like piss. It's nothing like Los Angeles or New York except in how it is unideal. Alex smiles to himself as the train rattles along. The city as adversary is something he will always understand.

He gets out by the Piazza della Reppublica, marvels at the semicircular plaza for a moment, then chooses a direction and walks. Narrow streets are deserted, but wider streets are chaos, full of honking and buses. People run into traffic if only to dodge a bewildered looking tour group diligently following a woman in impossible high heels waving a closed, hot pink umbrella over her head.

After thirty minutes of this Alex is sure that he must be getting close to something interesting with each block, only to find more of the same. He considers the possibility that he chose the wrong direction. Finally, however, he tumbles out of a narrow street and onto a massive rectangular plaza lined with cafés. Tiny tables and rattan chairs are set up in front of each business, and artists selling their work dot the plaza.

Alex isn't sure he is going to find what he's looking for here, a pessimism made no better or worse by his not even knowing what that is.

However, it's a long way back to his hotel, and he isn't sure he can get there efficiently or even at all. The prospect of trying at this moment seems less appealing than staying here, so he drops into a chair at one of the café tables. The tables are crowded more closely than Alex is comfortable with but people continue to not recognize him.

When a waiter comes to take Alex's order, a man at a table next to his turns around in his seat to stare in despair.

"Oh no," the guy says in Italian-accented English. "Why do Americans always do that to coffee?"

"I'm sorry?" Alex isn't sure whether to be amused or affronted.

"May I make a suggestion?" the guy asks, looking between Alex and the waiter.

Alex laughs nervously. He's not sure what else to do. Also, the guy is appallingly attractive – olive skin, black hair that curls against the nape of his neck, the barest hint of scruff. His dark eyes glint with amusement as he smiles at Alex.

"Sure," Alex says, waving his hand. "Go ahead." It's not any weirder than anything he deals with from Liam.

While Alex tried to learn some Italian in the weeks before he left on this trip, he's doing a lot better with street signs than with spoken language.

He can't follow what the guy is saying when he speaks rapidly to the waiter.

"You'll like this much more," the stranger says to Alex when the waiter is gone. "Or maybe not, but at least you will not be ruining decent coffee."

"I appreciate the rescue," Alex says. He's still captivated by the guy's eyes and smile. In some life he might want to pursue that captivation further. Paul's offer of *do what you need to do* still hovers at the edge of his consciousness, but Alex can't see how taking advantage of it will help. Still, there are ways to be interested in people other than physical attraction. Alex has never really been able to just make friends before. Maybe now is a good time to try.

"My name's Gianni," the guy says, extending a hand over the back of his chair.

"I'm...Jay," Alex says, with a hesitation he hopes the man – Gianni – doesn't catch. He hasn't thought of himself as Jay since he was eight and told his mom to call him Alex. Which was also, come to think of it, the same year he realized he was gay. Or at least the same year he realized he wasn't like other boys.

He's not sure why he uses the name now. It's certainly not about maintaining his anonymity. Rather, it's about separating this trip from his life back home.

"It's nice to meet you." Gianni's grip is firm and warm. Alex doesn't have to evaluate Gianni on the basis of threat or Hollywood usefulness. In light of that, Alex is suddenly aware of how good his hand feels in his own. "You too."

"So, Jay, other than ruining our coffee, what brings you to Rome?"

Alex struggles for a moment to find something to say other than the standard 'tourism' answer he delivered at customs.

Gianni nods to Alex's left hand, where his wedding ring glints in the sunlight. "Honeymoon?"

"Ah, no," Alex says awkwardly. He's not going to lie about Paul's existence, but he doesn't know how to explain him in this moment that doesn't make him seem like jerk.

"Divorce trip then?" Gianni hazards.

"Nooooo," Alex says, but his laugh is a little weak. "An incredibly long story, actually."

"Well," Gianni say, folding his arms over the back of his chair and resting his chin on them. "We sit in cafés here all day, so unless you tell me to go away or are very boring, I have the time."

Alex does not tell him the whole story. He can't. But he tells him a lot of it and more probably than he should. He tries not to sound ashamed as he explains how fast life seems to happen and how woefully unprepared he feels for his own.

He doesn't say *acting* or even *Los Angeles*, but he talks about the job he got when he was twenty, and how it's incredible and hard and like nothing he ever expected or wanted.

"And then I went home to visit my mom and my sister for the first time since I left as a kid, and it was a mess. Now I've got another big career thing coming up, that's going to make all the hard things harder, for a while or maybe forever, and it all just kind of hit critical mass, and I can't cope with any of it. My family or my job." Alex chuckles weakly. "So now I'm here. To reassess and just...take a break."

"Do you always tell strangers your entire life

story?" Gianni asks curiously.

"Almost never," Alex says. It's a lie. Because *actually* never is what's true.

◆

Alex talks to Paul and the kids late that night – afternoon in L.A. Paul is working from home to tag-team keeping an eye on the babies with Liam, who pops into frame for just a moment to wave hello before going to rescue Todd from Claudia.

Alex doesn't mention Gianni. He may eventually, but coffee and conversation is hardly a major plot point or anything like the adventures Paul told him to go ahead and have. Besides, Alex likes feeling like he has something that's just his. He sat in the sun at a café for hours and just talked to someone with no fear of being hassled or recognized. The revelation of it is a small and precious joy, one he suspects might threaten Paul far more than any stepping out on their relationship.

Instead, he and Paul talk about little everyday things, even though there are more pauses in the conversation than actual words. While it's as awkward as many conversations they've had when they've been apart and uncertain of their future, it's not angry or sad. Instead it's tentative and filled with the sort of tension that's interesting instead of dreadful. After they say goodbye Alex is happy to undress and crawl into bed at the reassurance that Paul is, as he always has been, on the other end of the phone line and utterly fascinated by what they can be together.

In the morning, Alex picks a site at random off his shitty tourist map and plots out what he hopes is the best route to it. It feels a lot like the pleasant challenge of planning a new climb. He'll probably need a better map at some point if he's going to be here for a while.

Alex eats an almond croissant from the bakery up the street from his hotel as he waits for the train. When he realizes he doesn't have to worry about eating it neatly in case someone with a camera is watching, he takes excessively large bites, laughing to himself as he does. He probably looks half-mad and doesn't care in the least.

He's off-put by how crowded his destination is. The Spanish Steps are packed with people. Alex waits for a few moments at the bottom for claustrophobia or general people-unease to set in. Somehow, though, it doesn't. He's not sure why. It may be the sheer scale of the place or the chaos of the crowd that asks nothing from him other than that he be a part of it.

Whatever it is, he's determined to enjoy feeling like a normal person, for however long it lasts. He takes the requisite artsy cell phone pictures. He'll send them to Liam later, to prove he was out and about and also because he can easily imagine Liam here, in the middle of this old stone in this old city. Something about the feel of the place reminds Alex of the all the strange and occasionally spooky places he showed him in Washington, D.C.

Alex didn't plan a route to the previous day's café in advance, but he's reasonably confident he can get there without too much trouble. He's wrong as it turns out, and he ends up getting lost when his every attempt to avoid the crowds at the Trevi Fountain somehow leads him back to it.

He gets there eventually, though, and stops on

the edge of the palazzo to skim his eyes over all the tables with their rattan chairs. Until this moment, Alex has been trying to convince himself he just wants the familiarity of a place he'd already been...and really good coffee. But now that he's here he's forced to acknowledge how much he'd been looking forward to the offer of another afternoon of conversation with Gianni. But he's not here.

The sensation of disappointment, or at least this particular flavor of it, is new. When Alex first hooked up with Paul, Paul was everywhere: at work, texting him, even at a group brunch, although that was an awkward accident. Alex never had the opportunity to miss him until they broke up. But here, Alex has had a moment of connection, now lost. He doesn't know Gianni's last name, let alone his phone number. He doesn't know if he's queer and mutually interested in Alex, or just friendly and kind. Alex sinks into a chair, touching the feeling gently, like a scratch he's fascinated by.

It's not that he has any specific plan or hopes for Gianni at all. Assuming he could even find him again. It's that Alex enjoyed a conversation with someone who isn't already enmeshed in his life in a hundred different ways. Gianni is interesting and attractive and curious. He also doesn't seem to be collecting every detail of their interaction as a bargaining chip in some status game that even after so many years in Los Angeles, Alex still doesn't even understand. He simply wants the conversation to keep going.

He orders something – not whatever Gianni saved him from yesterday, though he can't remember what Gianni ordered for him either – and sits at the table, watching the square. He avoids coffee shops in L.A. for all sorts of reasons. But even if he didn't, American coffee shop culture dictates that people bring a laptop or some other kind of work with them. Here only a few people choose such a distraction. Mostly everyone is simply enjoying the sunshine and conversation. Alex feels odd to just relax with his drink and nothing else to do, but he also feels good.

"Hello, Jay, how is your coffee ordering going without me?"

Alex is jolted out of his reverie by Gianni, who stands smiling at him. His hand rests on the back of the chair across from Alex and he has a questioning look on his face.

Alex nods at him to sits down. "Better than yesterday." His heart leaps at Gianni being right here in front of him. Did Gianni come looking for Alex, too, or is he just a regular here? He looks down at his cup, mostly empty now. "I still think I need help though."

"Well then, let us start."

This time after Gianni gets them drinks, Alex makes him repeat the order, slowly, so he can actually catch it.

"Yes," Gianni nods when Alex finally gets the pronunciation correct.

"Thanks," Alex says. "I try when I travel, but I didn't have a lot of time to prepare before I showed up here."

"All the language classes in the world cannot teach you what is good coffee."

Alex laughs. "Yes. That's true. I'm glad you found me here," he says, because it's honest and because he wants to see what will happen.

"You are hard to miss." Gianni touches Alex's hand on the table where it's lying next to Alex's first, mostly empty, cup.

"I try not to be."

Gianni tips his head from side to side, studying Alex's face intently. It's a lot, but it doesn't feel bad, and Alex smiles a little coyly at him.

"I like your hair," Gianni says. "But I suppose you could wear a hat."

Alex starts laughing and can't stop.

The conversation again lasts for hours. This time it's less of a one-sided info spill on Alex's part, which is a relief. Talking about the job and the family he needs a break from had been cathartic, but listening is good too. Throughout, Gianni touches his hands with an ease that could be casual interaction and could be something else. From what Alex has seen so far, men in Italy touch other men in public with an ease and intimacy that makes flirting somehow both easier and harder. And Alex has hardly ever flirted with strangers at all. Liam, he knew, and that affair involved very little flirting. Paul, he's known forever; whatever clumsy flirting they did at the beginning, Alex hardly remembers.

Gianni is a photographer. Alex has to stop himself from moaning softly at the revelation and wonders briefly if he'll ever get away from people who work behind or around a lens. But he also wonders, with an acute longing, if Gianni being a photographer means they can talk about the craft of film without touching on the truth of Alex's life at all.

"So I am going out this week," Gianni tells him, "to take pictures of the ruined churches of Rome. I would be happy if you would come with me."

Alex chuckles. "I've been here less than a week and am practically sick of the churches already."

"I live here, imagine how I feel. The pictures of the churches sell well, but they have their hidden virtues too. Would you like to see?"

Alex can't help but be drawn in. He smiles. "Sure."

"Good." Gianni nods, looking pleased. "When would you like to start?"

15

That night, Alex doesn't call Paul. He sends him a short email – *Hi, I love you, Rome is good, but I'm not up for talking tonight* – so Paul won't worry, then spends the rest of the evening alone, sitting in the big bay window in his room, one leg hanging outside. Gallivanting around Rome with a hot Italian photographer is not what Alex had expected to do with his break, and he wants some time to just turn over the events of the day and his plans with Gianni.

He's happy to take the next day to do nothing more but call the kids and sleep some more. The morning after that he shoves his new, not-actually-for-tourists map into his bag and heads out to meet Gianni.

Gianni takes him to part of the city that's an ordinary jumble of business people and chaos. If tourists come here, it is by accident. He's relieved, rather than disappointed, at the mundanity.

The church, however, is anything but mundane. Alex doesn't even notice the entryway – there are only so many soot-streaked buildings his eye can register at any one time – but Gianni shoulders the door open and yanks on Alex's shirt to push him in ahead of him.

It's dark inside, miserably so, and it takes Alex a moment to realize that the church has no electricity. There are no glaring exit signs or chandelier candles replaced with light bulbs. What light there is comes from votive candles and the little sun that can filter through the carbon-coated stained glass. When Alex runs his fingers over the back of one of the pews they come away almost oily with the residue of paraffin.

"Why doesn't anyone clean it?" he asks Gianni, who stands quietly next to Alex waiting for him to get his bearings.

"With what money?" Gianni murmurs.

"I've seen pictures of the Vatican!" Alex exclaims, which earns a snort out of Gianni.

"And you would wash away five hundred years of prayers?"

Alex shrugs. "Depends on if they worked, I guess."

It's quiet – they're certainly the only ones here – and while Gianni futzes with his camera Alex wanders around, slowly venturing farther away from him. He's afraid to touch the warped, worn wood of the ancient pew again and is almost surprised when he closes his hand around the back of one and his fingers don't go straight through it.

Liam would either love this church or be terrified by it. Either way, Alex doesn't want to pull out his phone to take pictures for him. He wants to keep this place, with its dank, pale light and ruined finery, to himself for now.

Victor, surely, would love it. Alex always thinks of him as still alive...just somewhere else. He wonders whether he ever came to Italy. He had the money, if not the time. Victor's diaries, that Alex found and read after the man died, rarely mentioned travel or anything else outside of the context of work. Alex suspects he never saw this place. The thought makes him suddenly, horribly sad.

"Jay," Gianni says, when Alex stops below a

carved statue of St. Sebastian.

The statue's head lolls against a tree in what Alex presumes is the ecstasy of martyrdom. Alex only knows who St. Sebastian is because that's the sort of thing Liam likes to babble about.

Alex looks back at Gianni over his shoulder. "Yeah?"

Gianni has his camera in one hand and is looking at Alex intently. "May I take your picture?"

For a brief moment Alex is tempted to say no. He barely knows Gianni, two sort-of dates aside, and his entire life, since he left Indiana at least, has been about avoiding the cameras of strangers.

But he came to Italy to leave L.A. – the inconvenience, the complexity, the paranoia – behind. Besides, he does like Gianni, and these photos won't end up on a shitty blind website or even Facebook. He's not yet sure Gianni knows who he is. But even if he does, this is something Alex wants.

So he says yes.

Gianni takes a few moments to put Alex where and how he wants him. It's almost like the work of a photoshoot. Alex can feel the tug that wants him to sink back in his own head and just go away while Gianni touches his arm and his chin to get him in the limited light the way he wants. But being present here and with this man feels good, so Alex does his best not to disappear.

Alex blinks when they step back outside into the noise and rush of the city.

"Do you have somewhere to be?" Gianni fingers the strap of his camera bag. He's still looking at Alex with that intent gaze.

"No," Alex says. Even if he did, he's not sure

he'd be able to walk away from the pull of Gianni's eyes. "Do you want to get food?"

They get arancini – fried balls of rice sticky with cheese and filled with mushrooms and prosciutto – and sit on the edge of a fountain to eat it. That they're surrounded by street kids hanging out and smoking cigarettes makes it perfect and like nothing Alex has experienced before. Neither of them are in any rush. After they finish eating, they sit together while it gets dark and the lights come on in the surrounding buildings. They talk about the church and Gianni's work and the random things Alex read about Italy before he came here. Gianni delights in correcting his misapprehensions and elaborating on things Alex is interested about. It's another new, strange pleasure when Gianni lets him click through the pictures he took during the afternoon. Normally Alex is never, and never wants to be, involved in that part of the process.

"Do you want to take a walk?" Alex asks eventually, looking over at Gianni who's leaning back on his elbows on the edge of the fountain, head tipped up to the sky.

Gianni nods, and Alex offers him a hand up. "Where to?"

Alex wonders what the hell he's doing. He has desire, but no clear plan and no real ability to even articulate to himself what he wants. He's wandering off into a city he still doesn't know with a man he just met. This might not be the smartest choice Alex has ever made. But he trusts Gianni. If Alex gets them lost, he'll be able to get them home.

Two streets over Alex grabs Gianni's hand again to pull him into the little niche formed by two buildings that don't quite align. Here, in this crevice of stone, they are out of the circles of light that spill from street lamps and windows.

"Jay," Gianni says softly, only partially a question.

"Do you know who I am?" Alex asks, breathless and chagrined. It's the worst sort of Hollywood question, one he has made sure never, ever to ask. Saying the words now is terrifying. But he needs to know.

Gianni hesitates before he nods. "Yes. Not at first, I didn't. But yes."

"Did you look me up on the internet to be sure?" Alex is still nervous. He's also grateful Gianni didn't lie. "Did you talk to me because I look like who I actually am?"

Gianni shakes his head. "No. And we don't have to talk about it."

"Now?" Alex asks. "Or ever?"

"Whatever you want, Jay. Whenever you want."

Alex smiles, relieved. He reaches out to hook a finger into one of the belt loops on Gianni's jeans. He barely has to tug at all before Gianni is curling his hand around the back of Alex's head, cradling it away from the rough stone of the wall to kiss him.

It's been years since Alex kissed anyone new and not in front of a camera for work. His first reaction is a surge of unfamiliar nerves and a peculiar shyness. He's fascinated. Until he forgets even that.

Gianni crowds him back against the wall as the kiss gives up any concept of chasteness. They probably should not be doing this here in the street where anyone could see. It might not be safe. It's definitely not sane. But Alex is half-hard in his jeans and just does not care. He doesn't know what happens next, but he doesn't need to. Right now he just wants this – the moment before everything – forever.

◆

The first night Alex is gone, Liam sends Paul a message – through the goddamn fucking app, which Paul finds hilarious – inviting him over for the evening in case he doesn't want to be alone in the house. Paul appreciates the thought, and tells him so, but as much as he hates Alex's absence he wants some time to himself. Besides, he has Claudia with him, so the place is hardly empty the way it used to be when Alex travelled.

Cool, Liam messages him back. *What about tomorrow?*

Paul chuckles at his determination. *Sure*, he replies, in part because he suspects Liam won't let up until he agrees.

The next day Paul has meetings that run long and a spat between writers to sort out. He doesn't get to Liam and Carly's house until well after any sort of reasonable dinner time. Liam's out, and Ali and the babies are already in bed. Vic and Claudia are asleep, or at least there's no noise coming from the baby monitor. Ali's huddled under her covers when he goes to peek through the crack in the door into her room, but he's willing to bet she's faking and has a book in there somewhere.

Paul gets beers out of the fridge for himself and Carly, and they sit together on the couch for a while in companionable silence. They've been there nearly half an hour when Liam finally rocks in looking exhausted.

"Date?" Paul asks. Liam's been going out with Minette regularly for the last few weeks and has not infrequently stayed the night at her place. He seems thrilled with the new relationship, and Paul enjoys seeing him happy.

But Liam shakes his head. "*Scism* drama. And not the fun award-winning kind."

"Do I want to ask?"

"You can, but I'm guessing no. Networks. Sponsors. Money. Standards."

With a squeeze to Paul's thigh, Carly excuses herself to get some work done. Paul feels a stab of guilt that he's kept her from more important things but appreciates beyond measure that he has friends that look out for him when he's likely lonely and capable of sinking into depression.

Liam grabs his own beer from the kitchen and sits down next to Paul in the spot Carly just vacated. He looks at Paul intently for a long moment. Paul wonders if that's Liam being Liam, or if he's about to get ambushed.

"What is this about?" Paul says cautiously.

"How do you know it's about something?"

"I know how you do communication. You've never been subtle."

Liam laughs and relaxes a little. "Okay. We know getting us all together and talking to Alex hasn't been working. So we didn't want to do the same thing to you."

"That's good," Paul says. He suddenly has more sympathy for Alex's inability to cope with their group communication style; it's hard not to feel like he's in the hot seat…and there's only Liam here talking to him. Liam's been getting more comfortable around him over the last few years, so he tries to take this now as a good sign, or at least not something he immediately needs to be worried about. "What's going on?"

Liam sits up a little straighter and starts counting off on his fingers. "I have three things. They're all really one big thing, but there's different parts."

Paul nods for him to continue.

"One. Ali's taking Alex being gone badly. Like…really badly."

"Oh?" Paul frowns, concerned. That Ali has been somewhat out of sorts since Alex left has been apparent, but he's not noticed any major behavioral changes in her. She must have been saving those for Carly and Liam.

Liam nods. "Two – even the babies are upset, but of course they are, they're babies and they hate when anything messes with their routines. They'll be fine in a couple of weeks. But I'm not so sure about Ali. Especially with the school year starting so soon. We know Alex needs to go do…whatever it is he needs to go do in Italy. To be clear, that's not, specifically, what I'm talking about. What I'm talking about is Alex not knowing whether he's going to be a part of this family. Or what it's going to look like if he does decide to stay."

Paul tenses. He knows Alex deciding to opt out of their family is a possibility and has been for a while, even before he decided to go to Italy. They've talked about it a little, but much of that discussion came from Alex's heat-of-the-moment frustration. Where he actually stands has been less clear. Liam saying the words aloud makes that possibility real for the first time.

Liam seems to sense his emotional reaction and

shifts closer to him on the couch. He pauses, as if waiting for Paul to stop him or move away. When Paul doesn't, he leans into his side a little.

Paul is touched by the gesture, even if it's awkward and he still feels rocked by what they're discussing. Liam has been educating him in the odd ways of Alex for over a decade now, but feeling at ease and intimate enough to try to comfort him physically is relatively new. It's very sweet, and Paul has another moment of appreciating just how close Liam and Alex are, and how much they mean to each other.

"What I'm saying, I think we all kind of knew," Liam says. "We just thought we could put off saying it. Or something. That things would maybe magically sort themselves out without anybody making hard choices. Or maybe that was just me," he says with a self-deprecating laugh. "Anyway. This is three. We've been talking for almost a year now about all of us becoming legal parents of all the girls. Whether we decide to go through with that or not doesn't matter. I mean, it does, but whichever the outcome, we can make it work. The uncertainty in the meantime is just…not good. I know Alex is going to have to figure his shit out before you make any decisions together. But you have to soon. Because this is not fair to any of us. Especially not your daughters."

◆

Despite Paul feeling – and agreeing with – Liam's urgency, he knows better than to call Alex about this issue, not now. It's everything Alex is taking a break from, and a discussion about the legal and practical structure of their future before

Alex knows his own mind is only going to freak him out. Paul will talk to him about it, but he needs to give him as much space and time as he can first.

Paul does need to talk to someone about it, though. And before he had Alex or Carly or Liam or anyone to work his shit out with, he had his sister.

It's not just that Sarah is Claudia's aunt and deserves to know what's going on, it's that she has put up with Paul and his issues longer than anyone. On his drive home the next day, he calls her.

"So," Paul starts in lieu of hello. "Remember when we had Claudia and you agreed to be the egg donor with the understanding that the co-parenting situation wasn't going to turn into a complete clusterfuck?"

"Yes?" Sarah says warily.

"I think it's about to turn into a complete clusterfuck. Or possibly already has," Paul says before launching into a summary of the last several weeks, including where Alex is and why, and the potential adoption situation.

He's worried Sarah will have concerns and would not blame her in the least if she does. While she silently processes everything Paul tells her, he stares at the seeming miles of brake lights on the 101.

"I get it," Sarah finally says. "Family's complex and society is just coming around to accepting the complicated way people actually live their lives. Will the rest of you get it now?"

◆

Another day, another coffee, another noontime of wanting more, and Gianni offers to take Alex to the Vatican. He is tempted by the offer, but insists on going alone.

"It's complicated for me," Alex explains, thinking of Liam and Victor and Gemma's attempts to get him involved with *Scism*.

Gianni shrugs gently. "Religion usually is. Especially here."

Alex gives a crooked frown, because religion isn't really the problem. "Maybe I'll tell you the story," he says. "But I have to figure it out myself first."

Their fingers skimming against each other, Gianni lets him go so easily.

Alex wishes, when he gets to St. Peter's Square, that he had company for the museum line. He fidgets with his phone repeatedly to text Gianni or Liam or Gemma. But the point of being uncomfortable is to actually be uncomfortable. He slips the phone back into his pocket over and over again as he watches the people ahead of him check to make sure they have enough skin covered to be admitted inside.

Once inside, he is less interested in the art in the Vatican museum than he is by the space itself. He wishes he could know this place empty and wonders what it would feel like to think of this strange city – the Vatican, not Rome – as his own. Without children, without women, it is a city of ritual and ghosts, a testament to eternity built out of the wildly temporary. If he took Gemma up on her offer regarding dead Victor's controversial show maybe he could at least get a tour after hours.

He frowns when he finally reaches the Sistine Chapel. He stares up at its ceiling with crowds jostling him and feels nothing. Alex flees, promising himself he will figure out why the place matters some other time.

St. Peter's Basilica is no less strange. Alex's conviction that it will be easier for him to deal with if he assigns himself a task is correct up until he realizes it's impossible to light a candle for Victor there. The votives have all been replaced by tiny light bulbs. He drops coins into the box and pushes the button to light one anyway, but it makes him furious.

♦

Returned from the Vatican back to his room, Alex composes and deletes half a dozen emails to Liam before he shuts his laptop and goes to sit in his window. He likes it up here above the street, partially hanging out over nothing. He tries not to think about how, once *Saga* is out, he may not ever be able to do something like this again. Not make out with the man who has somehow become his Italian lover – even if they haven't yet had sex – while he takes a break from his real life. And not sit here in a window and observe the world, instead of having it observe him.

As much as he wants to be processing this with Liam – after all, Liam has always been there when he's been in crisis – there's no good way to tell him. Certainly not before he tells Paul. And he doesn't want to talk to Paul about Gianni yet. He will. Probably. Eventually. Even if Paul made it clear Alex doesn't have to confess his adventures. But Alex isn't yet sure if Gianni is going to be the sort of adventure Paul meant. This new relationship doesn't feel frivolous or casual, mainly because it's the first thing Alex has had to himself in years. He wants to keep it close.

He and Gianni develop a routine of meeting every other day – at the café, for lunch, or at one of the random, run-down churches Gianni likes to mess around in with his camera. At each one he takes more pictures of Alex. No matter where they meet, they end every night making out in the shadows.

"Do you ever want to photograph me *not* in a church?" Alex asks from where Gianni has him lounged in a pew, his arm draped over the back.

"Yes," Gianni says simply, raising the camera to his eye.

The next time Gianni walks past him, Alex grabs his hand in the empty church and pulls him down into a kiss. Fleetingly, he wonders if his choices are dangerous, both to heaven and on earth. Mostly, however, he doesn't care; this world is only what we make it.

The second week they spend together, Gianni takes Alex to his studio apartment and turns him loose while he sits at an oversized monitor editing photos. Alex wonders if this is the kind of space Paul would have if they didn't live in L.A. with their three floors, basement offices, massive square footage, and life of celebrity. This place is small, but bright with natural light; two walls are almost entirely windows. There's a tiny kitchen in one corner, and in another there's a bed partially hidden behind a curtain. Something in Alex lurches when he sees the bed, his mind suddenly full of possibilities. He's not sure he'll act on any of them.

He wants to, though.

The question of modeling comes up that night, while they sit on the floor with a bottle of wine and panelle – chickpea fritters eaten stuffed between slices of rich, doughy bread. Alex pulls a portfolio of Gianni's photos from a shelf and flips through them. Some of them are like the ones he's been taking in the churches and are about space and architecture and odd little details of this ancient city. What isn't art he can sell for postcards and stock photography; it's a way to make money as an artist. But the ones that really catch Alex's eye are his photographs of people.

Specifically, models. Gianni watches him quietly as Alex pulls out a second book. This one is full of figure studies. The nudes are all stunning, and Alex pages through them carefully, as much out of respect for the subjects as the artist. They remind him of Victor's sketches. This time, he supposes, he at least has permission to look.

He tells Gianni, haltingly, a little about Victor – the man who somehow made his life into this thing Alex is no longer sure he wants or can cope with. He's never spoken of Victor's impact to anyone who didn't know the man, and he's not sure how to now. But he talks about sneaking into his house and all of the drawings he'd found there. He talks about reading his diaries.

He expects Gianni to be taken aback – Alex is vaguely aware that normal people do not break into dead men's houses and steal their drawings. Gianni, however, seems to shrug it off.

"You are hard not to let in," he says. "Even if Victor did not know exactly how. Or was dead when he did."

"And you do?" Alex wants to laugh in both outrage and delight.

Gianni nods. "Maybe. A little."

Alex takes a long time looking through the

nudes. There are as many of women as there are of men, and the ones of women are just as good. Alex isn't surprised, exactly, but he is relieved. All women, he knows, have something to lose very much the way he, as a celebrity and public person, does. That's what happens when the world makes the mistake of assuming you are an object. That women have trusted Gianni like this, and that Gianni has repaid that trust so well, makes him curious.

"Normally, I hate modeling," Alex says after he sets the books aside. He's lying on his back on the plain wood floor and swirling the wine around in his glass. "So many people touching me. It's like I'm not even a person."

"If it helps," Gianni says, smoothing a hand across Alex's forehead. "It is not actually about you. It's about the art."

"That's true," Alex allows. "But it's not art when it's me. It's marketing. And I could bear that, a little, when I had Liam in that mess with me. Even when we were on different projects, the work was the same. But now he's in development and I'm stuck in front of the camera all by myself. Every time someone takes a picture I think about everyone who will eventually see it. Sometimes they make them think they own parts of me. Other times the pictures make them think they don't own themselves."

It's not a thing he's ever really been able to articulate before. His struggles with fame in relation to Paul were always a slightly different issue. Liam, despite his compassion, never understood at all. "Also I still don't feel like a person. Or even alive. I never have."

Gianni nods and refills both their glasses.

"Would you like to see if it might be different with me?"

◆

Liam can't believe he didn't ask Minette out sooner. Aside from the thing where they were at each other's professional throats; that was a good reason not to. Over the last several weeks they've still had their disagreements both personally and professionally, but the hard edge of those arguments has softened. Liam has no small amount of shame about how much grief he put Minette through because he couldn't trust anyone else with Victor's legacy. But Victor's true legacy was about risk and, after a fashion, teamwork.

But as easy as things are with Minette when they're right in front of each other, Liam's struggling to fit their relationship into the mental map of his life when they're apart. Not the logistics of it – he likes Minette a lot, and Carly and Paul are both totally fine with Liam adding 'Date night with Minette' to his calendar – but rather, how it fits into his emotional landscape.

He tries to explain it to her one night a couple of weeks after Alex leaves town for Italy. They're in her apartment, sitting next to each other on her sleek leather sectional sofa, with Minette's feet in Liam's lap. Liam likes her place; it's got lots of clean lines and a minimalist feel that reminds him of Victor's house. But where Victor preferred bright whites and neutrals, Minette's home pops with color. There's an accent wall behind them that's bright red, the throw rug is striped in turquoise and brown, and the shelving in her kitchen, just visible around the corner from the couch, is a vibrant yellow. It feels so welcoming and warm, and the colors just make him happy.

"So thing," he says slowly, rubbing his thumbs across the arches of Minette's feet.

"Thing?"

"Content about me that you may have feelings about."

"I have all sorts of feelings about you. Go on."

"When Victor died, my world shrank. I lost Victor, and that was awful, of course, but I also lost everything else, at least for a while. Now, I can tell you this story and say that was just grief, and it wouldn't be untrue."

"But...."

Liam takes a deep breath and decides to just go for it. "I'm autistic. Which doesn't mean anything because it's just a word for how I am, which if you know me, you know. But when I get overwhelmed, when things are hard – and sometimes stuff you wouldn't even notice makes them hard – I lose the ability to do things that were hard-won for me."

"Like?" Minette, to his relief, looks nothing so much as mildly curious.

"Speech is the big one. My wife and I passed each other notes a lot during all that. I cover well, usually. This isn't public knowledge. It's very easy for me to hide it with being flakey and an actor and so Los Angeles. Until it isn't. And I don't know if it will ever be an issue around you, but if it happens, I don't want you to be surprised."

Minette considers him for a moment. "Do you know how nice it is to not be the person in the relationship who has to explain her body or her mind or her self and brace for terrible questions?"

Liam tilts his head from side to side for a

moment as he thinks about that. "I'm not sure. Do I need to brace myself for terrible questions here or not?"

Minette shakes her head at him and wiggles her toes. "I may have questions, but I promise to try to not be terrible about them."

"Thank you. So here's why the warning, other than I used to keep this a secret from everyone and that's worked out poorly. My family situation – Carly, Paul, Alex, the kids – is sort of a car crash right now. I don't know what Alex is doing in Italy; I don't know what decisions he's going to make about the future of our very weird family unit; and I don't know how I am going to react. So now you'll have context, I guess, if everything goes to shit."

Minette frowns slightly. "How about, we try not to have everything go to shit? Because I like you, I'm flattered by you, and I like being a part of your ecosystem. Because I care about you, I'm here for you if stuff goes wrong, but I don't exist just to be a foil to your pain and I don't want this relationship to be a constant reaction to the rest of your life."

"I agree with you completely." Liam nods. "I do. Call me on my shit. And I will do my best not to have shit to be called on. Okay?"

Minette gives the flirty shrug Liam has come to understand as agreement. "Sure. But only if you do my other foot now. I hate being lopsided."

Liam laughs and kisses her.

◆

Alex arrives at Gianni's apartment in the morning. Sunlight pours in through the southern-facing windows, and he blinks at the brightness when Gianni draws him further into the room.

Gianni kisses him gently before he pushes him away and retrieves his camera.

There's a screen Gianni waves Alex towards to change behind. Alex does so slowly. A bathrobe has been left for him draped over the back of a chair. He pulls it on before he re-emerges. Alex has never done a nude photo shoot – it was bad enough when *GQ* did shirtless shots of him – but other than the fact that he's naked, the process is pretty much exactly the same.

Except he's never had a photo shoot like this one. Gianni directs him gently, with quiet words and suggestions. It's the easiest thing in the world to follow the soft sound of his voice. The temptation to slip under, to fall into the passive place that is so near the small, submissive space he loves to go to in sex with Paul, tugs at the edges of his mind. Alex finds, somewhat to his surprise, that he has no interest in following it. He'd much rather be alert to enjoy the way the light catches in Gianni's dark hair as he raises the camera, or the way the floorboards squeak as he pads barefoot around Alex to get the best angles.

"How did you get that?" Gianni asks at one point, lowering the camera and pressing his palm close to, but not actually against, the broad, silvery scar on Alex's back.

"I fell."

"Tell me the story," Gianni says, stepping back and raising his camera again.

Alex obeys. It's ridiculous how vulnerable he feels, lying naked with his head turned away and his hair hiding his face, while he tells the story of how he'd gotten furious at Victor for torturing Liam, tried to punch the man, then nearly fallen to his death down a cliff when a knot in his climbing ropes failed.

Later, after they finish shooting they sit on the floor working their way through a bottle of wine. Alex is still wrapped in Gianni's bathrobe. The tension is delicious but also unbearable.

"You know, I just want to have you right here on the floor," Gianni says.

"I know."

Alex does know, because all he can picture is how easy it would be for Gianni to reach out to his bare ankle and trace his fingers up his leg. Or go, instead, right for the belt of the robe, folding it open and taking Alex into his mouth. But Gianni makes no move to do any of it.

"I like you because you do not know how to have a double life," Gianni says to the silence of Alex's unasked question.

"I told you my name was Jay."

"And then asked if I knew who you were."

"I didn't have a choice. Besides, I'm an actor," Alex tries, taking another tack.

"No," Gianni says. His fingers reach for Alex, but don't touch. "You are yourself. I'm sorry, but it's true."

Alex can only think of Victor.

◆

When his phone rings in the middle of the night, jolting Paul out of a fitful sleep, he hopes it's Alex. Both because Alex hasn't called in nearly a week other than to check in with the kids, and because if it's not, it's a work crisis or someone is dead, and he does not want to deal with either of those things at three in the morning.

"Paul," Alex sounds breathless and hushed when Paul answers, but he doesn't say anything else. It reminds Paul, jarringly, of the many strange middle-of-the-night phone calls they had the winter years ago when they were broken up. Whatever Alex is working out right now, they're solid.

"Alex," Paul prompts, after a full minute goes by without Alex saying anything.

"There's something I should tell you."

"Are you okay?"

"Yeah. Yeah, I'm fine. I'm great. Paul, I met someone."

Paul is aware that there was a point – many points, in fact – where Alex saying that would have thrown him into panic and despair. Now, although it's not entirely easy, it seems right and like anything but a threat.

He sits up in bed – Todd grumpily rearranges himself on Alex's empty pillow – and asks, smiling, "Do you want to tell me about him?"

"Yes. No. I don't know. I should." Alex gives a breathy little laugh that's clearly nervous.

"You don't have to," Paul reminds Alex. "Whatever you need. That's what I told you, and that's still true."

"Oh my God, Paul, I love you so much."

"I know. I love you too." Not everything in life is permanent, but some things are, and Alex is one of them. He's not going anywhere, no matter who he meets or what he does while he's away.

"I'm sorry I haven't called in so long."

"It's okay." It's not, really, at least not in the scope of things they need to be figuring out about their lives. But in terms of them, it is. Paul knows how much sometimes all Alex needs is patience.

The issue is just whether Alex's need for time and space will, reasonably, run out Carly and Liam's forbearance.

"How are the kids?"

Paul settles back against the pillows and tells him.

◆

Alex meets Gianni two days later at what he's come to think of as their café. He'd needed a day, after that photo shoot and calling Paul, to be by himself. Gianni had been understanding. They sit in the late afternoon sunshine, not talking much and just enjoying each other's company for more than an hour before Gianni folds his arms on the table and looks at Alex.

"What?" Alex asks, after a minute of Gianni saying nothing.

"There is an art installation in Milan I think you will like. I'd like to take you there."

"Why are you doing this?" Alex is baffled. He doesn't want Gianni to stop making the choices he is, but he also doesn't understand them. Whatever they are to each other, Alex is certain it is too ephemeral for this level of kindness and care.

Gianni just shrugs. "I want to see what happens next. Don't you?"

Alex nods. "Tell me about the art in Milan."

Gianni shakes his head. "You need to see it without anyone telling you about it."

"Did you run out of churches to show me?"

Gianni smiles. "No, it's Italy. We don't run out of churches. But this is different. I should warn you though, before you decide, it's five or six hours in a car. If you want to go, we should maybe make a weekend of it?"

Alex is overwhelmed by nothing so much as Gianni's shyness as he asks.

♦

Somehow, it's Carly that Alex calls. He still can't tell Liam about the invitation for a weekend away without telling Paul first, and he doesn't know how to tell Paul. Carly may not be the kindest to him, but she will be the most honest.

When she answers the video call, she has Claudia asleep on her shoulder, and Alex has a wave of homesickness so powerful he nearly hangs up right then to get on a plane. But home is hard, and aside from the painful degree to which he misses the girls, Alex still isn't sure what he'd actually do when he got there. L.A., and everything outside of the safe cocoon of Rome, feels terrifying.

Which brings him back to the reason he's calling. Carly listens to his whole story – she expresses no surprise over the existence of Gianni. Alex assumes Paul told her as much as Alex told him, which was just that there is someone.

"Okay," she says, when the trickle of words he can put together about any of it finally run out. "I have two things to say."

"Another list?" Alex says with a tired smiled.

"What did you think you were going to get? Okay. First up. Carly's Polyamorous Advice for the Incompetent. If you want to go, and do whatever with Gianni, and it's within the scope of agreements you and Paul have made with each other – go. I know you're obsessively in love with Paul. You don't have to prove anything to anyone on that front, including yourself. So if this is a thing that you want and is good for you – and your boyfriend – do it. But, and this brings me to point two, what are your plans for him long-term?"

"I don't know. I don't know what any of my plans are long-term. Which I'm assuming is part of the problem you're going to tell me about next?"

"You keep insisting you're not poly, and that's like, whatever, but the fact remains that you fall hard and pretty much completely for the people you do manage to make room for in your life. Liam was one, and now look how you two are."

"Not particularly speaking to each other while we fight over whether we share children or not?"

"Well, yes." Carly lets him sit with that for a moment before she speaks again. "Commitments you have made and are currently failing to keep impact our lives. Ultimately, the kids will be okay whether they have you in their lives or don't."

Alex opens his mouth to protest but she cuts him off. "I'm not asking you to make any declarations of anything right now," she says more kindly than Alex deserves. "I'm just saying when you make decisions about any of your relationships you should keep that in mind."

"I'm *trying*," Alex says. He knows he sounds petulant.

"I know, baby boy." Carly says. "But we were hard on Liam when he was in the middle of his crisis after Victor died no matter how much it wasn't his fault. We're willing to call this the fallout of your very real and clinical anxiety, but we still need to be hard on you too. Life goes on, even when we've been dealt hands that make it hard for us to do what we need to."

16

They leave before dawn. Gianni drives, because Alex isn't yet comfortable with navigating Italian traffic. Road signs and speed limits are clearly merely suggestions.

They drive north towards Florence, making a detour to have breakfast amongst the green terraced hillsides of Orvieto. Gianni starts to apologize for the tourists at one point, but Alex stops him with a glare. That he is not an excessively clumsy visitor to this place is due only to Gianni's kindness and the gentle but ill-advised nature of whatever they are doing with each other.

They're having sex this night, Alex guesses, after they see whatever it is he's being taken to see. He feels nervous about it like he did with Liam, an awkward destiny he's too brave and foolish to resist. After breakfast they turn for the coast ahead of the traffic snarl trying to reach Florence's outer edges. Alex tries to put the night ahead out of his mind. He takes refuge in the views passing by, the stunning peril of the cliffs and the sea. He's sorry to see it go when they turn inland again at Genoa for the final two hours into Milan.

When they get there, Gianni parks in front of a warehouse converted to a museum in what feels like the middle of nowhere on the dangerous industrial edge of the city. When they go inside the darkness of the space is nearly assaultive, and Alex reaches instinctively for Gianni's hand as he waits for his eyes to adjust.

"Come on, it's this way." Gianni leads him through the darkness, past other exhibits painted with light or showcased on televisions salvaged from another decade. "In here," he says, parting a heavy black velvet curtain and pushing Alex into the room ahead of him.

The space is cavernous, two or three stories high. A field of sand is laid out and, to Alex's chagrin, roped off. In it, built out of what may be shipping containers, are towers, each precarious, each filled with doors and windows with no stairs to reach them. It feels like a refugee camp and like something ancient and terrifying all at once. Gianni grabs his shoulders and pushes ever so slightly.

"Go on," he says. "Find what you need to find in it."

So Alex does, wishing he could be barefoot on that sand, even as he walks down the long length of one side and turns up the other to a tower littered with shards of glass covered in numbers at its base. He stares at them for a long time and tries to imagine how art works. Were they spilled from above, or arranged shard by carefully placed shard? He wants to know if there is a list of instructions for these ruins somewhere.

"What do you think the numbers are for?" Gianni asks, coming up behind him eventually.

Alex shakes his head, which is too filled with ideas he knows are close but wrong, and all some sort of horrifying. He can't make himself articulate any of them.

He must give Gianni a hopeless look, because Gianni brushes his thumb over Alex's cheek to get him to turn away from the glass for just a moment.

"They're stars," he says. "They're the addresses of stars."

♦

In the car, Alex leans his head against the window and stares blankly out at the city rolling by while Gianni navigates them to some less terrifying part of town.

"Are you okay?" Gianni asks softly when they stop at an intersection.

Alex shakes his head.

"I am sorry," Gianni says.

"No. Don't be," Alex says. "I'm glad I saw it, and I'm glad I was with you."

"But?"

"I'm going back eventually," Alex says, his heart sinking as he does.

Gianni says nothing, just gives Alex the space, as he always has, to find his own way to what's next.

"Sooner than eventually, and I...I feel ill at the thought."

"Then why?"

"My family. The fact that I belong there, even though it's not always a very good place for me. It's what I've signed up for, and it's what I have, and it's better than most things. Except you and your stupid stars."

Gianni reaches for Alex's hand where it's resting on his knee and squeezes.

"I could stay here with you so easily."

"But you don't want to."

Alex shakes his head. "No. Aside from the girls and my husband and my absolutely horrible, impossible friends who I am practically married to,

I like my work. It's the best type of running away there is. And I can run from all of them, but I can't run from it. And it *pisses me off.*"

♦

While they were looking at the art, Alex has been able to forget about their plans for the night - or rather, their distinct lack of explicit plans other than a hotel room booking. But now they're hauling their bags up the once-grand stairs of a pensione to an airy top-floor room with a view of the square below, and it all comes roaring back.

Alex realizes that not only does he have no idea what he's doing, he has no idea what Gianni is doing either. Because Alex is leaving. They both know it, they've both acknowledged it, and yet here they are. He spent a night like this with Liam once. The pain of doing it a second time is only lessened by the realization that this has to be a shittier deal for Gianni than it is for him.

They toss their bags maybe foolishly on the bed. When Gianni draws Alex into his arms, Alex goes easily. They're kissing before Alex can even think about it – it's not a topic change so much as a continuation of their conversation.

Alex's shirt is off and Gianni's is unbuttoned before Alex, his hands fumbling to get into Gianni's pants, steps back. "I'm sorry. I can't do this."

Gianni doesn't even look angry – with Alex or with the world. It's a trick Alex would like to learn.

"What do you need?" he asks, sitting down heavily on the bed.

"I need to go back," Alex says. "To Rome. Tonight. And I'm sorry, I'll get a train, but I am not made for what I feel for you."

"No no no no no, I'll drive, but what does that even mean?"

"That I have my shit together enough to be in love with Paul. But I don't have it together enough to be in love with you also. And I might be? I could be? I think I am? I did something like this once before, and it is the most exhausting miserable bane of my existence."

"Liam," Gianni says.

"I can't do it again," Alex says, shaking his head. "I can't be collecting people I can't keep." He runs his hands through his hair. "And the horrible thing is I'm saying all of this, and I feel like I'm breaking up with you, and I don't want to."

"Then don't."

"Gianni –"

"Yes?" He smiles in sad amusement.

"I can't tell if you're gentle or crazy," Alex lets his arms fall to his side, defeated suddenly by the absurdity of the situation.

"Do you want me to drive you back to Rome so you can call your husband, and feel safe, and get him to tell you what you need to do?"

Alex nods.

Gianni holds out a hand for Alex, who can't do anything but take it. Gianni wraps him up in his arms and Alex is left clinging to him.

"Will you just promise me you won't get on a plane without telling me?" he says softly into Alex's hair.

Alex, his head pressed into Gianni's shoulder, can feel the soft hum of his chest as he speaks. He nods, before leaning up to kiss him. It doesn't feel like saying goodbye to Liam. Somehow, that makes it even more heartbreaking.

◆

Paul's phone goes off in the middle of what he hopes is his last meeting of the day. It's more than a little worrying, especially since he hasn't heard from Alex in two days and it's well after midnight in Rome.

He excuses himself and picks up as soon as Alex calls a second time. "Alex?"

"You picked up."

"Of course I did," Paul says, fond but not really less worried.

"Somehow that still surprises me."

"You say that like I ever didn't."

"That was a really long winter. When I was in New York."

"I know. I remember. Alex, what's wrong?"

"I don't know. Nothing."

"You don't call me at three in the morning your time for nothing. And I'm at work so you may have to wait 'til I get home if you want phone sex."

Alex gives a breath of a laugh. "You're at work? What time is it there?"

"Six."

"Oh."

"Alex," Paul prompts again, when Alex doesn't say anything.

"I need you to get on a plane."

"Alex?" Paul asks. Of the many possibilities – all of them more or less stressful – he'd expected Alex to come out with, he hadn't anticipated this one.

"I. Need. You. To. Get. On. A. Plane."

"Yeah, that wasn't a small words issue. Are you okay?"

"I'm telling you to be a ridiculous jet setting celebrity and get on the first plane you can to Rome. No, I'm not okay." Alex chuckles wetly. "I don't even know if you'll make things okay. But I need you."

"I have…. Alex, I have my job. And the kids. And Carly and Liam."

"I know. I'm sorry. Can you make it work?"

Paul thinks and wants to bang his head against the wall at everything he's going to drop and reshuffle so he can go chasing after Alex. Carly's going to laugh at him forever. "I think so."

"So you'll come?" Alex sounds afraid. "I'll tell you everything when you get here, I promise, I just need to do it face-to-face."

"Yes. Yes. I will. Of course, I will." He has no fucking clue what kind of trouble Alex has gotten himself into, nor what it's going to cost either of them to get him out. He just knows that once he lands in Rome, he's not going to be able to avoid putting all his cards, and all the demands of their family, on the table. And once he does Alex – and Paul – may decide to end so many different things. Not with each other, of that he feels certain. But with the rest of their lives.

♦

After he calls Olivia, Paul calls Carly.

Given the amount of crap Carly puts up with on a daily basis from all of them, he should be less surprised than he is when she takes the news that he's going to Rome in stride. It makes him wonder if Alex called her first.

"I absolutely hate that I'm about to do this, because we promised each other we weren't going to dump our kids on each other...."

"Oh my God, Paul," Carly says. "We just spent the summer fighting with Alex over whether we're all a family or not. We *are*. Give us our damn baby and go bring Alex home."

"I don't know if that's what I'm doing?"

"Okay, Paul? Alex is nuts, but even he wouldn't call you to Italy just to break up with you."

"Point, but he still might ask me to break up with you and Liam."

Carly lets out a heavy sigh. "I know. We – Liam and I know. That was always going to be a possibility. We just decided it was a risk worth taking when we started building this life together."

"Why are you being so understanding about all of this?" Paul feels massively guilty, and he's not the one making everything hard for people right now.

"Because this is life," Carly tells him. "Life is complicated. That's true whether you call what we're doing polyamory or co-parenting or *whatever*. People get hurt or scared or can't live up to what we need from them. That doesn't stop being true once you have the wedding and get the kids and win the awards. Neither you nor Alex are getting special passes from us, so don't worry about that. You're just getting the same compassion and space we give everyone in our lives."

"You really are more enlightened than the rest of us."

"Not really. I mean, yes, I am, but no. I've just had a lot of practice. This is a family of choice. And whether Alex decides to stay or leave, he gets to choose that as much as the rest of us do. No matter how much it hurts or how hard it'll make logistics for a little while."

It's not until Paul's on the plane taxiing down the runway at LAX that it starts to sink in for him what, exactly, he's doing. If Alex asks him to leave this life – and Paul is unsure what's waiting for him when he lands – he's going to have to find a way to thread the needle of that disaster no matter how thin it spreads him. He can't refuse Alex any more than he can let Alex's inability to cope with his life take down the rest of their family with it.

Paul is overwhelmed almost as soon as he deplanes. Fiumicino is massive and seems to dwarf any part of LAX or the New York airports he's been to. Even the hellish transfer between the Reykjavik and Keflavik airports in Iceland with the chaos of the children had been mild by comparison.

The halls here are long, the enforced walks through duty free are endless, and the swarm of people waiting at customs doesn't even remotely resemble a queue. Paul despairs of being able to easily find Alex.

He also wonders whether he'll be able to communicate meaningfully with him once he does. He may have arrived in Rome, but he doesn't know how much longer he's going to have to wait to figure out what the hell is going on with their lives.

Alex is pressed up against the barrier at arrivals when Paul comes through. His hair is bright, shaggy, and uncovered. That and his stillness make him hard to miss. Paul rolls his suitcase up to him, more interested in greeting him than properly coming around the barrier. When he leans forward to kiss him, though, Alex recoils ever so slightly.

"So many people, Paul," Alex says, exasperated and apologetic. His eyes dart around the cavernous space of the terminal.

They walk out of the airport and bypass the cab line. "How are we doing this?" Paul asks.

Alex smirks at him. "I borrowed my boyfriend's car."

◆

No matter how much Paul encouraged Alex to take this trip and do whatever he needed, the admission is a little uncomfortable, especially after the aborted kiss. Paul spends a lot of time taking in the interior of the battered Fiat.

Paul feels stuck in a movie, and not one he would write, as Alex navigates them out of the tangle of roadways that make up the airport and into the harrowing traffic that is Rome. Alex points out sights – *Coliseum coming up on your left* – as he drives, calm, focused and never taking his eyes off the road.

"Am I here to meet the boyfriend?"

"Gianni," Alex says. "And no, you're here to take me home. But yes," he says. "Please." His eyes dart away from the road for the first time.

"Okay," Paul says carefully. "I'm not mad, and I stand by everything I've said to you about this, but full disclosure – I am not comfortable right now."

"We're in a car in Rome," Alex says as he curses at a driver who blows past him at a speed and proximity that almost take off his side mirror. "Of course you're not comfortable."

◆

Once Paul drops his bags next to Alex's suitcase in the hotel room, Alex kisses him, both needy and sure. Now that they're here he is remarkably present, and that goes a long way towards calming Paul down.

Alex sits on the bed. "We haven't slept together, and he's never come here."

"You can't have called me here to tell me that,"

Paul says, fond and incredulous.

"No." Alex echoes his tone and scoots back to lay down. He looks out the window, drawing Paul's attention to the noise of traffic below, as he speaks.

"I was so annoyed with you when you gave me that *do what you need to do* speech before I left. And, to be fair, I've been annoyed at Liam since Iceland for saying that rules can be different on vacation and that relationships can evolve. Even though you were both right...." Alex's voice trails off and he sighs. "Because what I needed to do, and what I still need to do, is uncomplicate my life to a point where I can fucking deal with it. Charming strangers from coffee shops are not uncomplicating my life. Neither is hanging out in Italy and pretending I can undo everything that's happened to me...and that I chose, I guess."

Paul smiles at Alex's hesitation about his own agency. Because while there are real truths in it, it's also a place where Alex's issues have caused a mountain of problems for both of them.

"You didn't have to say yes to the big blockbuster," Paul says gently.

"I didn't have to marry you either."

Alex's voice is easy and teasing, but the remark still slams into Paul with terrifying force.

"I also didn't have to agree to raise kids with our best friends that we've had too much sex with. And I certainly didn't have to be a knowing seven-year-old's only confidant."

"But all that happened," Paul says, attempting to tease back.

"Yup. It did. It still is happening. Just without me there. Which isn't fair to anyone."

"So what's the plan?" Paul asks.

Alex shrugs. "I come home. I keep loving you. I accept all the ways in which I'm never really going to be okay."

"Just like Liam," Paul says.

"Just like you," Alex corrects. "And Carly, even though she's more awesome than all of us. And yes, Liam too, and probably everyone on the planet including our daughters."

"Why did you need to tell me all of this here?" Paul asks. Alex is being so mature and wise, and it makes no sense juxtaposed with the *come-to-Italy-I'm-not-okay* panic in his voice just twenty-four hours ago.

"Because part of me is still hoping you'll tell me I'm wrong."

◆

Alex, it turns out, would like nothing more than to disappear into Rome. But he doesn't want to be a former movie star any more than he wants to be a movie star, and he certainly doesn't want to be without Paul just because he really would prefer to spend most of his time alone.

"He gives me space," Alex says once Paul joins him on the bed. "I didn't know how much I needed that until I had it. I didn't even know it was an option."

"We've always had space," Paul points out, possibly slightly defensively.

"If you and I could, we'd get into bed together and never get back out again. Regardless of how bad that would be for our relationship. We spend time apart because we like our jobs, no matter how much they suck, and we like our family, too. But that's always needed to be a choice. You and I, we're not wired for space. We never have been, and sometimes that's not very good for me."

"I love you too?" Paul hazards, because what Alex is saying sounds good but he still has no idea what he's doing here in Italy.

Alex smiles. "Yes. But it made me realize how I need to do things differently, when we get home. The whole family-meeting-ambush thing that you all swear is about clear communication? I get it, but it doesn't work for me. I love all of you, and I want to keep our family together, but I'd way prefer to be yelled at in private by any one of you than the solemn-discussion-all-in-a-group thing. I will fail way less at conflict resolution if I don't feel like the spotlight on me in my professional life continues at home too. With Liam focusing on production right now, all that light's on me, and it was easier when it was a burden I shared."

"Do you want to schedule a family meeting about that?" Paul asks lightly.

"As long as it involves no yelling, no ganging up, no booze, and no making out. I like having my boundaries pushed in certain contexts, but not by the three of you in our day-to-day lives acting like kids with a sack of firecrackers."

"We've behaved a little bit badly," Paul admits.

"Sometimes that's why I like you. You know, it wasn't easy to call." He reaches out to trace his fingertips along the collar of Paul's shirt.

"I told you, you didn't have to tell me anything."

"Not because of that," Alex says. "I knew you'd be okay with it. Thank you, by the way. I don't think I ever said that. But calling you meant walking away from my last chance for a life that isn't the one you're bringing me home to."

Alex smiles sadly, and Paul is only fascinated, as he always is, what time spent apart does to Alex and his understanding of his place in the world.

"When I first met Gianni I didn't know if I was ever going to leave him. But I get to do that and go home with you, because he was what I needed, and he gave me the space I needed, to figure the rest of my shit out. I wish there was a better way to repay that debt than just getting on a plane with you."

"I will totally understand if you say no," Paul says carefully. "Because I want this trip to keep being what you need and my being here to be a part of that. And I *really* want you to come home with me. But if it's an offer that you were serious about, I do want to meet him."

Alex smiles so widely his eyes crinkle up. "Yeah, so," he says grinning and looking up at the ceiling. He seems so young, like a kid with a crush and more emotions than he can contain. "I already made dinner reservations."

◆

Dinner is in Trastevere. To Paul's amusement what Alex frets about most is whether they should bring the car, which they have to return anyway, or worry about it tomorrow. Between Italian wine and the inevitable awkward of the situation, Alex suspects they may all want to drink copiously.

He finally decides to leave the car for tomorrow. Paul can tell he's nervous. And when they walk into the restaurant and Gianni is already there, Paul gets nervous too.

Gianni stands up to greet them, and Paul can't help but stare when Alex kisses him hello. It's brief and in public and Paul can't figure out if it's super European or super gay.

Either way, Alex wouldn't kiss Paul at the airport. And while this restaurant is dark and certainly far more private than any arrivals hall, but Paul is still, perhaps irrationally, stung. He tucks those feelings away carefully to examine later.

Alex makes introductions. Paul tries not to be too entertained by Alex's smugness at standing together with Paul and this man.

Gianni is incredibly attractive, with dark hair, a short beard, and a jaw that can only be called chiseled. Paul can't help but notice how much larger his hands are than his own when they greet each other.

"You're doing that thing you do," Alex hisses at him almost immediately.

"What thing?"

"The thing you do with Nigel!"

"What thing is that?"

"The thing where you get all moony because someone has bigger shoulders than you," Alex teases, his voice still a stage whisper and his eyes darting over to Gianni in amusement. Gianni, who is clearly listening to this exchange, looks wildly entertained.

"You did well," Paul tries by way of ever increasing awkward deflection.

Alex squares his shoulders and smirks. "Paul. I'm a movie star. Of course my boyfriend is hot."

Paul has never heard Alex state what he is – a movie star – before like it's not the worst thing in the world.

"Did you crash my car?" Gianni smiles as he puts a hand to the small of Alex's back to get him to sit down. The gesture is more gentle and intimate, somehow, than the kiss had been. Paul finds himself both fascinated and reassured. Whatever new and creative clusterfuck this evening is going to be, clearly Alex has been in good hands.

Once they sit down, the conversation is, somehow, not awkward. As the dinner proceeds, he's pleasantly surprised to find that it's not actually a disaster either. He's willing to admit the wine probably helps with that, but also, Gianni is easy to share space with. He either doesn't find any of this peculiar or has just been rolling with Alex for long enough that this doesn't strike him as any more strange than anything else.

They spend hours working through multiple courses. Alex, now that he's got his feet under him, is eager to tell Paul all about his and Gianni's adventures around Rome, and Gianni is happy to assist. Alex and Paul, meanwhile, tag team ridiculous Hollywood disaster stories, Paul updating Alex on what he's missed, and Alex providing context for Gianni that includes an utterly uncanny imitation of Darcy in network sales mode.

When Paul mentions casually that Liam had texted him the day before in the middle of a date with Minette, Alex stares at him.

"Wait, what?" he asks.

"What?" Paul says, caught off-guard by the suddenness of Alex's interruption.

"Liam and Minette?"

"Yes?" Paul doesn't know what the question is.

"Liam and Minette *are dating*?"

"Yesssss," Paul says slowly. "Like, for a while now. Since we were in Indiana. Did you not know that?"

Alex shakes his head slowly, his dark eyes huge. Gianni's eyes dart between them, smiling delightedly at the farce unfolding in front of him.

Paul gapes. "You didn't know that?!"

Alex gapes right back at him. "Minette and *Liam*?!"

"Oh my God." Paul laughs. "I thought Liam had told you."

"Noooo," Alex shakes his head. "Which, I mean, I know I've yelled at you for keeping information about Liam to yourself, but to be clear I'm not blaming you here. Minette and Liam," he says again, like the idea is unfathomable. Of course, if Paul hadn't been watching the relationship unfold in real time over the past few weeks, he'd probably feel the same. "I can't believe Liam didn't tell me. He always overshares. *Everything*," he adds, mostly to Gianni.

Alex's shocked expression softens to introspection. "Although, with the havoc I've been wrecking, I guess I can see why he didn't say anything." He still looks, not hurt, exactly, but sad. Paul says a silent prayer of thanks for what he suspects is Alex having a sudden illustration of the gaps his life will have if he chooses to leave their family of choice.

Despite that bump filled with laughter and heartache, the entire night feels, in a way it absolutely should not, normal. After all, thirty-six hours ago Paul was in L.A. and now he's having dinner in Rome with his husband and his husband's boyfriend. He's relieved that they don't have to have any serious collective conversations or relationship processing right now. Watching Alex, laughing and relaxed while out in public, is a joy. He's fairly certain that it's not the kind of thing Alex is ever going to be comfortable with at home, and Paul knows to enjoy it while he can.

The peace is interrupted by Paul's phone chiming.

"What disaster is it now?" Alex asks, when Paul sets down his wine glass so he can dig it out of his pocket. Paul wishes it felt like a joke; the way their lives go, this is either wonderful or terrible news.

Except it's neither, and Paul just smiles and hands his phone over to Alex so he can see the text, too.

"It's from Ali," Paul says.

Alex takes the phone with a wary look.

"She's demanding pictures of your boyfriend."

♦

Gianni swings by late the next morning to pick up his car. Alex meets him downstairs and awkwardly shuffles through the news that he and Paul are going to spend the day by themselves, maybe sorting things out, maybe just being together.

"I feel like I am stringing you along," Alex says.

"Yes and no," Gianni says.

It takes a long time for Alex to ask what he means.

"I knew you were married from the beginning. I spent all this time falling in love with you knowing I probably wasn't going to get laid. And you were always going back to Los Angeles. Maybe I just wanted to see how the story would go. Maybe now, I just want to see how it ends."

◆

Alex ends up talking, haltingly, about the exchange to Paul when they take a walk amongst the market stalls of the Campo de' Fiori. Alex shoves his hands deep in his pockets to stop himself from taking Paul's hand, which may attract more attention than he's interested in. They bump shoulders as they walk, and Alex struggles to put things into words, not because of the nature of the situation, but because this type of communication is still hard for him. But he and Paul have been doing this for years now. It's work, but it feels good.

"I have nothing in my life that's temporary or low-stakes," Alex says.

"Every movie you work on," Paul counters. "Every show."

Alex shrugs. "Not low stakes and definitely not temporary. Preserved on film and talked to death so that everyone knows what it was like except those of us who were really there. So no, actually."

They walk on in silence for a while until Paul speaks again. "Gianni doesn't seem low stakes. You had me fly out here to meet him."

"No. I had you fly out here so I could finish processing my shit." Saying so aloud, Alex feels like a jerk. He asks a lot of people. Too much maybe. But when he asks, they also show up. Now, more than ever, he needs to acknowledge that. "No one knows me better than you, Paul. No one puts up with me better."

Paul chuckles, but brushes the compliment aside. "You've cut quite a swathe of irritation through our lives back home."

"I know. And one of the reasons I need you here

to help me come back is I don't know how to fix a lot of that. With Gemma. With Carly. With Liam, apparently. With Ali. And I guess with you too."

Paul waves him off. "We'll be fine. We are fine. You're as certain as the sun to me, even if you are also sometimes a nightmare."

Alex chuckles.

"However, and don't get mad at me when I say this," Paul says. Alex scoffs. "But for a guy who keeps saying he wants to be a hermit, you sure do keep connecting to people and leaving a lot of damage in your wake when you decide that you – or they – can't handle it."

"Why do I feel like I'm being un-forgiven for our very first fight?"

"That was pretty epic," Paul muses.

"I was not the only crazy one in that room," Alex says.

"No, you really weren't."

"Gianni knew what he was getting into."

"Is that what he said?"

"Yes."

"Okay, I am all for taking people at their word...." Paul says.

"But?" Alex asks.

"But I find that hard to believe since you had no clarity on what you were doing or what your plan was. And I feel like you still don't."

Alex looks evasive. And maybe a little guilty. "What's that supposed to mean?"

"We're still here. We have intent, but we don't have plane tickets. You haven't described to me what you want us or our lives to be like when we go back."

"Impatient much?" Alex asks, with only the

slightest edge to it.

"Maybe a little. This is a nice bubble out of time I get why it's seductive, and I'm enjoying being here. But you running away is one thing. We can't both do it. Not with my show and your movie, and our family in whatever shape it ends up being waiting for us back home."

"I know. And I'm working on it. The family question, and what I'm going to do with *Scism*. Both in terms of what I can handle and what I owe a lot of people who are, fairly, pissed off at me. But also I'm just...I'm trying to figure out how to wrap things up here."

"Do you need to?"

"Our whole lives revolve around story and you ask me that?" Alex says. He stands aside from the path and turns to face Paul.

Paul smiles sadly. "And you still keep saying you're nothing like Victor."

♦

"I want to sleep with Gianni."

Paul makes a noncommittal sound. He's doing a crossword puzzle from an old issue of the International edition of the New York Times he found in the lobby of the hotel. Until his pronouncement Alex has been resting his head on his shoulder and staring off into space for hours. Paul is unsure how serious Alex is or what he wants from him by way of response.

But Alex doesn't say anything else.

"What are you looking for from me?" Paul eventually asks.

When Alex gives a little annoyed huff, Paul is not the least bit surprised, but he's done trying to be a mind reader in this particular situation. In another forty-eight hours, he's going to have to give Alex an ultimatum, simply because he can't be away from work or family this long with no discernable plan to come back.

"I need you to be there," Alex eventually says.

"Have you talked to Gianni about this?"

"No," Alex says petulantly. "I'm talking to you. First."

"Okaaaaay." Alex is not actually giving terrible answers. They're just coming out very slowly. If he doesn't speed up soon, Paul is going to get caught out at having exhausted his ability with the crossword and now just using it as a prop to mask his myriad concerns. "How do you need me to be there?"

Alex sits up enough to fix Paul with a sharp look.

"Do you want me to watch?" Paul asks, his tone reasonable. "Do you want me to participate? Do you want me to drop you off and pick you up when you're done? Now that I'm here, and you're asking me to be involved, the thing where you don't have to tell me what's going on doesn't really work anymore."

Alex mutters something. Paul can't believe the ways in which his husband can still be so reticent when it comes to talking about sex. It is, as it's been for a decade, inappropriately appealing.

18

Gemma looks up from her computer at the sound of a knock on the doorframe. She finds Minette is leaning in her office doorway.

"Are you doing anything tomorrow?" Minette asks.

"I don't think so. Why? Unless this is your way of asking me if I can take another meeting with that reality TV nightmare you should have never taken on, because I am so done with them and I am way too busy with everything to ever talk to them again."

Minette laughs. "Nothing like that. I promise. Do you want to get drinks and dinner?"

"Sure." A break from the office, and some time hanging out with Minette to talk smack about their mutual work headaches, sounds perfect.

"Actually. Let me be slightly more clear. Do you want to get drinks and dinner with me and Liam?"

"Uh...." Sure, they're both her friends to varying degrees, but being asked to tag along with the weird that is them dating each other has the potential to be awkward in six different ways. Gemma's still getting used to the idea that Minette and Liam are no longer sworn enemies. That the situation has now evolved into Liam overlapping his personal and professional circles, she can almost deal with. What this invitation is, however, she's almost afraid to ask. "I don't want to cut into your couple time...."

"You wouldn't be." Minette is smiling broadly

now. "Do you want to get drinks and dinner with me, Liam, and a friend?"

Gemma stares at Minette. Maybe that's less awkward. But maybe it's not. "Are you or Liam dating this friend, or…?"

"What? Oh, no! No, he's for you. If you want. Double date?"

Gemma narrows her eyes. "Was this your idea or Liam's?" She's relieved the situation is less bizarrely awkward that she had feared, but blind dates are almost always perilous.

"Liam's idea. In broad concept, at least. The friend is mine. Because as I'm sure you're aware, most of Liam's friends are unbearable."

"Believe me," Gemma says drily. "I'm aware. Now, swear to me he's not in the industry."

"Is that a deal breaker?"

"Yes!" Gemma clasps her hands together beseechingly. "Swear it!"

Minette gives a little bounce of excitement. Really, she and Liam are so well suited it's terrifying. How had no one predicted that match before? "I swear it. I'll send you the details."

♦

That night, Alex can't sleep. Paul doesn't even stir when he gets out of bed.

"That," Alex whispers to himself, "is the sleep of someone who hasn't pissed off everyone he knows." He then reconsiders. It might just be jet lag.

He sits down at the small desk in the corner. This room feels far more cramped now that he has Paul's things to trip over too. There's a familiarity to it at least; his real life is filled with the chaos of parenthood and the unavoidable sloppiness of overworked adults with erratic schedules.

He flips open his laptop and logs into his email with some trepidation, but there's no real reason for his fear. It's not filled with angry messages he's been ignoring because it's not filled with anything at all. Begrudgingly or not, everyone in his life has given him the space he's asked for, and now he has to live with the resulting silence.

He glances over at Paul again.

Or…he could ask for something different. From them. And from himself.

He emails Gemma first. She's been so clear with him for so long, he's fairly certainly he can finally figure out how to reply in kind.

Hey. Still in Italy, but back within the next week. Didn't come here to think about Scism — or rather, I don't think that's why I came here, but of course I did. If your offer/favor request is still on the table, I'm interested. And I won't be a hardass about the negotiations either. It's the right thing to do, personally and creatively. Let me know what you need on your end for the business stuff, and maybe we can work on the rest when I get back. I know the ball's in my court, but I want to make sure you're still interested in playing first, otherwise that might just be annoying.

Emailing Liam is harder, because anything he says about Minette or finding out about Minette from Paul sounds accusatory when he just wants to be funny. Liam deserves happiness and the courage to let new people into his life. If Alex wants to feel left behind over it, that's not Liam's fault.

Eventually he does the only thing he can, and dives in.

The problem with you and I, he writes, *is that we never need to use words, except when we do. Pencil me in somewhere, but I'm still not using your shitty app.*

◆

Several hours, a nightmare commute home through L.A. traffic, and two panicked calls to Minette because seriously *what should she wear* later, Gemma is seated with her, Liam, and a frankly insanely attractive guy who introduces himself as "Robby Morales Who Is Most Definitely Not Industry."

Gemma hasn't been on a real date in a while. She has no interest in anyone she works with, and randos on dating apps in L.A. are more objectionable, somehow, than randos on dating apps anywhere else in the country. Everyone's always looking to get ahead in the business, and Gemma got sick of dates that felt like pitch meetings a long time ago. It's been ages since dinner with anyone actually felt like fun.

Until tonight, at least. Sure, there's the little voice in her head shrieking *I am on a double date with Liam Campbell and my boss HELP,* and there's some awkwardness at first, of course, but Liam pulls out his most charming social skills and gets the conversation going. Before she even realizes it, Gemma's deep into a debate with Robby over the relative merits of different video game systems.

The entire night feels less like a date in L.A. than dinner with friends in literally any other industry in any other city. Gemma's life will never be normal, which is something Alex forgets when he's angry about all the ways fame makes him show his scars to the world. But the work here takes something from everyone, whether or not they ever appear on film. Gemma doesn't want Alex's life, but she also doesn't get its more tangible awards. Something so simple as a meal with people she likes is as much a relief as it is a revelation.

After dinner they stand together in the parking lot for a few minutes, still talking and laughing. Robby keeps meeting Gemma's eye with a look somewhere between shyness and determination.

"I'll walk you to your car," Liam announces, putting an arm around Minette's shoulders. Gemma sends a silent vibe of thanks his way. Once Minette and Liam are a few yards away, Robby kisses her softly.

"You should give me your number," Gemma says when they finally break apart.

◆

Do you think you'll see him again? Minette texts Gemma later that night.

Definitely, Gemma replies. Although, all things considered, that's not entirely the point. Maybe she'll get a boyfriend out of this, maybe she won't. What matters most is that she feels seen, for the first time in so long, as something other than a job title or an unwelcome ghost from someone else's past. Alex may be one of her oldest friends, and one of her best friends, but he's far from a *good* friend. Their day-to-day lives hardly intersect anymore, and Gemma's made her peace with that. But it still hurts, and that hurt makes her have even more gratitude for a night so simple and kind.

◆

Once Alex is actually able to tell Paul what he wants from him – and from Gianni – in the current circumstances, setting up the rest is just a matter of Alex arranging a time and a place with Gianni via email. Which is how, two days later, Paul finds himself in Gianni's apartment with him and Alex on a random Tuesday afternoon.

"Hi."

"Hi."

Pressed close up against each other, standing in the middle of Gianni's room, all Alex and Gianni can manage to do is hold hands and greet each other over and over again. At least they're smiling. Paul knows he shouldn't enjoy their awkwardness as much as he does, but at least it's not about jealousy. He wants this to work, for Alex's sake. It's so sweet and as if all of them are much younger than they are.

"Is this okay?" Alex asks Gianni.

"I'm good." Gianni glances at Paul.

Paul shrugs and smiles a little helplessly. Their awkward might be charming. He's a little less certain of his own.

Gianni cups Alex's face with one of his palms before he kisses him. Gianni's hands really are huge. Alex tilts his head up easily for him. There's no hesitation. But of course, Paul realizes, they've done this before. Often, if his impression of the situation is correct. And he's sure it is.

They go from careful to heated fast. Paul wonders how they managed to hold off for so long. But Alex is strange, and Gianni seems like a gentleman – whatever that means. When Alex starts to fumble with Gianni's shirt, Gianni hooks a hand around Alex's waist, fingers sliding up under his T-shirt to bare skin. Gianni isn't careful of Alex like he's fragile – Alex would despise him if he were – but he treats his body like it's precious. Paul's own carefulness looks different than his version of the same, but he's still glad to see it. Especially when Gianni goes to his knees, not to get immediately into Alex's pants, but simply to run his hands over every inch of him, even through his clothes.

Alex meets Paul's eyes. Paul thinks he might actually be about to get a request or at least some instruction, but all Alex does is give a shuddering breath. He closes his eyes again as Gianni starts unfastening his jeans.

Paul has no idea what to do. None of them are even drunk, and the bottle of wine Alex insisted they bring is still unopened on the table. That's probably for the best, but if Alex wants something specific, Paul hopes he'll ask. Otherwise, he doesn't want to interrupt. He feels clumsy, to be here in the middle of this.

So he wanders around the room. The question of what it is and is not polite to touch or pick up seems absolutely absurd in the face of what's now happening on the bed, but it's there. He settles for running a finger along the top of a camera case on a shelf and repositioning a book on an end table. After a shocked moment, he recognizes it as one of Alex's, loaned – or perhaps given – to Gianni. Gianni, who now has Alex naked on his bed. Alex, who is gasping Paul's name.

At least that – Alex's voice – is something like an instruction, and Paul kneels by the bed. They're beautiful together. Alex's freckles match the tawny hue of Gianni's skin, as if he's always been marked by this man, before he'd even met him. Paul finds that oddly reassuring.

He kisses Alex to say as much, and he responds eagerly. Who wouldn't, with Gianni's mouth around their dick? Paul is keenly aware that all three of them are in this moment like they are starving and none of them feel like they really belong there. Because, of course, they don't. Under other circumstances, Paul would be all in on a threesome like this, but right now he's an interloper, no matter how invited.

19

After that first rush of hunger, of Alex crying out, of Paul and Gianni trying to desperately make the other feel welcome with their bodies, the day passes lazy and dreamlike. Paul stores it all in his memory, less for his own sake than for Alex's. This afternoon is precious and strange, and whatever feelings Alex is going to have about it, tomorrow or for the rest of his life, Paul wants to be able to honor them properly.

They all nap for a while, piled together on Gianni's bed. Alex's head rests on Gianni's shoulder. Paul's arm drapes over his waist. When they wake the room is cool in the shadows of early evening, small squares of sunlight lingering high on the walls.

They each get up slowly, making quiet and easy conversation as they get dressed. Gianni makes food for them with Alex's assistance. Paul can't stop marveling at how good Alex looks in this home with this man, his long red hair loose around his shoulders and a bruise darkening at the base of his throat where it's just barely hidden by the neck of his T-shirt.

By the time Paul and Alex leave – they both kiss Gianni goodbye at his apartment door; anything else seems absurd – and walk back to their own accommodations, the sky is the deep, vibrant blue of twilight. Lamps shine in windows and on street corners, throwing their golden glow against the encroaching dark.

Back in their room, they tumble into bed again together. They don't do much other than kiss, but Alex seems to be seeking some sort of reassurance and Paul is happy to give it to him. They fall asleep as the moon rises outside their window over the roofs of Rome.

♦

Paul wakes in the middle of the night to noise from the street outside. Alex left the window cracked open before they went to bed. He rolls over towards him because he wants to cuddle before they both wake up for real and have to talk about an actual plan. If Alex doesn't have one, Paul's going to have to be a hardass about it, and anything they come up with may very well mean a longer and much scarier separation.

Alex, however, is not asleep. He's sitting up in bed, his computer open on his knees.

"What are you doing?" Paul asks groggily.

"Buying plane tickets."

"To where?"

"Home."

"Both of us?"

"Yes."

It's everything Paul wants to hear, in outline at least, but in classic Alex style and with too few words to actually be informative. "What are you going to do about Gianni?" he asks, sitting up next to him.

Alex looks at him sharply. "Stop using the fact that he's wonderful to run away from the rest of my life?"

"Okay. But what does that mean?" Paul leans his head on Alex's shoulder.

"I guess we'll find out," he says as he finishes with the airline website and shuts his laptop.

Alex doesn't say anything else, and he may be fine now, but Paul knows this – both leaving Gianni and returning home – is going to hurt like hell later.

◆

They stay in bed late, unwilling to get up and have the conversation they really need to. Paul knows it shouldn't feel ominous, not when Alex has said he's coming home and they even have plane tickets. But there is still so much to decide – or at least articulate clearly – lest they fly back with no plan and into a mess that can only grow.

Alex gets up first and pulls Paul out of bed and into the shower. The mood is pensive as Alex makes Paul wash his long hair and talks about he should probably get it cut when they get back to L.A. Sure, the tangles are getting annoying, but a haircut will also be a nice external marker of the new phase of his life he's about to embark on. Also if Gemma still wants him to play an evil bishop in *Scism*, the long hair will have to go.

He doesn't talk about anything of substance until they go out in search of food, and Paul wonders what it is about this city and Alex that he keeps wanting to have these conversations out in the world.

Once they're actually having it, the discussion is not a painful or drawn-out negotiation. Alex's goal is clearly a family structure that works for him while not blowing up the rest of their lives, which is all Paul ever wanted from him in the first place. Most surprisingly, to Paul at least, he wants out of the movie business. As much as Alex talks about hating fame and being away from home, he's always loved the work and has never talked seriously about a change. But he makes it very clear that he's increasingly concerned with the isolation movies bring him. He enjoys it too much to preserve everything else that matters to him. Returning to TV, he says, feels like a better choice.

The conversation spins out over lunch at one of Alex's haunts and lasts through a walk back to their room. As much as they talk and sort things out between them, they don't actually fix anything. Among other things, they still have to negotiate all these issues with Liam and Carly and even Ali to an extent. After the drama of the last six months, their patience with and trust of Alex is, understandably, not what Paul's is. Though he is relieved to hear that Alex has already reached out to Liam and Carly and to Gemma. Because talking is one thing, but actions are what drive their lives.

♦

Alex still has to wrap things up with Gianni. He brings him up only once, haltingly, to tell Paul he wants to say goodbye to him before they leave. Paul, to his relief, agrees immediately.

So Alex texts Gianni and arranges to meet him later that day. He's glad when Paul doesn't ask any more questions about him; Alex feels like he's already run out of words with which to plan his life and what he wants. Which may not make this the ideal time to do this, but there is no other time.

"You can stay the night with him, you know," Paul says when Alex kisses him goodbye.

Alex doesn't say that won't be necessary. It's been a lie every other time he's said it in regard to this trip, and he'd prefer not to continue that streak.

◆

Gianni kisses him hello at the door. The air is heavy and sad between them immediately, and they skip the small talk to discuss whether they should fuck, just the two of them, while they have the chance. But neither of them are really into the idea. They day with them and Paul had been joyous if a bit complicated, and it's clear that whatever this is wouldn't be.

So they sit, shoulders pressed together, on Gianni's couch and look through the pictures he took of Alex. They drink a bottle of wine and talk, as they always have, for hours. When Gianni finally levers himself up to hand Alex a stack of prints he made and a poster tube to carry them in, Alex nearly loses it right there.

And then, Gianni asks gently, as he's always been gentle, for space.

Alex finds it a relief, in a way, to give it to him.

Before he goes, both of them lingering and not-quite-touching at the door, Alex says, "I could really use someone who isn't a part of the rest of my life, but I don't want to use you. If you're not furious with me once I'm gone, please still be here? Please write me emails and tell me about your photographs and your friends and whoever you're going to fall in love with –"

"Next."

"What?" Alex doesn't understand at first. But then he does. "Next? Oh. Yeah. Okay. Next. Fuck."

◆

By the time he and Paul slip into their seats on the plane, Alex is already numb and exhausted. The fact that they're going to have to do eight hours in the air to New York before hitting customs and immigration, switching terminals, and doing another six on to Los Angeles is overwhelming. Alex doesn't want to think about it, but he can't stop, although that is in some ways better than the alternative.

He leans against Paul as they take off and lets Paul deal with the flight attendant about beverage and meal choices. Even though he could probably use a drink, he's glad when Paul asks only for water; air travel is so drying, and Alex can't help but laugh a little hysterically at his very L.A. thought.

After the meal service is cleared, he twists in his seat so his back rests against Paul's arm as he stares out the window.

It takes Paul a long time, but eventually he asks if Alex is okay.

"Not really."

"What can I do?"

Alex doesn't know where to start, and he isn't aware of making a sound. But he is aware of Paul unbuckling his seatbelt and curling around him to gather him up, as much as is possible in the confines of the cabin.

"It's okay if you're sad," Paul says from over his shoulder.

Alex hopes it sounds pathetic to his ears too. Sad is definitely an understatement. "It's not okay if I'm sad here." His focuses on being stubborn because that's a lot easier than explaining how hard he's working not to be distraught.

He can feel Paul shake his head against his

shoulder. "Fuck that."

"That's very nice of you to say."

"How about," Paul whispers insistently in his ear, "you do what you need to do, and I worry about your precious public image and assholes with smartphones."

Alex gives a weak laugh.

"We are going home. To our baby, and our other babies, and our co-parents who are very concerned about us –"

"– and Gemma who still kind of hates me and who I asked for a job –"

"– and Olivia who probably didn't enjoy being the only adult on deck."

"Oh God, it's all a mess," Alex says, half laughing.

"A little bit, yeah. But you just broke up with someone, so why don't you just worry about that right now."

"Nothing to worry about anymore."

"I don't know." Paul's voice is wry. "I mean, Liam's your best friend."

And that's when Alex loses it completely, because the situation with Liam has always been weird and hard and is a hot mess right now, but it has been a constant. Liam may be a confusing fact in Alex's life, but like Paul, he is a fact. Gianni is just gone. And promises to email and exhortations to have a wonderful life aside, it's just fucking awful.

Alex twists around, presses his face into Paul's shirt and cries, grateful for Paul's hands on his back, soothing and a little useless but there anyway, the constant of the ground even when everything is up in the air.

◆

"I feel like we're never going to get there," Paul says as they wait in the interminable traffic on their route from LAX home.

Alex nods without saying anything. His leg jitters a little as he sits in the passenger seat. That might be restlessness from being on a plane for the last day, but Paul suspects Alex is nervous. And rightfully so. Their first stop isn't their own home, but Carly and Liam's. Alex wants to see the girls, and, perhaps even more importantly, wants to start fixing things tonight.

Carly didn't sound entirely enthused about that idea on the phone when they called from the baggage claim, but she wasn't unwilling. If Paul had his way, Alex would get some sleep first, but this isn't his show, and he's proud that Alex doesn't seem put off by Carly's totally earned wariness.

When they arrive at Carly and Liam's house they ring the bell instead of using their keys. Alex stands on the doorstep waiting to be invited in when Carly pulls the door open. Paul watches in fascination. He's never thought of her and Alex as particularly alike, but as they test each other, suddenly they seem like exactly the same species.

"Liam isn't home," she says.

"I know," Alex says. "I was kind of hoping to talk to you."

"And see your girls?" Her tone is incredibly sharp.

"And see my girls."

"Are you waiting for my permission?" she asks.

Alex smirks. "I am still standing on your doorstep," he points out.

"What are you, a vampire?"

Alex shrugs like it's as reasonable as anything else. "Could be."

With just a hint of a smile, Carly waves them in.

No matter how much Paul wants to save Alex from himself – and Carly – he knows he needs to let Alex speak, not just on this mess of issues between them, but in regards to life in general. Just because he can make it easier for Alex to move through the world in the short term, doesn't always mean that's the right answer. His husband has always desperately needed to feel like he has agency and is still learning how to exercise it without running to the other side of the planet.

At least Paul finally knows why.

Carly relays to Alex the message that Liam wants to talk to him at some point.

"Not tonight, you're exhausted and he's going to be late. But soon."

"Yeah," Alex says, nodding nervously. Paul can only imagine what Alex and Liam sorting out their current mess is going to look like. "Yeah, of course."

With a gesture to Carly, Paul slips upstairs. The babies are presumably asleep, and Ali certainly should be too, but Paul knows that's unlikely in actual fact. She's a voracious consumer of media – books, television, movies – and disturbingly adept at discussing how to adapt them into her own personal starring vehicle. Sure enough, Paul finds her in bed, using her phone as a reading light. She's been lying in wait.

"You're home," she declares.

"Yup."

"Alex too?"

"Alex too."

"Is Mom yelling at him?"

"Mmmmhmmm."

For a moment, Ali goes back to her book and frowns. "She better leave some for me."

"I don't think he's going to dissolve from the yelling," Paul points out.

"No," Ali says like Paul is being particularly obtuse. "But it's not fair that everyone else always gets to go first."

Paul makes a brief detour to check on the babies, asleep in their respective cribs in the room across the hall from Ali's. He can hear Carly and Alex's voices from downstairs; they're not yelling, but there is an intensity to both their voices that clearly means they're going to be at it a while.

Back in Ali's room, he pulls a small, white, overstuffed armchair closer to her bed and holds out a hand for her book. "Want me to read to you?"

Ali looks at him consideringly. "I don't need you to."

"I know you don't. But sometimes it's nice to let people do things for us. It's an important skill to learn."

She considers him for a moment. "Why's that?"

"Because otherwise you might end up like Alex."

That seems to delight her, and Paul reads to her for a bit from *James and the Giant Peach*. But while he gets lost in it, eventually she gets restless enough to climb out of bed and tug the book from his hands. "Let's go see Alex."

"You're supposed to be asleep."

Ali rolls her eyes. "You're up here. She knows I'm not asleep. Did you buy me anything in Italy?"

Paul feels vaguely alarmed. He has no idea if

they did. He's praying Alex has various souvenirs stashed in his luggage. "Everything's still packed."

Ali huffs. "Fine," she says. Then, "Alex."

Paul knows her one-word demands are a terrible habit picked up from Liam at his less verbal, but he's not going to nag her about it now. Instead he scoops her up in his arms as she shrieks with what is likely baby-waking laughter and carries her downstairs.

Alex and Carly look up from their mutual hunched-over dismay, and Paul hopes the fact that they're still talking is actually a good sign. Ali twists out of his arms like a cat and rushes headlong at Alex, hugging him tightly.

"Hey," Paul says. "Guess you're forgiven."

Carly side-eyes him. "Not likely."

♦

Alex and Carly finally finish talking close to midnight, when even Ali has fallen asleep curled against Paul's side on the couch. Paul carries her back upstairs and tucks her into bed, relieved when she doesn't wake up. Then he waits in the doorway of the babies' room while Alex steps quietly across the floor and picks Claudia up out of her crib. Her eyes blink open, but only for an instant, and her head flops forward onto Alex's shoulder as she gives out a contented sigh. Alex's smile, as he drapes a blanket over her for the short walk back to their house, is beatific.

Somehow Claudia miraculously remains asleep through the transfer to her room at home. Alex makes sure she's settled, then joins Paul in their bedroom.

"It is so damn good to be back in my own bed,"

he says, sliding under the covers. By the time Paul crawls in next to him, he's asleep.

20

Alex meets Gemma the next day at her office because it's the only way she agreed to see him. Frankly, he's a little surprised – though relieved – she agreed to see him at all. Her reply to his email from Italy had been a curt *If you're serious, we can talk about it when you get back*, which had not felt propitious.

But he's fully aware that the Gemma stop on the Alex Apology Tour is a thing that needs to happen whether he gets something out of it or not. He's glad to not drag it out, and that's aside from the conversation they need to have about *Scism*.

She keeps him waiting in reception. And while on some level that might just be L.A., Alex can't help but be aware of it as a power play. He's J. Alex Cook, usually other people are kept waiting because of him. He's not annoyed though; he's impressed. But also a bit nervous. After all, he's been counting on the role in *Scism* still being there for him.

He needs it for so many reasons: To provide the proof of concept for his willingness to stay close to home. To be a far more responsible parent than he has been since Claudia was born. To make things right with Liam. Even, in a very real way, to make things right with Victor. If the role isn't there anymore, or the project has evaporated while he was busy having his Italian crisis, he's going to have a problem.

"Sorry to keep you waiting," she says when he's finally shown in to Gemma's tiny starter office by a too-crisp intern who asks him if he wants tea or coffee or a presumably designer water. Gemma doesn't get up from behind her desk.

"No you're not," Alex says genially. And, because he is aware that this is a test much like his very different and still unresolved conversation with Carly, he doesn't sit down until she invites him to do so. For a moment, he doesn't even think she's going to, possibly because this is not a performance she's engaged in before. Gemma is very good at her job, Alex knows – she has always worked at anything she's wanted obsessively and with passion. But she doesn't necessarily know this script.

There's an awkward moment once Alex is seated where they both shuffle and stare at each other. Gemma has to remind him that he asked to see her and ostensibly for very specific reasons.

"I know you are totally pissed at me...." He trails off when she raises an eyebrow. "Oh man, you're going to make this hard, aren't you?"

"I really hope this is a business meeting," she says. "I don't have time for anything else."

"Look, I've been an asshole, and I know that. And I'm more than happy to say I'm sorry and –"

"Then say it, Alex. Don't describe it."

"I'm sorry."

"Thank you."

The silence stretches. "Is *Scism* still happening? Because I'm interested. Really, really interested."

"You sure didn't sound interested when we first talked about it."

There's no petulance in her tone, just a cool disbelief, and Alex is once again impressed. He continues to be a little intimidated. "I know. But I thought about it a lot, and now I am."

"What changed your mind?"

"Well, for one, this is Victor's last great project and I still have unfinished business with him. Being in Italy, being at the Vatican, telling the story of Victor and *Fourth* and my whole life to someone new made that clear. But I'll also be far less of a failure as a human being, a father, and a friend if I'm not away six months out of the year working on movies because I'm terrified of human connection not written and directed by other people. But most relevantly for this conversation, I've disrespected your career and not offered you help where I probably could have."

"Go on," Gemma says when he pauses.

"I know I can't buy your trust in me, but that doesn't mean I don't owe you. So if you would like to call in some favors while I am earning back your emotional trust, I would be super okay with that."

"You understand that you're not carrying this show, right? I mean, yeah, you are, but I am going to use you to get a whole bunch of other big deal people in it, some of whom may get higher billing than you for half the time on set."

"I know," Alex says. "I also know that's a my-people-talking-to-your-people thing, and that at this point we're just being ridiculous. So is it there if I want it?"

"Yeah," she says, leaning back in her chair. "It's there if you want it."

♦

As soon as Alex leaves, Gemma puts her head down on her desk. She's not quite sure whether she wants to laugh or cry. Alex has always been a lot, but this is a new level.

There's a soft tap on the door, and Minette peeks her head in.

"Well?" she asks when Gemma lifts her head from her arms.

"Come in." Gemma straightens up in her chair. "And shut the door."

Minette does, warily.

Gemma says, "He said yes." It's so strange a thing to say, after how long – and through how much shit – she's known Alex. Especially after his confession, years ago now, that his last-ditch plan to escape Indiana had been to marry her.

Minette grins and claps her hands. Gemma has to smile. It really is a very good thing. She can hardly believe it's happened.

"So how fun was that?" Minette asks.

"Playing the ice queen for him?"

"Uh-huh."

"*So* much fun. Oh my God, you have to call your boyfriend!" Gemma says, finally bouncing out of her chair to hug Minette and do a little victory dance.

Eventually, they settle down enough for Minette to dial Liam. Alex being on board changes everything. He's the leverage they need to get to a series order.

"Hey, what are you doing?" she asks when Liam picks up.

"I've got something Downtown. Why?"

Minette sets the phone on speaker. "After your thing do you want to come over and celebrate? At the office I mean."

"What are we celebrating?" Liam asks warily.

"Alex agreed to do *Scism*," Gemma says.

"Shit. Seriously?"

"Seriously," Minette confirms. "The goal over here is to get it on paper this week."

"Hot damn."

Gemma wonders briefly what Liam's doing Downtown. Visiting Victor, maybe.

"So are you coming over or what?" Minette asks again.

Gemma hopes he does. They have a lot to celebrate.

"I thought we were trying not to mix business and pleasure," Liam says cautiously.

"You have a very valid point," Minette says with a wink to Gemma, "but a win is a win."

♦

That night, Alex is back at Carly and Liam's house, along with Paul and all the kids, for the Big Family Meeting. It doesn't feel as terrible as all the others have, which is probably just because he knows this has been coming and has already had his big breakdown. This style of confrontation is still not one he wants to continue with in the future, but for tonight at least, it's necessary. With any luck they'll all come out of it with some real, tangible agreements about how to move forward.

They keep things light and easy at dinner while Ali and the babies are still up, but once the kids have been put to bed and the adults are gathered back in the living room, no one wastes any time opening discussion.

"Okay," Carly says, settling herself regally in the big armchair across the room from the couch where Alex and Paul are sitting together. Liam has his legs tucked under him on the loveseat adjacent to the couch.

"Item the first," she says, while Liam twists a bracelet around his wrist and looks nervous. "Alex, how many children would you like to have?"

Alex says, immediately, "Three."

That Carly is pleased is evident. What is also evident, is that while that's the outcome everyone *wants*, no one is sure that outcome is still appropriate.

Alex has spent so much of his life since Victor plucked him out from behind a clipboard and dropped him in front of the camera negotiating for things even when he's been wildly out of his depth. But he's never had to negotiate for his family before. He doesn't think that Carly is going to refuse to let him and Paul adopt Ali and Vic, or refuse to adopt Claudia herself. But she makes it clear that outcome may be longer in coming now than it would have been in the past. He's going to have to work for this.

One of her and Liam's biggest concerns is Alex disappearing, unexpectedly or otherwise, again in the future.

"The shit you pull," Carly says, "is really not good for Ali. And it's not going to be good for Vic and Claudia when they're old enough to be aware of when you're here and when you're not and, mostly importantly, the why of that."

"What if I promised to stay around more?"

Carly brushes her hair back over her shoulder. "You make a lot of commitments, Alex. You promising that doesn't necessarily mean much to me."

"Well," Alex says, while Liam avoids his eyes. "I have an offer. Have had. For a while. Series regular on *Scism*. Clearly, film is bad for me and fucks me up, and I know I'll still be gone for like a month to do the *Saga* junket. And maybe in a few years I'll have to go back to do a sequel to that movie or whatever. But if I do *Scism*, and it survives the absolute fury it's going to unleash, I can't disappear for eight months at a time, and I can be around in a really consistent and predictable way at least until the babies are in school."

"I knew I did the right thing in not getting involved with that show," Paul observes mildly.

"Yes, Alex," Carly says dryly. "Take on the hardship of starring on a network TV show to prove what a good parent you are."

Alex takes a deep breath. He's earned that snark from Carly, and she has a point, but he also knows she is also making sure he hurts and seeing if he can take it when the going gets hard.

"Okay, that's totally valid. But I recognize that there is actually nothing I can do to make you trust me right now. You can take or not take the leap, and I understand that that is a huge ask to make, but I am. If there's something I can offer you, you need to let me know what it is so I can. Because frankly, not only do I not enjoy being a punching bag, it's not really going to solve any of this."

"What about Delilah?" Liam asks.

Alex tenses, because he has no idea what Liam is about to say and can only imagine terrible things.

"No no, hear me out," Liam says earnestly. "If all the girls are going to be like, legally, all of ours, then our extended families become related too."

"That's a scary thought," Alex mutters.

"But I don't actually know anything about your sister," Liam presses on. "Except that she scares you and bad things happened in Indiana. I don't need to know what happened, but I do need more data than I have, so we can collectively decide what to do, because like, no offence, I don't trust your read of the situation. Also," Liam says, holding up a hand when Alex opens his mouth to speak. "I have feelings of extreme caution about someone who you say tried to stab you twice being around my children. But I'm not convinced she's the villain of this piece any more than the rest of us ever were. So I need you to help me figure that out."

"Also, therapy," Carly puts in.

Alex restrains himself from rolling his eyes at her; he is aware how bad that would be for his case right now. Carly, clearly, can read it off of him anyway.

"We are all rich, famous people in Hollywood with an incredibly unconventional family structure," Carly says. "Even if all of you were mentally healthy, which you are not, we should all be in therapy. For fuck's sake, *I'm* in therapy, and I'd like to remind you Team I Haven't Had a Breakdown Yet consists entirely of me and the kids."

◆

Eventually, the pressing issues are as resolved as they are going to get that night, and Liam asks Alex to take a walk with him. The night is cool, and in this car-obsessed city, other than the occasional jogger or dog that needs walking, the sidewalks of their neighborhood are always empty. Warm light flickers at the edge of Alex's vision. The glow of houses, of other families and other lives – rich, well cared for, and likely messy – are layered in the hills and canyons.

"Why do I feel like I'm not going to like whatever this is?" he asks.

He and Liam walk side by side, arms brushing, hands not finding each other's as they had in Iceland.

"I'm mad at you," Liam says.

"Everyone's mad at me," Alex says. "I'm mad at me."

"I'm glad you're back though."

"Are you?"

Liam makes a noise of assent that reminds Alex of nothing so much as Victor. "Do you remember when I asked you, about Bjarki, if you were angry it wasn't you?"

"Yeah. That was an asshole question," Alex says.

"Maybe that's because I'm an asshole."

"You are." Alex knocks into Liam's shoulder. "But what's your point?"

"Maybe I'm angry it wasn't me."

"What?"

"You. Your Italy fling. Whatever it is you felt like you could do there."

"Carly told you," Alex says. It's not really a question.

"Since you weren't talking to me. Yeah."

"It wasn't intentional. I just couldn't. And it's not like you were talking to me either."

"Because you were doing with someone else exactly what you did with me."

Alex shakes his head. "That's not fair. You dumped me because I was a mess and using you to be a mess, which was decidedly not what I was doing in Rome."

Liam sighs. "You're so brave. With everyone

but me."

"No," Alex says softly. "It's not like that at all. I'm so brave with everyone but *me*. That's the thing I need to deal with. And it kind of sucks. Like, I can handle my trauma, but I can't really handle my own damn company as a person who has had that trauma. It's easier when I run. But that just means there's a way for it to be easier when I stay too."

For a long time, they walk in silence. Alex is dimly aware that they will soon reach the bottom of the hill, at which point they will encounter a major road, businesses, and the noise of traffic. The spell of this moment will be broken, and then, to their mutual misery, they will have to trudge back up the hill together.

When they can see the green, yellow, red of the traffic lights at the intersection below Liam stops and grabs Alex's wrist with a quiet urgency. "Can you do me a favor?"

"Probably. What is it?" Alex knows not to agree entirely until the request is actually named. Liam can be like the Devil sometimes, too easy to make bargains with before the shape of them is fully known.

"After you figure out how to have the nerve to face yourself, can you find the nerve to face me and whatever this has always been?"

"Shit...Liam...." This is why Alex hesitates when Liam asks for things, because he asks for things like this.

"I'm not asking for anything other than for you to be present one hundred percent when we're in the same place alone together. It doesn't have to be about sex or romance or anything more than whatever we are. I just want us to be more skilled at it. Because I am so sick of us being about conversations we can only have in the dark or when one of us is in pain. Whatever we are, we're better than this."

Alex swallows. Then nods. "Yeah. Okay. I guess."

"Cool. No rush."

"Bullshit," Alex says with a little laugh.

Liam echoes the sound. "Yeah, okay. True. Wanna go back?" he asks, pointing down at the intersection and all the lights they aren't ready for yet.

"Sure. But only if you tell me about Minette and how that hell that happened. Because, last I checked, you two hated each other," Alex says.

"Yeah, well. That's what you get for running away to Italy." Liam snaps his fingers and turns to face back up the hill. "Turns out I had to learn how to trust myself too."

♦

Eventually, Alex figures out that his return to Los Angeles and being present in his own life is a marathon, not a sprint. Trust doesn't grow out of a single conversation, and forgiveness – from himself and others – takes time. No one doubts Alex's ability to be present and kind when he wants and is able to. Rather, it's the day-after-day, year-after-year that everyone questions. Alex doesn't blame them, but he can only take it one day at a time. Life, he is coming to accept, is also a form of work.

He starts therapy – again – even though it's wildly tedious to explain the backstory, both recent and not. He knows everyone is used to having celebrity clients, but it's still weird to pretend that there's no assumed knowledge when he walks in the door. He knows how important it is not to keep score in any of his relationships. He also doesn't understand how anyone actually. manages that.

Least of all Gianni.

He gets the email late one night when he's been up dealing with a teething Claudia. Messing with his computer isn't good for going back to sleep, but now that he's trying to be present and engaged in the whole of his life he likes the privacy of these hours when Paul is asleep and no one in the world can possibly want anything from him.

Except, of course, the man he left in another time zone. Gianni must have sent the message over breakfast, and Alex pictures him in his studio full of morning light, the scent of coffee, and ghosts of the not-yet-dead captured in photos.

Alex debates deleting the email unread.

He doesn't want to be yelled at.

Or tempted.

But not running away from his life in Los Angeles also means not running away from his life in Indiana or Iceland or Rome. He takes a deep breath and holds it as he clicks on the message.

The email is long and nothing like he expected. Because other than asking Alex how he is, it's not about him – or what happened in Italy – at all. It is, instead, merely an account of Gianni's life since Alex left. Friends seen, an update on his photography projects, a meal at a new restaurant…all of it filling in gaps about the man's day-to-day reality that Alex had, of course, never actually been a part of. He finds the thought as reassuring as he does depressing. Perhaps they had both been running from something. Or, making up stories that could never have come true.

But this, the simple account of a day without condemnation or request, is somehow more real. Alex hopes it's the bid for friendship he suspects it is. He hasn't made a friend in any way that is natural to him since Indiana. Since Gemma. His life in Los Angeles has never allowed for the intimacy of near-anonymous and desperately ordinary confessions typed in the dark. But now, suddenly, it does.

Alex finds himself replying to Gianni long into the night about his own ordinary days since his return. When he hits send, he finally understands: Every life is ordinary, and every life is extraordinary, and most everyone – even Alex himself – is trying to do their messy best.

♦

"So what do you think?" Carly asks as she and Liam go to bed together. It's the same question she's asked every night for the last month. They know what their answer is ultimately going to be, but they also know that they haven't quite been ready to give it.

Liam smiles. There is something to talking about Alex and his place in their family while in bed with his wife that makes him happy. His family doesn't quite have any shape he ever expected – Victor is dead, his relationship with Alex is complex and mostly nonsexual – and he doesn't always get to communicate with people the way he wants. But he has Carly and the girls and Paul and Alex and now Minette, too. It all feels right to him. So does talking about Alex and not having to feel sad anymore.

"I think we say yes."

"Really?" Carly asks, not that she sounds surprised. Liam knows she's been at yes too, simply because the other option is too terrible to contemplate. But, as much as everyone thinks Carly is the reasonable one of the pair of them she, like Liam, has been waiting for some sort of sign.

Liam nods.

"Why now?" Carly's expression isn't challenging, just curious, and she snuggles down under the covers to lie face-to-face with him.

Liam shrugs. "Why not?"

"Liam!" Carly's laughing, but she sounds scandalized. "It's our children! All two-and-a-time-share of them."

"Okay, but you asked Alex to stop playing games. And he did. And now we're playing games because...why?"

"It's fun?" she offers.

"You're deflecting," Liam says. "And you're still pissed."

"Yeah. Aren't you?"

"Sure," Liam grins. He takes her hands and starts playing with her fingers. "But you know how I need you to hold me to the same standards as everyone else?"

"Yes?"

"You're not really doing that if the standards for Alex are totally different."

Carly groans. "Liam...."

"Don't say math, you're perfectly good at math, and you only say you're not when I'm annoying you. If we're going to get this done, let's get it done. Because it's going to take forever, and it doesn't matter how long we wait, everything that's already happened…Iceland and Italy…isn't going to change."

"So are you going to tell them," Carly asks, "or am I?"

Liam grins wickedly. They may be saying yes, but he can't resist one last little jab at Alex in the process either. "Oh no, we're totally having another family meeting."

21

The paperwork doesn't get completely finalized until December, the week after Alex gets back from his press junket for *Saga*. The night before they go to the lawyer's office to sign everything, they all gather at Carly and Liam's house. Minette is there too, at Liam's invitation. The mood is festive and the house is, predictably, chaotic. Liam is lying on the floor in the middle of the living room entertaining the babies at their own eye level. Minette sits on the corner of the endless kitchen counter kicking her legs and chatting with Carly while Paul and Alex cook.

"Hey, are you excited about tomorrow?" Alex asks Ali as she sets the table and he checks the vegetables roasting in the oven.

"I don't know," she says. "Are we all going to get jewelry out of this thing?"

Paul snickers.

Ali looks at him. "I *know*. Dad is totally running out of fingers."

"No. No jewelry," Alex says firmly. He's amused but expressing that feels dangerous.

"I have eight fingers left," Liam calls from the living room.

"Thumb rings are stupid," Ali yells back. "Pinky rings are also stupid. You have four left."

Carly looks over at Alex. "Welcome to autistic parenting. Everything's a goddamn math joke."

"I still want jewelry," Ali notes.

"*Maybe*," Carly says, "if everything tomorrow is not a complete cluster, we can get your ears pierced afterwards."

Earrings are a new thing for which Ali has been advocating since Alex got home from Italy. He's amused that it's taken Carly this long to give in. It's so much better than Ali's desire to be a child star.

"Cool," she says to her mom. Then she turns back to Alex. "I'm going to be on TV next."

Suddenly he understands why Carly hadn't wanted to give in.

"You're going to be on *Scism*." Ali bounces on her toes. "I can be your bastard daughter!"

Alex stares at her. Minette, from her perch on the counter, is clearly exerting a huge amount of effort not to cackle.

"Yeah," Liam says, entering the dining room carrying Claudia, Vic toddling behind him. "We'll talk to the writers' room about that one."

"Really?" Ali asks hopefully.

"Nope," Liam says.

"You can't be my bastard daughter if I'm legally adopting you," Alex points out.

Ali stares at him and screws up her face into her best super mean sarcastic elementary-schooler look. "Do you not know how TV works because you're from Indiana?"

◆

Dinner is convivial, and Alex enjoys himself immensely. Ali eats both vegetables and salad without complaint or references to the diets half her classmates are already on. Neither of the babies intentionally pitch food at anyone. Liam manages not to drop anything. Paul and Minette have an amazing conversation about their own personal blacklists of unbearable people in the industry. Alex and Carly entertain themselves by kicking each other under the table.

Whatever they're play fighting about, Alex loses, because when they're done eating, he clears the table and loads the dishwasher. Dessert passes with only the minor incident of Vic upending her small bowl of ice cream all over herself, which she at least finds hilarious. Then everyone gathers in the living room for comfortable low-key conversation and board games.

Eventually, Minette gets up to go, and Liam walks her out to her car. When he's gone more than about a minute, Alex starts looking at the clock. He knows Liam, and he knows what he's likely doing right now.

After about ten minutes have passed, Carly catches his eye after he looks at the clock yet again. He knows she knows exactly what he's thinking. Every time he starts to giggle, she raises a judgmental yet amused eyebrow, which just sets him off more.

When Liam finally comes back, Alex takes one look at him and collapses sideways on the couch, his face buried in a throw pillow. Liam's not mussed in any telltale way, but Alex can't help himself.

"...What?" Liam asks, confused.

Alex is sure he won't be able to clarify.

"Alex is being immature about you making out with Minette in the driveway," Carly says matter-of-factly, as if she hadn't been just as bad as him.

"I didn't make out with her in the driveway!" Liam protests.

"In her car. *Whatever.*"

"Ugh kissing," Ali pipes up, counting her

Monopoly winnings. "All because our neighbors are not that interesting for you to stare at for that long."

Alex is relieved when Carly takes on the task of responding to that one.

Finally he regains his composure and straightens himself up to sit on the couch. "You really like her, don't you?" he says quietly to Liam.

Liam sits next to him, pressing their shoulders together. He gives a small, gentle smile. "Yeah. I really do."

Shortly after that they start the process of putting the kids to bed. Ali grumbles, as she always does, but Alex finds it an immensely familiar and comforting backdrop to the routine of getting Claudia cleaned up and into pajamas and settled into her crib. Paul sits on the floor talking quietly to both him and Carly, who's putting Vic to bed.

After that, the adults spend a long time sitting together downstairs, chatting and laughing quietly and triple-checking that they have everything they need for tomorrow. Finally, after Alex has tucked himself closer and closer into Paul's side, Paul finally leans over and whispers in his ear, "Do you want to go to bed?"

Alex nods.

♦

Staying over at Liam and Carly's has, historically, been something Alex tried to avoid. He and Paul haven't always been successful. There's been nights when they drank too much and others when the babies were too fussy to move and everyone was too exhausted. There was also the family-wide norovirus incident, but Alex tries not to think about that; children are really gross.

Mostly, Alex prefers to be at home in his own bed with marginally decent privacy and clear boundaries. Until recently, neither boundaries nor privacy felt like something he could have at Liam and Carly's. But tonight had been comfortable and kind in a way that makes Alex view as silly his past insistence on not sharing labels about polyamory and partnership with Liam and Carly. While he's still grateful they don't all live in a weird hippie commune of Sarah's worst fears, tonight he really doesn't mind being under the same roof with everyone else. It just makes sense and even feels a little sweet.

Alex sits on the bed with his back to Paul. From here he can see out the window and down the canyon to where the lights get more frequent and roads cut through the electric landscape like runways.

"What are you thinking about?" Paul asks.

"Victor's house," Alex says, more than aware that he sounds quizzical.

"God, why?" Paul asks.

"Because we're in Liam and Carly's guest room. And it makes me think of Liam's room at Victor's. I was so horrified by that, and now I just feel foolish. Being alive – being a person – is complicated. I wish it hadn't taken so long for me to understand that that's okay."

Paul is silent, staring at him fondly, making the moment both bright and heavy.

Alex recognizes the occasion may call for that sort of happy solemnity, but he can only take so much. He lets a look of mock horror slide over his expression. "What have we done?" he says in a stage whisper.

Paul chuckles at his antics, but refuses to break the spell. "So much wrong," he says looking at the ceiling. "But everything right."

Special thanks go to Giulia Caruso, the Italian artist who introduced us to Anselm Kiefer's The Seven Heavenly Palaces (2004) designed for and permanently on view at HangarBicocca in Milan. This book could not exist without her.

You can visit her online at https://www.giuliacaruso.com/

More by These Authors

Visit www.Avian30.com to join Erin and Racheline's mailing list and get information about new releases.

The Love in Los Angeles Series
Starling, Book 1
Doves, Book 2
Phoenix, Book 3
Cardinal, Book 4

Love in Los Angeles is a queer romance series, with elements of magical realism, set in and around the TV and movie industry.

When J. Alex Cook, a production assistant on *The Fourth Estate* (one of network TV's hottest shows), is accidentally catapulted to stardom, he finds himself struggling to navigate both fame and a relationship with Paul, one of Fourth's key writers. *Love in Los Angeles* is the story of Paul and Alex – and of their friends and family – as they navigate love, and life, both in and beyond Los Angeles.

A Queen from the North

A widowed prince in need of an heir, a not-so-united kingdom in need of healing, and an ancient prophecy that still lingers in the modern world are about to conspire to make Lady Amelia Brockett A Queen from the North.

The Art of Three

Two men. One woman. No love triangles.

The Love's Labours Series

Midsummer, Book 1
Twelfth Night, Book 2
More coming soon!

42-year-old John Lyonel has never been attracted to men before, but falling for 25-year-old Michael Hilliard is actually the least screwed up thing that's happened to him in years. Even if sometimes he thinks Michael's a changeling.

Short stories

Sample and Hold
Off-Kilter
Lake Effect
Snare
The Omega's Reluctant Alpha
Alpha Bodyguard
The Hart and the Hound